THE CARD SHARP

THE CARD SHARP

Bob Gust

NORTH STAR PRESS OF ST. CLOUD, INC.

Saint Cloud, Minnesota

I wrote this book for my sister, Jolene. I hope this is the kind of character and type of story she had in mind.

PROLOGUE

Transcript of U.S. Coast Guard Emergency Broadcast
Illinois River Station

Caller: Mayday! Mayday! This is the Captain of the M/V Kay Drabeck. All boats stand clear. We're on fire. We're somewhere around mile marker 280, just south of Joliet. We're cutting our barges loose. Everyone down river needs to get out of the way.

Operator: This is the Coast Guard Emergency Channel Operator. Can you force your tow onto the shore?

Caller: I don't think so. We'll be lucky to get ourselves onshore.

Operator: Have you already . . . have you already cut the lines?

Caller: No, but we're moving as fast as we can.

Operator: How many barges in the tow?

Caller: Twelve. Get notice downriver. Clear everything out. And get us someone to help with the fire.

Operator: Any casualties?

Caller: None that we know of from the fire, but this is far from over.

Operator: Thanks for the warning. We're sending out a full alert. Good luck.

Operator: Attention all watercraft on all frequencies. This is the Coast Guard. We have a towboat on fire at about mile 280 of the Illinois River. We will soon have a raft of twelve barges adrift below that. All non-emergency vessels clear out. All emergency vessels and available towboats and switch boats are asked to head to the scene. This is not a drill.

CHAPTER ONE

"AMY, I NEED YOU TO DROP everything and do something for me."
The man standing in the doorway was the most senior partner in
the law firm of Schreiber, Marko & Meath, and a young associate
like Amy Prescott couldn't afford to do anything but comply.

"Of course," she said. "What is it?"

"We have a client that we do a little work for, and we have a chance
to do a lot more if we can handle this. Minnesota Marine Transport is
one of the top barge lines in the country. One of their towboats caught
fire on the Illinois River. The crew is cutting the tow loose, so right now
there's a towboat burning somewhere south of Joliet and pretty soon
there'll be a raft of barges floating uncontrolled down the river."

Amy's mouth hung open with a look of confusion. She was generally
uncomfortable around Mr. Schreiber anyway, but now felt lost. "I'm
happy to help, but I don't really know much about admiralty law. What
is it you want me to do?"

"I need you to get to the scene. The main thing is to act like you know
what you're doing. The barge companies generally hire lawyers who are in
cities on the Mississippi River because that is where most of the traffic is. You
need to convince the client that a Chicago law firm can handle their admiralty
work. We already handle some of their work at the Commodities Exchange,
but we need to show them that we can handle everything."

Amy wanted to give the appearance of someone springing into action, but really she just looked confused. "Okay, but how will I know
what to do when I get there?"

"Like I said, just be on the scene. The fire department or the Army
Corps of Engineers will make all the decisions. You just need to be there
to take it all in. The client called us because we're closer than any of their

other lawyers and they have a big investment on fire. Call me from your car and I'll give you as much information as I have."

Amy stood up and grabbed her briefcase. "I just hope my roommate didn't take the car." She turned toward Schreiber. "Y'know, by the time I take a cab home and drive to the scene, it could be a couple hours."

"That's okay. The company is flying someone in from Minneapolis. You should be able to get there before they do."

Amy breezed past Mr. Schreiber and down the hall. When she reached the lobby, she turned to the young black man at the reception desk. "Valiant, I'll be gone for the day."

"Yes, ma'am," he said with a smile. "Ms. C. Amanda Prescott is gone for the day."

Within minutes, she was in front of the Illinois Center hailing a taxi. *Admiralty*, she thought to herself. *They didn't even teach that when I was in law school. Or is it called "Maritime Law?" Come to think of it, why would anyone need to know the "law of the sea" if they were just dealing with a river?* Her intellectual confusion was combining with her haste and resulted in the look of someone who was coming apart. Once in the cab, she closed her eyes and took a few deep breaths.

The taxi driver either sensed her need for speed or had his own appointment to reach, as he drove as though they were being chased by the paparazzi. Amy was happy for his focus on the mission, but would have been equally happy if he had stopped for the red lights. Fortunately, her apartment in Lincoln Park was not far away and mid-day traffic was light.

She bypassed her mailbox and went straight to the garage. She still had no idea what she would do when she got to the river, but she wanted to be able to at least tell Schreiber about the effort she made. Once on the interstate, she pulled out her cell phone and called in for more help.

"Jim Schreiber," announced the voice on the other end of the phone.

"It's me," Amy said. "Can you give me a quick primer on admiralty, or maritime, or whatever the heck I'm going to be doing?"

"Sure," he said. "Admiralty law is really just a question of whose insurance pays for the loss. The barge company transports product for one or more customers, and the only question is whether a loss is considered a general average loss or a particular average loss."

This wasn't helping Amy. "What are you talking about?" she said with exasperation.

"It's old English law. If a boat is in danger of sinking, they throw cargo overboard. The cargo thrown over is usually whatever happens to be on top, so it's only fair that everyone share in the loss and it's called 'general average.' If, on the other hand, someone's cargo is damaged because it is just too susceptible to the elements, it is a particular average loss. You don't really need to make any determination, just use those phrases and they'll think you know what you're talking about."

Amy took little comfort in his words. She didn't know much about the law of the sea, but the barge business was not entirely new to her. In a part of her life she didn't advertise, she had grown up in a river town in Wisconsin named Prairie du Chien. As a girl, she'd sat on the bluffs and watched the towboats chugging downstream with their barges strapped together in big unwieldy masses. She fantasized about jumping aboard and escaping her agrarian existence, but the same towboats inevitably returned.

"Any more information on where I'm going?" she asked.

"My latest information is that the towboat went aground south of Joliet. The barges have been set adrift. Head for Joliet."

Amy pushed a little harder on the accelerator. She was in a hurry to get there, but, at the same time, was not eager to get there. After an hour or so, she noticed a plume of thick, black smoke filling the sky. This was clearly an industrial fire, and it appeared to be large. *What was the point?* she wondered. *The towboat will burn beyond repair and, once it sinks, the fire will be out.*

The smoke had signaled the curious, and the road leading to the river was clogged with vehicles lining the shoulders. Assuming she couldn't drive any closer, Amy parked and got out of her car. The crowd was gathered behind a police line that had been established by yellow tape and fire trucks. Amy made her way to the front to see what there was to see.

Pushed onto the shore was a three-story maritime vessel whose normal function was to push barges up or down the river. The structure was designed so that the captain was high enough above the water to see past the front edge of the front barge, which might be three football fields in front of him. In the spot where someone might imagine a smokestack, a black cloud gushed upwards like a waterfall turned on its head. The acrid smell of burning diesel made breathing unpleasant.

The most striking part of the scene was not, however, what was happening. The most striking thing was that nothing was happening. The fire burned and the rescue personnel kept the crowd back, but nobody appeared to be taking any action to arrest the blaze or even to protect the shore. Amy didn't really know what she was doing at the scene, but she was more consumed by the fact that nobody else seemed to know why they were there either.

Amy walked to the area that appeared to be the entrance into the restricted zone. A County Deputy stood guard. Amy flashed him a business card. "I'm Amy Prescott of Schrieber, Marko & Meath. We're the lawyers for Minnesota Marine and I need to talk to the people in charge. Could you tell me where I can find them?"

The deputy gave her an accommodating smile. "I'd be happy to help you, but I'm not too sure myself. Y'see, that boat is burning in the middle of a navigable water. As a result, it's on federal property and the local fire department doesn't really have jurisdiction. Of course, the Army Corps of Engineers doesn't maintain a fire crew in every port, so it's anybody's guess who's in charge. The best I can do is to tell you that the guy over there in the seed corn cap is the local Fire Chief."

"Thanks," Amy said with an appreciation for his candor.

Amy pondered her best approach. She was only seven years out of law school, and the chief looked like he'd held the job since before Amy was born. She had always made a point to project strength and confidence, but she didn't want to appear threatening to "old school" men.

"Chief," she said in even tones, "I'm the attorney for Minnesota Marine and I'd like to be briefed on the situation."

The chief, to his credit, did not patronize her. "What we have is an engine fire. Right now, the boat isn't really burning. It's the engine and the fuel. We can't spray it with water because it'll just spread the fire. We thought about sinking it, but I don't know whether that will put out the fire or cause a big fire on the surface of the water. We have things to put out chemical fires, but I'm nervous about having the EPA on my ass if we start introducing chemicals into the water. I don't like looking like a dummy, but this isn't what we're trained to do. I'm waiting for someone with experience in this type of deal to give me a little help."

"So, you're going to do nothing?"

"No, Minnesota Marine is flying their Harbor Captain in from Minneapolis. I'm hoping he can give us some advice."

"Where's the crew?"

The chief pointed toward the rescue vehicles. "The captain is over there being treated for smoke inhalation. The cook is in the ambulance being treated for a broken leg."

"How about everyone else?" she asked. "There must be other crew members."

One corner of the chief's mouth turned up. "They're riding the barges downriver."

"You're kidding! You mean they're just out there floating toward a big crash?"

"From what the captain told me, it seemed safer than staying on a burning towboat."

She shook her head in frustration. "Well, Chief, I guess the only thing I can worry about is this burning boat. I'm not an expert, but won't this boat be toast by the time the company guy gets here?"

The words had barely escaped her lips before the thundering buzz of a helicopter rotor could be heard overhead. "I don't know for sure," the Chief said, "but I think the Cavalry might have just arrived."

The helicopter settled in a nearby clearing. The engine ground to a halt and the lone passenger flung the door open and stepped out. He looked to be in his thirties, but had the air of someone who had been calling the shots for fifty years.

The Chief and Amy were the only other people inside the police tape, and the helicopter passenger wasted no time finding the man in charge. "I'm looking for Chief William Monroe. I assume that's you?"

"That's right," the Chief responded, extending his hand.

"I'm Tucker Sheridan," he said with a clasp of hands. "I'm the Harbor Captain for Minnesota Marine Transport. What's the situation?"

Monroe smiled with relief. "To be honest, the situation is a fire that we don't know what the hell to do with. I'm basically at your disposal. Tell me what we can do to help you."

"It looks like it's an engine fire, am I right?"

"I don't think there's any question," Monroe responded. "It's been burning for quite a while, but the boat itself doesn't seem to have caught fire."

"Fair enough," Sheridan said. "Do you have an asbestos suit for me?"

"Why?" the chief said with a hint of trepidation in his voice.

Sheridan furrowed his brow and looked at the chief as if he'd just asked how he knew the earth was round. "Because I need to go aboard to turn off the fuel line."

"Wait a minute!" Amy interjected. "Are you saying that you're going on board? That's too dangerous. I can't allow that."

Sheridan gave her a look of incredulity. "You can't allow that? And who the hell are you?"

"My name is Amy Prescott and I'm the attorney for the company. Walking on to a burning vessel is not a risk worth taking. Furthermore, if something happens to you, it would be treated as a regular average loss and your customers wouldn't appreciate that."

Sheridan looked at her for a long time. "Do you mean 'general average loss'? In any case, isn't it our job to minimize any loss?"

"Yes, and that's exactly what I'm doing by preventing you from going on that boat."

"I'm sorry," Sheridan said, "who are you again? You're the new *lawyerette* that represents the company?"

Amy's blood pressure was rising. "I was sent here to manage the situation. My job is to protect the interests of Minnesota Marine Transport. As far as I'm concerned, its interests are that it suffer property damage, but not personal injury."

"That's really nice, sweetheart, but we've got important business to take care of, so you better get out of the way."

Amy expected that attitude from the older generation, but Tucker Sheridan was young enough that she thought he would have been more enlightened. She was momentarily speechless, but then said, "So, I guess you're part of that segment of the population that's still pissed that women have the right to vote?"

Sheridan had been looking past her, and didn't acknowledge her statement. He then directed his attention to the chief. "So, do you have an asbestos suit for me?"

"Absolutely," the chief said before leading Sheridan to the back of one of the rigs lining the perimeter. He pulled out an asbestos suit and mask and Sheridan stripped down and suited up.

Sheridan then walked toward the boat. It wasn't clear whether his swagger was the result of the suit or his attitude. As he went past Amy, he said, "Y'know, I used to think that, but now I'm much more enlightened. I'm willing to let you ladies continue to vote, but I think you should meet me halfway. If women are going to be allowed to vote, I think they should surrender their right to drive. I mean fair is fair."

Amy was not amused. "Did I say you couldn't go on board that burning boat? I misspoke. Please go on that burning boat. Whether you wear protective clothing or not is of no concern to me."

He smiled and then headed for the boat. When he reached it, he vaulted the gunnel and headed toward the fire.

The middle of the boat was a flame topped by a plume. Sheridan walked into the heart of the beast. He didn't sneak or hesitate. He walked in as though he were walking into a bar. The spectators suddenly stopped talking and, for that matter, breathing.

Amy was as transfixed as the rest when her cell phone rang. "What's happening?" The voice was Jim Schreiber's.

"You won't believe it," she responded. "The boat is just burning away, not bothering anyone, and this load of testosterone from the company shows up and insists on boarding the thing. I tried to prevent it, but he just ignored me."

If she was hoping for sympathy, it wasn't forthcoming. "You're there to assist the client," Schreiber said. "Arguing with him won't help anything."

She was silent for a moment. "I appreciate your advice, Mr. Schreiber. I'll do my best." She looked at her watch, but she wasn't really sure why. "What's the word on the runaway barges?" she asked.

"I heard a report that they went aground, but that may not last. Just because the front barges are hung up doesn't mean the river's current won't push the back barges until they come loose and head downriver backwards."

Amy thanked him for the update and hung up her phone. She folded her arms across her chest and stared at the boat. Sheridan hadn't said how long he'd be gone, and she wondered at what point she should get concerned.

Monroe stared into the fire and shook his head. "Crazy son of a bitch," he muttered.

More minutes went by and the silenced crowd began to murmur. Sheridan had not taken any tools, so it was logical to assume that he was merely going to throw a switch or turn a valve. Unfortunately, he'd been gone too long for that.

Amy started to pace. She was having regrets. Not because she failed to prevent him from boarding. Instead, she couldn't help but think that the last thing she might have said to a dead man was that she hoped he would die. "What's taking him so long?" she said to nobody in particular.

She had just looked away when she was startled by a loud bang. She thought it was an explosion, but realized it was more of a crash than a boom. She looked at the boat and saw that the antennae had collapsed. The heat apparently melted the steel and it fell to the deck of the boat. "Chief, we have to do something," she pleaded. "What if something fell on him and he's trapped?"

"I don't really know what we can do," he said with a mixture of panic and exasperation. "We only have the one suit."

Amy's arms began to flail as she spoke. "Well we can't just stand here, for God's sake! Can't you at least start spraying the hose on the fire?"

Suddenly a cheer went up from the crowd. Sheridan walked out of the fire with the same swagger with which he'd gone in. Once off the boat, he pulled the mask off to take in some fresh air. He walked to Amy and the chief. "That should take care of it," he said. "I turned off the fuel, so it should burn itself out in a few minutes."

"What took so long?" Amy said in a voice that betrayed her anxiety.

"Did you worry about me?" he said. "I'm touched."

"Don't flatter yourself," she sneered. "I was just worried that I'd be held responsible for your idiocy."

Sheridan smirked. "I'm lucky I've still got this suit on. I need something to protect me from you." He turned to the chief. "Do you have some paperwork that we should complete?"

Monroe nodded.

Sheridan turned back to Amy. "Well then, I guess I'm done being the object of your scorn. You let me know if you need anything from me for the insurance claim or anything else for that matter." He winked at her and then walked away.

CHAPTER TWO

AMY WAS LATE TO THE OFFICE the next day. "Good morning, Ms. C. Amanda Prescott," Valiant said with a smile. He always called her by the name the way it appeared on the firm's letterhead, and he always said it as though there was something amusing about a woman choosing to use her middle name. The fact of the matter, however, was that the mailroom staff had come up with their own name for Amy. They effectively changed the punctuation in her name and referred to her as *C'Amanda Prescott*, the way a southerner would pronounce "Commander Prescott." She'd overhead some of them giggling about the unflattering sobriquet, but hadn't decided what to do about it.

It was Wednesday, and that meant the day started with the weekly litigation meeting. The firm of Schreiber, Marko & Meath had more than fifty attorneys, but only about fifteen were trial lawyers. The meetings were designed to share information, report on cases, and balance the workload. Another objective was to foster camaraderie, although the meetings sometimes had the effect of promoting competition among the younger lawyers who were hoping to make partner.

Jim Schreiber had stopped trying cases years earlier, but he was still the head of the litigation department and led the meeting. After welcoming everyone, he was quick to sing Amy's praises. "As many of you know, this firm has done some work for Minnesota Marine Transport for many years, and we'd been itching to get a piece of their river litigation. Yesterday, they had an emergency and we got the call. I sent Amy to Joliet to be on the scene at that towboat fire that was on the news. She must have made quite an impression on someone, because I got a call asking us to set up a meeting to review all of their litigation matters."

The other attorneys offered their praise and some even clapped. Amy was a little embarrassed, and said, "I can't imagine who would have been there who would have made such a recommendation. As far as I know, the only person from the company that I spoke to was a total Neanderthal, and I all but told him I hoped he'd die in the fire."

Mr. Schreiber chuckled. "Well, you must have said something right. In any event, that's why I want to assign you to the client. It seems their losses are way out of the ordinary and they're afraid someone's deliberately causing them. We'll have a lot of work to do."

"Thank you," she said, "but this isn't really a very good time for me. I have a trial scheduled for next month."

One of Schreiber's titles was "Litigation Coordinator," and he always felt compelled to live up to the title. "We'll get someone else to take it or to help you. What's it about?"

"Employment discrimination," she said.

"Is it discrimination based on race?"

"No."

"Sex?"

"No."

"Religion?"

"No."

"Age?"

"No."

"Sexual orientation?"

"No."

"Well, that seems to cover the spectrum. What is it?"

"The Plaintiff claims Zodiacal discrimination."

Schreiber furrowed his brow. "What?"

Amy smiled her own disbelief. "Zodiacal discrimination, as in signs of the zodiac. Plaintiff is a Pisces, and he claims that his supervisor discriminates against Pisces in favor of Virgos or Capricorns."

Schreiber's eyes widened and he leaned forward as if he couldn't believe his ears. He'd been in practice since before employment discrimination claims even existed and now saw it brought way past its logical extreme. "There's no such thing," he said. "How can that be a protected class?"

Amy raised her eyebrows to acknowledge his frustration. "There are some laws that say you can't be discriminated against because of the circumstances of your birth. You know, the ones that were designed to protect illegitimate children by making sure they had equal rights to inherit from their parents. The plaintiff's lawyer just got a little creative."

Schreiber wasn't amused. "That's the dumbest thing I've ever heard."

"Tell that to Judge Bradford. I think he must be a Pisces as well, because he exhibits all the classic signs of indecision that are characteristic of that sign. I think maybe he's hoping to pave the way for a future claim of his own."

Schreiber shook his head in disbelief. "Well, we'll get someone to help you out on that one."

Amy wasn't going to go easy. "I appreciate the opportunity," she said, "but are you sure I'm the best person for it? It sounds like there might be some sort of sabotage going on and I deliberately left criminal law behind me long ago."

The statement was only half true. After law school, Amy had worked for the District Attorney in Marathon County, which was in the middle of Wisconsin. She was an up-and-comer, and she presented herself so well that she quickly became the media contact for the office. When asked to comment about a particular claim of police brutality, she smugly responded: "Well, if the Defendant didn't like the way he was treated while in our custody, perhaps next time he'll try one of our competitors." Her boss confided that he thought her statement was "funny as hell," but the outcry forced him to ask her to start looking for a new job. Ultimately, the strain of the criminal justice system was starting to wear her down anyway, and that was her private justification for her statement.

Schreiber wasn't taking no for an answer. "Well, at least you have some experience with that sort of thing. You're clearly the best choice, so get used to it. We've got a meeting scheduled with the client next week."

While Amy had her doubts about the upcoming project, she tried to look on the bright side. Big clients meant big bills, and that usually translated to a partnership in the firm. She sat through the rest of the meeting without absorbing much of what was said. Her practice was likely heading for a change, and she was trying to prepare herself for it.

CHAPTER THREE

Amy met her roommate Jasmine for Happy Hour on Friday. "I don't know how you talked me into this," Amy said upon arriving. "I mean, I don't mind girls' night out, but the Four Farthings has been Chicagoland's number one pick-up bar for the last four decades."

"I'm sorry about that, but some of us are still trying to find our sugar daddies. Thanks for being a good sport."

Jasmine was the yin to Amy's yang. They were opposites in virtually every way. Jasmine believed that dressing for a night out meant positioning her clothes in a way that assured that her red thong panties were at least slightly exposed. Jasmine rarely went anywhere without a supply of condoms "just in case." For all of her show, she wasn't overly promiscuous – but she was ready to be so if the occasion presented itself.

"Don't get me wrong," Amy said, "I like the atmosphere, but I'm not sure how I'd explain it to Chadwick if he knew I was here."

"Just tell him you're here to spend time with me. Or tell him you thought it would look worse if we were in some secluded bar somewhere. I mean think about it. If you got picked up by some guy here it would be about the same as if you got picked up at second base at Wrigley Field. Given the crowd and the number of people here who know us or at least recognize us, everyone would know. So you tell Chadwick that this is such an obvious *meet* market that we came here because we were basically drinking in the open."

Amy smiled and shook her head. "I guess that's why you're in product branding. Because you can rationalize just about anything."

"Thanks, but just the same, if anyone does hit on us, play along at least for a while."

"Just so we agree that 'playing along' doesn't include inviting them back to our place."

"Please!" Jasmine said. "Since when do I want them to know where I live? I'd rather have sex in a taxi than let a stranger know where I live."

Amy was leaning against the bar and let her head drop against her arm as if she had fainted from disbelief. "Nice to know that you have such high moral standards. Or are you just embarrassed about your housekeeping deficit?"

Jasmine gave Amy an angry look, but decided to let it slide. "Speaking of Chadwick, where is he tonight? How do you know he's not hitting on women somewhere?"

"He had some sort of work function. Some contact from Europe is in town and tonight was the only night they could get together."

Jasmine paused while pondering her next question. "How are things going with you two? Have you been ring shopping yet?"

Amy shrugged her shoulders. "Not yet."

"Well, if he asks, will you accept?"

Amy thought for a moment. "Hard to say."

"What's the problem?" Jasmine asked. "I would think it's a sure thing."

Amy looked around the bar as she looked for an answer. "I guess I'd probably say 'yes,' but I haven't really thought about it."

"Girl, if you haven't thought about it, then there must be something missing. Every woman I know fantasizes about the moment he asks, and if you haven't even considered it, then you must not be that keen on the idea."

"Jasmine," Amy scolded, "don't say things like that."

"What? To tell you the truth, I think you're crazy if you're not dying for Chadwick to ask. I mean, yeah, that 'call me Chadwick not Chad' bullshit of his is kind of annoying, but you can just call him 'honey.' A girl could do worse."

"That's because of the 2000 election."

"What is?"

"That's why he goes by Chadwick. After the Florida recount, people started calling him 'dimpled Chad.' He got mad and started with the 'Chadwick' thing."

Jasmine smiled at the explanation. "Okay. I guess I can live with that. How's everything else?"

Amy wasn't sure this was the time or place for the discussion, but kept it going. "I'm not complaining. Just because we're not talking marriage doesn't mean something's missing."

Jasmine squinted her eyes as a signal the tough question was coming. "How's the sex? I mean, I never hear too much noise coming from your room when he stays over."

"Jasmine!" Amy said. "Do you lie awake trying to listen?"

"No, but sometimes I have trouble sleeping."

"Did you ever think that maybe I'm just not the type to put on a show, and I'm trying to be considerate of you?"

"That might be the case, but now it sounds like you're trying to avoid the question. Is the sex okay or not?"

Amy drew in a deep breath and let it out. "I'm afraid I don't have as much to compare him to as you do, but, as far as I'm concerned, it's just fine. Chadwick is very considerate and our time between the sheets is very nice."

Jasmine's face lit up like the "idea" light had just gone on. "There's a problem right there. Do you always have sex under the covers?"

"What are you talking about?" Amy said.

"Sex under the covers is fine if it's winter, but don't you ever do it a little rougher?"

"What?" Amy said with exasperation. "Are you telling me sex is better with a little physical abuse?"

"That's not what I'm saying at all. Have you ever been with a man and his desire for you is so strong you could cut it? I'm not saying he rapes you or does anything against your will. I am saying that, just maybe, he might rip off some of your clothes along the way. He can barely control himself and you know you're the one driving him there. It may be animal desire, but being the object of that desire can be pretty awesome."

Amy decided she wasn't going to win the argument and that she wasn't sure she wanted to win it. "I'm afraid that I haven't had enough sex in my life to have gotten bored with the conventional stuff. Maybe I'll get Chadwick some handcuffs and a whip for our anniversary."

"Suit yourself, but don't underestimate the ability of passionate sex to supercharge everything."

As Jasmine finished her sentence, she raised her eyebrows to signal something was going on. Amy felt someone sliding up to the bar behind her and Jasmine's gawking look suggested he must be good looking. Amy stopped talking in order to listen to what was being said.

Whoever it was, she heard him talking to his friend. The curiosity was killing her, but she didn't want to turn and look or even turn to try to see their reflection in the mirror behind the bar. The bartender finally arrived and Amy heard one of them order a glass of Chopin vodka on the rocks, while the other one ordered an Amaretto Sour. At that moment, Amy decided that if she was going to play along, it was going to be with the Chopin guy. In fact, she wondered whether she'd have to play along at all in light of the fact that any man who would order an Amaretto Sour had to be gay.

Finally, she turned to take a look. The Chopin guy was decidedly elegant, while his friend looked like he was pining for the return of disco. Her turn apparently provided enough encouragement for Chopin to strike up a conversation.

"How rude of me," he said. "Can we offer you ladies a cocktail?"

Amy turned to Jasmine, who glanced at her empty glass as a way to signal an obvious response to the question. Amy turned back to the pair. "Who could refuse such an offer?" she said. "We're drinking Dom Perignon."

"Really," Chopin said. He made a deliberate glance at their Martini glasses and said, "Do you always put olives in your champagne?"

Amaretto Sour proceeded to laugh so hard through his nose that people around him began to fear what would come out.

"Oh that," Amy said. "They say champagne is for celebrating, and we want to celebrate that some guys offered to buy us drinks."

Chopin turned to Amaretto Sour and said, "Sounds like all of the women we know in Minnesota. Always complaining that guys aren't forward enough when it comes to buying drinks."

Amaretto Sour shook his head and pretended to be discouraged. "I can't imagine why guys aren't more eager to buy drinks for women they don't know. I mean, look how they respond. More than happy to screw us now, but not likely to screw us later on when it counts."

Chopin let out an involuntary laugh, but quickly contained it and pretended not to notice the remark. Amy stared at Amaretto Sour as though he were on the witness stand and she was about to disassemble him.

Amy took a deep breath and smiled at Amaretto Sour. "We're going to assume that your little remark somehow slipped by your internal filter, but that similar remarks will not make the great escape." Turning back to Chopin, she said, "If you're still offering, my friend Jasmine is drinking a Cosmopolitan and I'm drinking a dirty Martini."

Chopin smiled at her. "Gin or vodka?"

"Gin," Amy said. "I like to taste my booze."

The bartender was delivering the vodka and the Amaretto, so Chopin added the other two drinks to his order. Chopin proceeded to introduce himself and his friend. Amy was confident that she'd never need to know their names again in the future, and didn't make an effort to store the information in a part of her brain that she'd be accessing again. She did, however, play along for Jasmine's sake. The problem was that a true friend would try to get Chopin talking to Jasmine, but the result would be that Amy would have to talk to Amaretto Sour. Perhaps this would have to be a group discussion.

"So," Amy said, "what brings you gentlemen to Chicago?"

"A little business and a little pleasure," Chopin said. "We had meetings yesterday and today, but decided to stay in town for the weekend. The airfare is cheaper if we stay over the weekend, and we thought we'd go to Comiskey or Cellular Field or whatever you call the ballpark here and watch the Twins thump the local boys."

Jasmine was doing what she could to insert herself into the discussion. "I'm afraid we're Cubs fans. If you were hoping to incite an argument, it won't work because we probably hate the White Sox as much as you do."

"Well then," Chopin said, "I guess we have something in common. Perhaps those drinks won't be the worst $20 I've ever spent."

A four-way conversation soon ensued. Chopin seemed to have a personal interest in Amy, but he was sensitive enough to the group that he didn't try to co-opt her. What had started with a tense moment soon became four people laughing heartily at everything any of them said. Chopin was charming and, after a while, Amy even warmed up to Amaretto Sour.

"I want to be fair," Amy announced. "I appreciate you guys buying us a round – particularly in light of the fact that you're from Minnesota where that's apparently unheard of – but I need to buy this round. The fact of the matter is that I have a boyfriend and I feel a little guilty letting you buy me a drink. I don't want to be accused of being either a gold digger or a teaser, so let me get this one."

Chopin sat with his arms crossed. "You don't need to apologize," he said. "We wanted to meet good-looking women. The two of you have helped us achieve our goal. If it had gone farther, so much the better, but we don't consider a day without sex to be a day wasted."

Amaretto Sour let his filter slip again. "Says you," he said. "Some of us have urges that need to be met."

Chopin and Amy ignored him. Jasmine took up his cause with a simple, "No shit," and proceeded to drag him onto a makeshift dance floor that had been set up in the corner. That left Amy and Chopin alone.

It was awkward for a moment, and then Chopin said, "I hope you aren't expecting me to ask you to dance."

"No. Why?"

"Don't get me wrong, I'd be happy to dance with you, but it seems a little forward under the circumstances."

"Agreed," she said.

They stood without speaking for a long period. Amy performed well when she had an audience, but was a little uncomfortable when the two of them were alone. Amy kicked herself for not trying harder to get him interested in Jasmine. She decided to take a direct approach and started telling him about all of Jasmine's good qualities.

Chopin took it in stride. It didn't seem to take hold, but he wasn't running away. After a couple dances, Jasmine and Amaretto Sour returned. They talked some more as a group, but the two people most interested in sex weren't that interested in each other. The night was not a waste, but the acquaintances made were not going anywhere.

CHAPTER FOUR

O N MONDAY, AMY AND JIM SCHREIBER boarded a plane for the Twin Cities. Flying with the boss meant sitting in First Class. Amy didn't need the extra room, and they wouldn't be partaking of the free cocktails. Still, she liked flying first class. Her perseverance in seeking to better herself was rewarded by the recognition that goes with riding up front. That was almost enough to offset the discomfort of being with Mr. Schreiber.

"I'm glad we could get seats together," Schreiber said. "It will give me a chance to brief you before our meeting."

"I hope the flight is long enough," she said sarcastically.

"You'll be fine," he assured her. "This is what's great about our job. It's always something new."

"I guess I can't argue with that," she said. "Where do we start?"

"Let's start with the client. Minnesota Marine Transport is really just a family operation. We're going to meet with Tony Drabeck. The company was founded by his father. Originally, it was just a little switch boat operation, but Tony took it to the next level."

"Okay," Amy interrupted, "we already need to stop for an explanation. What's a switch boat and what's a switch boat operation?"

Schreiber smiled. "River traffic is done with barges. A towboat will push as many as fifteen barges at a time on the upper Mississippi and three times that number on the lower river. Switch boats are used to move the barges around one at a time when they're being loaded or unloaded. You don't want any downtime with the big boats, so they just push barges downriver to their destination and then pick up a new tow and push it upriver. The switch boat operators take care of everything else."

"Makes sense," Amy said. "There was something like that up the river from where I grew up, but I never knew what it was called."

"Anyway, Tony's father ran a switch boat operation in a small Minnesota town called Winona, but Tony decided to roll the dice and buy some towboats. A lot of the big players were getting ideas about ocean shipping and running barges to South America, so Tony went after the United States brown water market in a big way and became a big player."

Amy wrinkled her nose. "The *brown water* market?"

"I know that doesn't sound as appealing as the 'blue water' label given to the ocean marine market, but what are you going to do?"

"This is helpful," she said, "but what do you think we can do for them?"

"Apparently their losses are way out of whack. The insurance underwriter is threatening to terminate coverage if something isn't done."

"Shouldn't they just put some safety programs in place?"

"I think they tried that, but the problem's much worse. They think some of the losses may have been intentional. For example, there's a concern that the towboat fire might have resulted from sabotage."

Amy shook her head with disbelief that she had been the one asked to work on this file.

A TAXI TOOK THEM FROM THE AIRPORT to St. Paul. As they approached the downtown, Amy noticed only a few buildings that would qualify as skyscrapers, and even they were barely in that category. One in particular had a large neon sign that said "1st." That turned out to be their destination.

The offices of Minnesota Marine Transport might have been considered swank about the time the building went up, but it didn't appear anything had been done to update them. Some might call the furnishings "retro," but that word usually connotes an attempt to copy something old. These furnishings were simply old.

Drabeck looked to be in his seventies and had a fatherly, if not grandfatherly, demeanor that seemed inconsistent with a man who had built an inland shipping business of the magnitude of Minnesota Marine Transport. Drabeck and Amy shook hands and exchanged greetings. "I'm sorry about your loss," Amy said.

"Thank you," he said. "It may sound funny, but when you name a boat after a member of your family, the loss seems to hit you a little harder. Fortunately, it looks like we'll be able to salvage her. Thank God for men like Tucker Sheridan."

"Yes, about that," she replied, "I don't think it's a good idea to have your men risking their lives to save a boat. Your liability exposure is too great."

"Actually," Schreiber interrupted, "with admiralty law, a seaman's claim for injuries is generally limited to the value of the vessel causing the injury. Y'see, an injured seamen doesn't sue the company; he sues the boat. If the boat burned up, the liability would be limited to its salvage value."

"That seems a little harsh," Amy said.

"Don't worry," Drabeck said. "We take care of our people and, if necessary, their families. But we can do that on our own terms. We don't like having personal injury attorneys telling us what we can and can't do."

"I understand," Amy said. "What is it you want us to do?"

"We've been experiencing an abnormally large number of losses. The fire was the worst yet, but the damage to barges and cargo has been growing at an alarming rate. Furthermore, the number of injuries to seamen has been escalating. I think there's something going on and I need you to help me find out what it is."

"You don't think it's just a series of misfortunes?" Amy asked.

"I'd be fine if that's what it was," Drabeck said. "Unfortunately, I've been in this business a long time and our loss ratios are way out of proportion. I've come to your firm because I need a fresh look from an objective point of view. We have lawyers up and down the river, but they make money every time we have a loss. So, we decided to get someone new."

"This sounds interesting," she said, "but I don't know how we can help."

Schreiber answered her. "Mr. Drabeck wants us to study all of their loss files to look for patterns or preventative measures."

"Okay," she said, "but maybe we could start with a little education about the company."

"Sounds good," Drabeck said. "What do you want to know?"

"Give me the Cliff Notes version of your company," she said. "What it does? How many people work for it? Why it succeeds at what it does? Things like that."

"Okay," he said. "We're primarily in the towing business. We own some barges, but primarily we just push other people's cargo up and down the river. We have twenty towboats right now, and we have an excellent reputation. As for what makes us successful, I'm afraid I have to be immodest. It's me. I built this business and it's my pride and joy. If I had a son to pass it on to, the business could probably live on and even grow. Unfortunately, I have two daughters and they grew up before it was common for women to work. Their husbands both worked for the company at different times, but I'm afraid they're not management material. Furthermore, one of them isn't even my son-in-law anymore."

Amy was jotting notes but stopped to ask a question. "Is that why you're not retired and living the good life in Florida? Because you don't have anyone to take over the business?"

Drabeck smiled at her insightfulness. "I suppose that's it. I'm afraid that my future heirs see the company as the vehicle that has allowed us all to live well. For me, it's much more than that. You'll think this is corny, but loading up farmers' grain from the Midwest and bringing it downriver and then bringing other staples back upriver just makes me feel – I don't know -- patriotic or something. I love the way this country works and I love the way I feel like I'm right in the middle of it."

Amy smiled at him. "That's a work ethic that we usually only find in the history books."

"Look," he said hiding a trace of embarrassment, "I don't want to blow smoke about the 'Greatest Generation' or anything like that, but one of the best jobs I ever had was when I was a kid working in the K-Rations plant during World War II. We didn't make much money, but we showed up nights and weekends to assemble K-Ration kits for the army. We were all part of something extraordinarily big. Even the supervisors were tiny pieces in that big puzzle, but we were all working for one thing and not for our own personal gain."

"I'm obviously too young to know about that," she said, "but I think an event like a war might help unite people."

"Maybe," he said. "But I never wanted to run my business any other way. Yes, I make by far the most money in this company, but I do it by treating the employees as though we're all in a great venture together. Ultimately, my people tend to make more than they would elsewhere and, because I have the best people, I have the best reputation. We tried hiring MBAs, but they thought the way to make money was to spend less. Any dipshit can tell you that you'll increase profits for a year or two if you hold revenue steady while cutting costs. What they don't know is that cutting costs usually leads to poor performance and, in turn, lost revenue in the future."

"Well, if you have all the best employees, how come you have such high losses?"

He hesitated and then shrugged. "That's what makes me consider sabotage. My people are too good to be that sloppy."

"Who would want to sabotage you?"

He hesitated again. "This is confidential, right? I mean, I can't get sued for telling you what I think, can I?"

"That's right," she said. "Our communications are protected by the attorney-client privilege."

Drabeck still seemed uneasy discussing it, but showed some level of relief. "We have a prime operation and our competitors are jealous. Some of the other companies probably figure that if we go out of business they could step in and take over."

"I hear what you're saying, but I'm not connecting it to the sabotage theory. How would they accomplish it?"

"Well, maybe we have some malcontents that slipped through the cracks and want to hurt the company."

"That's possible, but I thought you had losses throughout the system."

"I guess that's true," he said. "But I can't really think of anything else that could explain it."

After an hour or so of questioning, Drabeck appeared to grow weary. "Ms. Prescott," he said, "I built this business up from next to nothing and it's the legacy to support my heirs. I may choose to sell it – on my terms – but I couldn't bear to just lose it. I need someone to help me get to the bottom of this before my company is destroyed one boat or deckhand at a time."

Schreiber had been watching quietly but finally spoke up. "We understand, Tony. We'll do what we can to get to the bottom of it. Y'know, it could turn out to just be a series of bad coincidences, but, if we can prove that, we should be able to persuade the insurance company to renew your coverage."

CHAPTER FIVE

AMY ARRIVED AT THE OFFICE EARLY Saturday morning. Mr. Schreiber was fond of saying that, in his day, Saturday was better known as "casual day." Back then, most of the lawyers came into the office on Saturday for at least a half day, but, because they weren't meeting clients, they treated themselves by going casual. Generation X seemed to shy from the tradition, while Generation Y acted indignant at the mere suggestion of working on a weekend.

Minnesota Marine Transport had delivered several boxes of legal files. Some were active cases and some were historical records. Amy's job was to learn the history, look for patterns, and make suggestions. Work this tedious demanded time without distractions.

After about an hour, she heard the front door open and slam shut. She normally felt some trepidation when she knew Schreiber was coming, but was hoping it would be him so he would see her working on a Saturday. She wasn't disappointed.

He stopped in the entrance to her office. "Nice to see someone else is helping to keep the lights on," he said.

"Well, there's a lot to digest in these files, so I figured I should start as soon as possible."

"Anything of interest so far?"

"Just one. The file I'm reading involves a collision with a railroad bridge, and . . ."

Schreiber held up a hand to stop her. "Actually," he said, "when a moving vessel hits a stationary object it's called an 'allision,' but I'm sure you'll pick that up soon enough."

She nodded her surprise. "Well, in any event, the captain of the towboat apparently lost control and smashed into the bridge. That's not really that remarkable, I guess, but now the company is suing the railroad because its bridge was in the way."

Schreiber smiled. "Does that seem strange to you?"

"Of course."

"Well, I think it has something to do with the law of navigable waters. If the railroad is going to build a bridge, it can't unreasonably restrict the vessels that want to use the river for transportation."

"So, you think the barge company can win that claim?" she asked.

"Maybe. Or maybe the attorneys knew the railroad would sue and just decided to be proactive. If the accident occurred in a spot where the river was the border between two states, it would be logical to bring the lawsuit in either of those states. By being the first to sue, perhaps the barge company got the case venued in a state that they thought would be more favorable to it."

"I see your point," she said. "Still, I think it would take awfully creative lawyering to blame a bridge because you ran into it."

"Well, you might be surprised. Guiding a tow down the river can be a tricky process. The river twists and turns, has shallow spots and islands, and can be affected by current, wind, and weather. To turn a tow requires that you start turning long before the actual curve. As a result, even an experienced captain can make all the right decisions and find himself in a situation where it's impossible to change course."

"Y'know, Mr. Schreiber, I find this all very interesting, but are you sure I'm the right person for this client. We have several male attorneys that are about my age and I think they might be a better fit."

"Nonsense," he said. "You'll get it down in no time. I thought about it and I'm sure you're the best person for the job." He turned to go, but then turned back. "I'll be around all morning. Maybe we can talk before lunch to see what else you've found."

"That would be fine. In fact, maybe we should have lunch together."

He put his hand to his chin to consider the matter. "What would people say if they saw an old goat like me out to lunch on a Saturday with a pretty young woman like you? I'm not sure I'd be comfortable."

"What do you think they'd say if they knew we were alone in this office? I think a restaurant might be a better setting. Besides, I'd like to talk to you about some other business."

He pondered it a moment longer. "Okay," he said. "I guess if anyone wants to think that we're romantically involved, they'll think I must have an awful lot of money. I suppose I can live with that."

Amy smiled and turned back to the files on her desk. She didn't need to learn the details in depth, but she needed to develop a working understanding. While the subject matter was new to her, she had to admit that it was holding her interest. The employment law issues she normally dealt with usually involved the same story – the marginal employee who insists that the failure to get a promotion was because of race, age, sex, national origin, sexual orientation, or something that they did or didn't do at the office holiday party. She found herself a lot more sympathetic to seamen who suffered serious physical injuries than she was to office workers who wanted a large payout for emotional distress every time something didn't go exactly their way.

At Schreiber's suggestion, they walked to The Palmer House for lunch. A restaurant in a hotel seemed like the last place to go for someone who was trying to avoid the appearance of having an affair. Apparently, Schreiber had warmed to the idea and thought it would actually be fun to have people thinking he could be in a romantic relationship with someone Amy's age.

"What else did you find in the files?" he asked.

"A lot of injured deckhands, a few collisions, and at least one allision. I don't know if the number of losses is unusual under the circumstances. I think I should probably meet with the insurance broker."

"Well, the loss numbers must be unusual. Otherwise the insurance company wouldn't be threatening to cancel the coverage. I agree, though, that you should arrange to see him. How about the lawyers?"

"I'd like to meet with some of them as well, but they're all over the map."

"Well, I think you should start with the loss over in Joliet. Someone needs to investigate it anyway, and, if you're on it, the company won't feel compelled to hire anyone else."

"Fair enough," she said. "What do you suggest?"

"Get the boat records and investigate who was on board and who could have been responsible. In fact, you should probably interview the crew as well."

"Okay," she said. "I think we're going to have to cover a lot of ground. Is it okay if I hire an investigator?"

"To do your job, or something else?"

"I'll do the interviews and everything, but I'd like to have someone to dig up criminal records, conduct surveillance, and things like that."

"That makes sense. Do you have someone in mind?"

"I don't think there's any reason to hire someone from Chicago because I don't think there's anything relevant in this area. I have a guy that I used to work with when I was doing criminal law in Wisconsin. His name is Ken Scouten. He was a cop then, but now he's retired and doing investigative work on the side. He's a known quantity, and his charges are fair."

"Sounds good," Schreiber said. "Let the client know, but make sure the investigator is paid directly by the firm – it helps preserve confidentiality."

Schreiber stopped talking for a while and turned his attention to his meal. Not talking made it look even more like they were a couple. After a pause that Amy found uncomfortable, he spoke. "So, what was the other business you wanted to discuss with me?"

"Well," she said hesitantly. "I've been here for five years and pretty soon I'll be up for partner. As you may have noticed, we don't have any women partners. So, I'd like to get some idea where I stand."

"We've had women partners in the past," he replied. "They left for various reasons, but I can assure you that we have no problem making women partners."

"It's not so much that," she said. "It's that I don't really feel like I have a mentor who I can rely on to keep me informed, to advise me, and to go to bat for me."

"Well, I'm not sure what I can do about that," he said. "I can tell you that we're all happy with your work."

"So, what does that mean when it comes to partnership?"

"Good work is a good place to start, but partners generally have clients of their own. If things go well with Minnesota Marine Transport, you could be doing yourself a real favor."

"And if they don't?"

"Well, you should be doing what you can to enhance your other opportunities."

"That's fine," she said, "but it doesn't seem like I get the same chances as the men."

"What do you mean?"

Amy felt like she was competing with two male associates who were at her same level of experience in the firm. "I don't think I get the same opportunities as the Tom-Tom Twins," which was her nickname for Tom Bethany and Tom Jackson. "They get invited to do *guy* things with clients. It seems like they're being given clients just because they go drinking and golfing, while I have to earn my stripes in the library."

"Amy, we entertain our clients in a way that they like to be entertained. If you can find prospects that want to go to the ballet or the opera, we'll pay for the tickets. For that matter, if you want to come along when we take clients hunting or to the football game, you're more than welcome. But don't think we're going to stop doing what we like to do just because you don't want us to do it."

Amy wasn't happy with that response. On the other hand, she didn't expect or even want them to change their marketing techniques. She just wanted to make sure she was getting some recognition. The Tom-Tom Twins were, in her opinion, suck-ups who couldn't hold a candle to her when it came to the practice of law. Yet, they seemed to be in tight with the powers in charge.

"Amy," Schreiber said, "maybe you should reconsider your *pro bono* and philanthropy projects. Most people work at the local food shelf in order to increase their visibility in the community. I keep seeing reimbursement requests from you for something called *The Manumission Commission*. What the hell is that?"

"Manumission is the word for the legal process for freeing a slave. *The Manumission Commission* is a network of legal professionals around the world dedicated to ending human sex trafficking."

"That's what I mean," he said. "I'm sure fighting human sex trafficking is a fine cause, but maybe you should start with your neighborhood before trying to solve the problems of the world."

Amy wasn't sure how she'd come to choose her battles. Chadwick thought it was her nature to choose the most impossible causes. For her part, food shelves were an unpleasant reminder of her childhood, so she opted for something else.

"I meet other professionals working with The Manumission Commission," she insisted.

Schreiber wasn't persuaded. "Most of those type of people work full time at their cause. You need to interact with business people who spend *some* of their time on civic and charitable causes. Why don't you join Rotary or the Junior League?"

"Mostly because those organizations don't need me. The Manumission Commission needs people with my skills to make a difference."

"No offense, but you've been working with them for quite a while and I don't know of any evidence that anyone's been saved. Maybe you need to start with smaller goals."

Amy didn't respond. She hadn't expected him to be sympathetic, but she didn't have any other good options. Finally, she just dropped it.

When the bill came, she grabbed it and insisted on paying. Anyone in the restaurant who might have thought she was Schreiber's trophy mistress would have been quickly disabused of that notion. Amy would have let him continue the illusion if he'd given better answers. Under the circumstances, however, she decided to deny him of that pleasure. She wasn't mean about it, but she was deliberate in her attempt to make it look like a business lunch.

CHAPTER SIX

AMY ARRIVED AT THE OFFICE EARLY ON MONDAY. It wasn't early compared to the rest of her working life, but it was early compared to her peers. Valiant was sitting at the reception desk and gave her a big smile. "Good morning," he said. And then, turning to the roster that he used to keep track of the office personnel, he said, "Ms. C. Amanda Prescott has reported for duty," and made a notation.

Amy had thought she might need to confront him and the rest of the mailroom staff about their unflattering nickname for her, but decided Monday morning was not the best time. She was generally recharged after the weekend and had some of her most productive moments on Mondays. Using her energy for a petty personal matter didn't seem like a good idea.

As it turned out, her intellectual energy would be in demand. There was a note on her desk from Schreiber that said, "See me, ASAP." She grabbed a note pad and proceeded straight to his office.

"You wanted to see me, Mr. Schreiber?"

"Yes. Thanks for coming right away. Minnesota Marine has a new problem. The longshoremen's union is picketing its operations in Paducah, Kentucky."

"What's it about?" she asked.

"I think it's mostly about the fact that Minnesota Marine isn't unionized."

Amy had a look of surprise. "What?"

Schreiber smiled. "There's something about seamen. Longshoremen might be the most unionized group anywhere, but the guys who work on the boats have never shown much interest in the unions."

"Why do you suppose that is?"

"Well, some of it probably has to do with the fact that they are already pretty well protected. Admiralty courts have always had a special

33

place in their hearts for seamen, and Congress apparently did too, because the Jones Act gives injured seamen rights that longshoremen don't have."

Amy's face pinched in as she thought. "If the seamen don't want the union, that's pretty much the end of the argument. I don't think a union can picket if it doesn't represent the workers," she said. "I mean, we don't do much of that work here, but my recollection of labor law is that unions have to be invited to the party. If at least a few of the employees don't ask for a union, the union can't go in and just demand to represent the employees."

Schreiber had a look of relief. "I think you're right about that, but, more importantly, I know you're right when you say that we don't do much of that work here. The fact that you seem to be familiar with it is a big help."

Amy pondered whether her zeal to show her breadth of knowledge had just earned her a trip to Paducah. "So, what do you want me to do?" she asked.

"I think we need to get a temporary injunction to stop it. You'll have to go to Paducah. I have a law school classmate who can act as local counsel, but I think we want to be in the lead on this."

Amy was right. She had talked her way into a trip to Paducah. She stood quietly for a moment and then something occurred to her. "Do you think the union could have anything to do with the losses? I mean, maybe there are some employees who want the union and they're doing things to make the job seem more dangerous and, in turn, one that requires a union to protect the employees."

"That's a good insight. I hadn't thought of that, but it's entirely possible. In any event, the client wants the picketing to stop. No it's not necessarily hurting business, but Paducah is a small town and the employees don't like the situation."

Amy thought about how she had planned to use the day to catch up on some miscellaneous matters that had been neglected for too long. "I'm on it," she said with resignation.

CHICAGO TO PADUCAH WAS NOT A ROUTE over which the major airlines battled. Amy booked a flight on a regional airline offering propeller plane service. If it didn't storm, she might not throw up. Fortunately for her and the other passengers, it was a calm, sunny day.

Arguing for a temporary injunction involved a peculiar balance. On the one hand, you wanted to present a well-written memorandum and supporting documentation. On the other hand, the thrust of such a motion was that bad things were happening and that you couldn't afford to wait another minute to have the matter resolved. The question, therefore, was always why you bothered to write a memorandum and other documents instead of going to court the minute the problem arose. Fortunately, trial court judges rarely raised that dichotomy.

Amy managed to schedule an emergency hearing for the next day. She had enlisted one of the new associates to draft briefs while she was in transit. She wasn't generally comfortable leaving that responsibility to someone else, but, under the circumstances, she had little choice. Ultimately, if the work product stunk, she could just pretend that the problem was so egregious that she came straight to court without the benefit of briefing. Fortunately, the memoranda satisfied her standards. It was a basic recitation of the standards for obtaining a temporary injunction – a strong likelihood of success on the merits at trial and irreparable harm if relief isn't granted in the interim.

She had spent plenty of time reviewing the arguments and her confidence showed in her stride as she walked to the courthouse. She met local counsel in the lobby, and then a surprise awaited her. The client, Jim Schreiber, or someone else had decided to send Tucker Sheridan to help persuade the Court. Amy suddenly felt a little nervous. "What are you doing here?" she asked.

"My title is Harbor Captain, and that makes me the contact person for union activity. If any employees want to hold an election to see if the employees will be unionized, they're supposed to bring it to me. That never happened." He held her gaze for a moment before saying, "Besides, now I get to watch you work."

"Do you think a *lawyerette* like me can handle the matter?" she said sharply.

His response was meek. "I guess I'll find out." By his tone, he seemed ready to be more of an ally than he had been in their previous encounter.

When he had defied her at the towboat fire, she resented the fact that she found him handsome. Now that he seemed to be on her side, she didn't feel bad about being attracted to him.

"Have you ever testified in court before?" she asked.

"No. I've had my deposition taken several times, but we never made it to court."

"Okay, I might need to call you as a witness. The most important thing is that you lose a little of your *machismo*. I know when you're on the job it's important for you to look like you're in complete control. In court, the judge is in control, and you can't do or say anything that appears to challenge or threaten that control."

He made a face like he'd bitten into a bitter lemon. "Are you saying judges all have some sort of complex that requires everyone to bow to them?"

"That's not what I'm saying. There are probably some that do, but what I'm saying is that court involves a protocol, and it's not a good idea to go against it. When a judge enters a courtroom, everyone is required to stand. Furthermore, everyone's required to address the judge as 'your honor.' Everything else we do needs to be consistent with that paradigm. The judge is in charge."

Sheridan still wasn't satisfied. "Maybe you better give me some examples of what I should and shouldn't do."

"For starters, don't try to be funny. Sometimes a little humor cuts the tension, but it's dangerous because the judge might not think it's funny. And don't try to show up the other side. Just answer questions. Try to act like you know what you're talking about, but don't brag about being an expert. Finally, if you don't understand something, politely tell the judge that you don't understand."

"That doesn't sound too hard."

Amy hesitated and gave him a saccharine smile. "And try not to refer to any of the female court personnel as 'honey,' 'sweetie,' or worse."

He looked a little embarrassed. "Point taken."

She led the group into the courtroom. Court was already in session, so they took seats in the gallery to wait their turn. Amy hadn't had a chance to do much research on the judge, other than to learn that his name was Paul Olson, but he was better known as "Bear" Olson. She didn't know the source of the nickname, but it certainly suggested someone with whom one should not trifle.

Federal district court judges are regularly called upon to sentence drug offenders, and Judge Bear Olson was doing his best to make sure the defendants would remember the day. He was loud, but he wasn't yelling. His word choices were enough to make the point. He seemed to be relishing the abuse he was inflicting on the defendants he was sentencing.

Amy gave Tucker a sideways look to reinforce the preparatory comments she had made in the hallway. Finally, Judge Olson did raise his voice. "I have to follow the sentencing guidelines, so you're not getting nearly as much time as you should. I'm making a note for the records, however, that I want to preside over any future proceedings if you decide to return to a life of crime. Next time I'll do what needs to be done." He paused and glared at the defendants. "Is that understood?"

Both defendants nodded.

"Is that understood?" he yelled.

"Yes sir," said the one, and "Yes, your honor," said the other one.

"Bailiff," the judge said. "Take these men away. Madam clerk, call the next case."

"Minnesota Marine Transport versus The International Brotherhood of Longshoremen and Harbor Workers," she said.

Amy led Tucker and her local counsel to a table on one side of the courtroom. Another group got up and took seats at the other counsel table. The recently-sentenced convicts were being led out a side door with Judge Bear Olson glaring at them as they left.

After the defendants and their lawyers were gone, Olson looked at his court reporter. "Let's go off the record," he said. Then, turning to his law clerk, he said, "How'd I do?"

She smiled. "You had me convinced."

The "Bear" smiled and shook his head. He looked at the lawyers and clients who had just been called for the next matter. "I'm trying a new strategy with criminal defendants. If those guys get convicted again, it's three strikes and I have no choice but to sentence them to life. I used to plead with defendants to get their lives in order, but that didn't seem to work. By making this day as unpleasant as possible, I'm hoping they'll get the message."

Amy thought about mentioning her own frustrations from her time handling criminal prosecutions, but thought that might be assuming a level of informality that would not be welcome. Instead, she just tried to make a thoughtful nod of approval at the strategy. At the same time, she felt relief that his ornery mood was apparently an act.

"Okay," the judge said. "Back on the record. Counsel, state your appearances."

Amy had made the motion, so she felt comfortable standing up and going first. She introduced Tucker Sheridan and the local attorney who had been hired to assist. One of the lawyers from the other team did likewise, and the hearing began.

Amy was brief and to the point. The right to unionize was a right granted to the employees. The union didn't have a right to force itself on the company or its employees. The picketing was illegal and had to be stopped immediately.

Opposing counsel quickly wrapped himself in the Constitution in an attempt to defend the union's actions. "Your honor, the First Amendment protects the right of assembly and the right of free speech. My clients were merely exercising their Constitutional rights. Our forefathers . . . *blah blah blah*, and our ancestors died defending . . . *blah blah blah*." Amy had heard these arguments before, but they were ordinarily made in "letters to the editor" written by people who apparently struggled to pass ninth-grade civics. This time, the argument was coming from a seasoned lawyer from one of Paducah's bigger firms.

Amy rose for rebuttal. "Your honor, the First Amendment says 'Congress shall make no law abridging freedom of speech or association,' and we're not dealing with an act of Congress. These people are just trespassers. They are free to speak and they are free to assemble, but nothing in the Constitution gives them the right to do so on other people's property."

Opposing counsel had apparently never learned that interrupting was impolite. He jumped up and yelled, "What about the entire civil rights movement? What about civil disobedience? We're just doing the same thing."

Amy let her mouth hang open and turned her palms up in a silent gesture to the judge, who quickly admonished opposing counsel for his failure to follow hearing protocol, much less his lack of manners. "Ms. Prescott," the judge said, "I apologize for the way you were interrupted, but why don't you address that issue before you're done."

"Gladly, your honor," she replied. "Civil disobedience is about disobeying unjust laws when you are politically powerless to affect the laws in any other way. Civil disobedience, as taught by Thoreau, and practiced by Martin Luther King, calls for the people disobeying the laws to acknowledge that they have broken the unjust law and then accept the punishment as a means to bring attention to the fact that the law is unjust. Civil disobedience does not let you break laws simply because you claim some sort of moral imperative."

The judge was nodding and seemed to appreciate how thoroughly she was dispatching an argument that had just been thrust upon her.

"What is the law that is unjust in this case?" she continued. "We're simply trying to enforce our basic property rights. Does the union honestly think that they're going to generate a groundswell to abolish trespassing laws so that anyone claiming a cause can come on your property in order to try and force that opinion on you or others? Furthermore, if they want to claim civil disobedience, let them all plead guilty to trespass and accept the punishment the way they're supposed to. Then we'll find out if there's public support for taking away basic property rights so that other people can use your property to speak and assemble." As she spoke, she became more and more animated, and her voice was getting louder.

Judge Olson held up a hand to get her to stop. "Let me interrupt you for a moment." Turning to opposing counsel, he asked: "Are you making any claim that the National Labor Relations Act gives you any rights, or is your argument based entirely on the Constitution?"

"We're not claiming a right under the existing language of the NLRA. We are trying to get that changed, and we're using civil disobedience to bring attention to that."

"Okay," the judge said, "but your clients all have normal political processes available to them, don't they?"

"Your honor?" the lawyer replied with confusion.

Judge Olson continued. "What I'm saying is, when civil disobedience was used in the civil rights movement, African Americans were frequently shut out of the political process by being denied the right to vote and things like that. In your case, your members are not part of a particular ethnic group, but are joined merely by their allegiance to the union. And there is no systemic barrier keeping them from trying to elect candidates who support their causes."

"That's true, your honor, but union workers are the little guys. They don't have as much power as some other people."

"Well, sir," the judge said, "that's why they join unions. And if you're saying the International Brotherhood of Longshoremen and Harbor Workers has no power, I'm afraid you're not going to have much credibility with this Court. I don't see any civil disobedience. I see only lawlessness. There are procedures for delivering your message and electing your candidates. If you are politically unpersuasive, that's just the way democracy works. Personally, I'd really like to see the city build a new stadium for our minor league baseball team, but breaking into the mayor's office to protest his lack of action on the subject does not immunize me from prosecution just because I claim it's the only way to get my message across."

As he spoke, Amy realized the battle was won. Still, she wasn't sure she wanted the war to end. So long as the Court granted her temporary relief, the lawsuit might help her if it continued. Specifically, if the union was causing the losses, the lawsuit might provide a means to investigate. In the end, the judge ordered the picketing to stop until further order. He left it to the parties to decide whether the lawsuit needed to go forward.

Amy left the courtroom with an adrenaline rush. She was so pleased by the forceful way the Court grasped her argument that she almost hugged Tucker Sheridan. Instead, she smiled at him. "I hope you were as impressed with the way I handled that as I was impressed with the way you handled that towboat fire."

He smiled. "I'm not sure I even understood half of the legal mumbo jumbo that was being said, but I could tell you kicked some ass."

She took his answer to mean "yes."

CHAPTER SEVEN

THE CREW OF THE M/V KAY DRABECK was temporarily reassigned to a towboat that had been chartered for it by the insurance company. Fortunately for Amy, the replacement boat was on its way to Moline, and she'd have a chance to start her investigation before they embarked.

When she arrived at the river, the replacement boat was already at the dock preparing to go. As she walked down the pier, she could feel the seamen's eyes on her. Nobody was saying anything, and that was almost worse because she imagined them doing coarse pantomimes behind her back.

As she stepped onto the towboat, she was startled by the sudden presence of an old man. His weathered skin made him look like he could have been a hundred. His salt and pepper hair was matted down by sweat, and several of his teeth were framed by gold. "Hello, sweetie," he said with a leer. "What can I do for you?"

"I didn't see you," she said in an attempt to persuade him that it wasn't his appearance that startled her. "I'm looking for Captain Murphy. Can you tell me where I can find him?"

"Are you sure you aren't here to see me? I have a lot more to offer a girl than the captain."

Amy bristled at his advances, but took some comfort that it was the old fashioned kind of harassment that men of a different generation did for amusement. Somehow, his comments weren't threatening and were almost entertaining. "Yes," she said dryly, "I can see that you really have quite a bit to offer someone like me. Is there a phone somewhere so I can call my mother and tell her my search for a husband is over?"

The old man was taken aback slightly by her answer, but then smiled. "Follow me," he said.

He led her onto the boat and up the stairs to the bridge. When they arrived, he said, "Captain, this lady says she'd rather see you than me."

"Captain Murphy," Amy said, "it's nice to meet you. I'm Amy Prescott from the law firm that's been hired by the company and I'd like to ask you some questions about the fire."

Murphy shrugged. "They said someone would be coming, but you should have gotten here sooner. We're about to get going."

"I apologize for not getting here earlier, but I came as soon as I was told you'd be here. This is pretty important, so I think you'll have to make some time."

"Well, I'm afraid that, in this business, there's nothing more true than the saying that 'time is money.' If you want to ride along we can let you off at the next lock, but I have a tow to pick up and it can't wait."

None of the available options appealed to her. "Perhaps if you could just give me the names of everyone who was on board at the time and who was on duty. That way, I can use them to reference the company's employment records and find out if any of them have been involved in other significant losses."

"That seems fair," he said. "You just met Ray. He's pretty much always on duty. His rank is first mate, but he's never really stopped being a deckhand."

"Okay. What's the rest of his name?"

"Dudley."

"How about the rest of the crew?"

"Tell you what. I'll give you a copy of the duty log. That has everyone's name and it shows when they were working and what they were doing."

"That would be great," she said. "Since we're trying to do everything in a hurry, can you tell me your understanding of what happened?"

Captain Murphy was flipping pages in a notebook and gave her only half his attention. "Not much to tell. We were coasting along and all of a sudden one of the engines was burning hot. I sent someone below to look and the whole thing was on fire. We needed to get the boat ashore, so we had to cut the tow loose. After we did that, I beached her as soon as I could."

"Why did they have to call in the Harbor Captain from Minneapolis to go onboard?"

The Captain glared at Amy. "Do you mean: Why didn't I put on the asbestos suit and go onboard?"

"I guess that's another way of putting it," she said apologetically.

"For starters, because I'm not crazy. More importantly, I'm hired to navigate and drive. The engines aren't my responsibility. The way we handled it was the policy. I think it has something to do with insurance. I think different rules apply if management gets killed or hurt."

"Was anyone on board doing anything to cause suspicion? I mean, is there any reason to think it was sabotage?"

"I haven't noticed anything unusual amongst the crew, if that's what you're asking. On the other hand, fuel lines usually don't just break. So, the accident does look a little suspicious, but I can't think of anybody on the crew who would be a suspect."

"Does everyone on board have access to the room where the fire started?"

Captain Murphy's focus went back to other things. "Yeah, it's not locked. But your average deckhand wouldn't likely know enough about engines to sabotage them without getting hurt."

He was now checking and writing entries in a book. "Look," he said, "I'm not kidding when I say we're pulling out. I'll walk you down to the dock, but you really have to get off."

"Okay, but what about my last question. Who knows enough about the engines to sabotage them?"

"Well, I suppose I know enough to sabotage them. The engineer would know 'cause that's his job. Ray would know on account of he's been on boats so long that there isn't anything he doesn't know. After that, nobody else would be required to know anything about the engines. Some know more than others just from past jobs or working on their own cars, but, as far as I know, none of them really know anything about boat engines."

The Captain led her down the stairs. When they got to the dock, Ray was waiting with his metallic smile. He held up a hand to help her off the boat. At that moment, she noticed he was missing the two smallest fingers on his left hand. She thought again about how workers in some industries suffer maiming or debilitating injuries, but get less compensation than those who claim that they once overheard their supervisor say the word "fuck."

"Come and visit us again soon," Ray said with a smile.

Only if my life doesn't improve, she thought to herself. "Thank you," she said, "but don't keep a light on for me."

CHAPTER EIGHT

A S SOON AS SHE GOT BACK TO THE OFFICE, she called Ken Scouten. When he answered, she said, "Sergeant Scouten, this is Amy Prescott calling."

"There's a voice from the past," he said. "Nobody calls me Sergeant anymore."

"Just habit, I guess. I heard you were doing private investigations now, and I need to hire someone."

"You heard right," he said. "I'm still in the business, but now I have a little more control over my schedule. I get to decide when I'm going to work and when I'm going to go deer hunting. Where are you working now?"

"I'm in Chicago. It's mostly corporate law, but we need someone to help with a corporate client with a lot of problems."

"Do I have to come to Chicago?"

"Probably not. The client is in the barge business, so it's more likely to be cities on the Mississippi, like Minneapolis or New Orleans."

"Can you get a Brandy Old Fashioned in those places?"

Amy chuckled at Scouten's devotion to the unofficial state cocktail of America's Dairyland. "I'm pretty sure you can," she said. "I might even buy you one."

"That sounds like a deal," he said. "Frankly, it'll be good to work with competence again. Once you left the Marathon County Attorney's office, it went to shit. I might not have taken early retirement if there had been anyone there who could actually convict the scumbags I worked my ass off to arrest."

Amy absorbed the flattery. Scouten was old school, as he'd been in law enforcement since before the time the Supreme Court determined that the first responsibility of the police is to try to talk criminals out of confessing. She had originally expected he would have difficulty working with a woman, but her conviction record quickly caught his attention and respect.

She proceeded to give him the background of the problems and the names of the crew. "I don't know exactly what your role will be, but I know I need help," she said.

"I'll get started right away." For all of the flattery he had directed at her, the fact that she tracked him down for this assignment was perhaps the most flattering thing of all.

CHAPTER NINE

THE LEGAL FILES THAT SHE HAD reviewed were interesting, but they generally only contained information on disputed claims. The insurance files would be more comprehensive. That meant a trip to St. Louis.

Minnesota Marine was insured through one of the big insurance brokerages, and it had a St. Louis office that specialized in river traffic. Amy arranged to spend a day at their office meeting with the main broker and his staff. She wasn't sure what she needed to do in order to make sure people took her seriously, so she just hoped.

The broker's name was Ted Hollerback. He met Amy in the lobby and enthusiastically escorted her to a conference room. Ted was middle aged and dressed like fashions hadn't changed since he joined the working world. He wore a short-sleeve polyester shirt with a tie that came about halfway down his stomach. He looked like someone who was seriously disappointed that he could no longer find white dress shoes.

"Here's the stuff," he announced. "I don't think you'll find it very interesting. Did you bring golf clubs along? I think you'd have more fun at the club."

Amy smiled at the offer. "I'm afraid I didn't. And I don't have a hotel for tonight, so I have to get through all this stuff today."

"Suit yourself," he said. "Do you want to talk to me first, or do you want to look at the files?"

"I guess we should talk first. Otherwise I don't think I'll know what's here."

"Sounds okay," he said as he poured himself a cup of coffee. He nodded an offer to her, but she shook her head to decline. "Drabeck has only been my client for a few years," he said. "There was a guy in our Minneapolis office that had all the big barge accounts, but he retired. Guess he wanted to play more golf."

"That's odd," Amy said. "I thought that the main thing insurance brokers did was play golf. Why would someone retire from playing golf in order to play golf?"

Hollerback smirked. He didn't seem offended by the comment. In fact, he seemed proud. "Probably got tired of having to let his clients win."

He took a seat at the conference table. "If you want to exchange barbs about professions, I think I might know a few lawyer jokes."

She smiled in an attempt to soften her earlier jab. "I'm sure I've heard them already."

"How about the lawyer with the ethical dilemma. Did you hear that one?"

She shook her head. "I don't think so."

"An old woman comes in for legal advice. At the end, she's told it will be $250 and she decides to pay cash. After she leaves, the lawyer realizes that she overpaid by $50. Now, he has an ethical dilemma."

"Why's that?"

"He doesn't know whether he should split the extra money with his partner!"

One of the people in the room laughed uproariously at the joke and, perhaps not surprisingly, it was the person who told it.

"Okay," she said with a smile that was more submission than amusement. "Let's call it even and get down to business. What can you tell me about Minnesota Marine and its loss records?"

He raised his eyebrows in an attempt to foreshadow the magnitude. "From an insurance standpoint, they're hitting on all cylinders. They've had cargo losses, pollution claims, injured seamen, collisions and allisions, and now a boat fire. If there's insurance for it, they've probably had a claim."

"Do you have any theories or ideas as to why the claims have taken such a jump?"

Hollerback rubbed his chin, as though looking thoughtful would help him actually be thoughtful. "It's really across the board. You can't just blame one thing or one area. Some things can be blamed on the captains, but other things happened without explanation."

BOB GUST • 49

"Would you say it's atypical?"

"Certainly. The losses are well above what the bean counters at the insurance companies expect, and that's why the insurance coverage is in jeopardy."

"Well, my job is to figure out why. Any ideas about who would benefit from all of these losses?"

He again tried to look pensive.

Amy didn't wait for an answer. "Perhaps we should start with you. Aren't you paid a percentage of the premium as a commission? As a result, as losses go up, don't rates go up and, in turn, doesn't your commission go up?"

Again, Hollerback looked more proud than offended. "Is this a great country or what?"

Amy barely smiled. "It's true, isn't it, that you benefit financially when your clients have bad losses?"

"That's true to a point, but this case disproves it. Too many losses and there's no coverage at all. So, yes, if you think I could somehow be on all those different boats sabotaging things, then I do make more money for a while. The problem is that it's sort of killing the goose that lays the golden eggs. Furthermore, losses create work for me. If I can sell an insurance policy and never hear from the insured until it's time for the renewal, I'm as happy as can be."

Amy had her doubts, but couldn't reasonably expect a confession under these circumstances. "Well, who else would benefit from so many losses? If this can't be explained as typical, then we have to look at who might be trying to influence the situation."

"The question isn't who benefits from losses – because I admit that I do. The question is who benefits from so many losses that the company is driven out of business."

Amy hadn't been holding Hollerback in high regard, but she appreciated his ability to frame the issue. "Yeah," she said, "I guess that's right."

"Do you know about the buy-out offer?" he asked.

Amy suddenly had a feeling that this meeting wasn't going to be the waste of time she had feared. "No. I met with the owner and he said other companies wanted to buy him out, but he didn't mention anything in particular."

"I think that's because he's in denial. Amalgamated Grain wants to acquire Minnesota Marine, but Drabeck doesn't want to sell out. Tony probably didn't mention it because he wants to pretend the offer doesn't exist."

"So, would these losses lower the purchase price?"

"Maybe, but the more important thing is that they might lower Drabeck's resolve. He has shown no interest in selling even though he should retire, but this might force the issue."

"Okay, but how could Amalgamated Grain be causing the losses?"

"I didn't say that they could. I just said that they were possibly benefiting from the losses because it might help the purchase to go through."

"I don't understand why Drabeck doesn't just sell," she said.

"Don't underestimate the desire for immortality. If the business lives on, he feels like he lives on."

"I suppose," she said.

"Make no mistake about it," he said, "that's one of the great things that drives the world. Think of all the museums, theaters, and university buildings that exist because people decide they want to be remembered by people other than their heirs. Tony Drabeck is a prince. He doesn't want to die and have his business die with him. He wants a legacy."

The discussion with Hollerback continued far longer than Amy expected. His insights into Tony Drabeck seemed logical. Unfortunately, she still didn't have any clear leads.

CHAPTER TEN

AMY RETURNED TO HER OFFICE TO find that Scouten had already sent the criminal records of the crew of the M/V Kay Drabeck. The reports were unremarkable, with one exception. Few of the crew members had completely clean records, but the crimes were what you'd expect from seamen on leave. The exception was Raymond Dudley. Scouten indicated that he couldn't find any evidence that Ray Dudley even existed.

Amy called the personnel department at the company and asked for his file. She was told that no such file existed. Exasperated, she called Tony Drabeck. "Mr. Drabeck," she said when he came on the telephone, "this is Amy Prescott and I'm calling because I'm investigating the crew and I can't find any information about this guy Ray."

Drabeck paused for a moment. "You don't need to investigate Ray. There's nobody that I trust more in this company."

"I understand," she said, "but getting to know things about him might help me know things about people he knows."

"Look," he said with some impatience, "I didn't hire you to investigate people who pose no threat to me whatsoever. Checking out our employees is fine, but save your energy with Ray. He's been with the company forever and, if I know anything about people, he's not an issue."

His response was only raising Amy's concerns, but she didn't want to be difficult. "That's fine," she said. "In fact, maybe that's the best reason to talk to him about what happened. It sounds like he's your most trusted guy, so I don't have to worry about getting the runaround." She didn't believe her own statement, but it was the best way to continue her investigation of Raymond Dudley without upsetting her client.

"That would be okay," Drabeck said with less than full enthusiasm. "His boat will be in the Quad Cities in a couple days. He'll have a little time while they go through the lock. You might be able to call him, but it might be easier to go see him."

Amy got the details and was determined to be there when the tow arrived in order to make sure she didn't get short-changed the way she had the last time. "Thank you, sir. I'm doing my best to help you figure this out, and he may hold some answers."

"I'm sure you are," he said, before abruptly hanging up the phone.

CHAPTER ELEVEN

AMY WAS WAITING WHEN RAY walked off the dock. He was walking with his head down, but caught a glimpse of her. "Hi there," he said as if he were a sailor in any port addressing a "professional" woman waiting at the docks for guys like him. "Are you here to see me this time?"

"Actually, yes."

That response took him a little by surprise, but he quickly recovered. "Don't let the captain see us," he said with a wink.

As unappealing as she found his advance, she was mildly amused by his banter. "I'm afraid I'm just here for some conversation," she said. "Can we go somewhere so that I can ask you a few questions about the M/V Kay Drabeck and your long career at Minnesota Marine Transport?"

Ray was trying to act crestfallen, but his act wasn't generating much sympathy. "Buy me a cup of coffee and I'm all yours."

Amy led him up the dock. They found a suitable coffee shop and went inside.

They sat down and Ray stared at her. He was enjoying being in Amy's company and, more importantly, being seen in her company. "What can I do for you?" he said.

"For starters, I need to know who you are. We ran a routine background check on the crew of the Kay Drabeck and we couldn't find anyone who could possibly be you. We found a lot of Ray Dudleys, but, when we cross-matched them by age and geography, there was no way any of them were you."

Ray raised his three-fingered hand up and rubbed his eye with the knuckle of his forefinger. "That's probably because you got my name wrong."

"What?" she said.

"My name's not Ray Dudley. It's Dudley Raymond. People call me Ray because I don't really care for the name Dudley. Something about having the nickname "Dud" just doesn't work for me."

Amy wondered how she could have missed that possibility. She didn't want to look like a rookie, however, so she decided to act like that was only the start of her questions. "Well, that clarifies some issues, but I have a lot more." Amy wanted to get as much information as possible to make sure that her investigator could find everything that was possibly relevant. "How old are you?" she said.

"Sixty-eight on my next birthday," he announced with some pride suggesting that he had lived longer than people would have thought.

After getting his precise date of birth, she asked about his marital status and his wife's name. "And how old is your wife?"

"Sixty-four," he said.

Her line of questioning was of marginal relevance, but she decided to close the loop. "Any children?"

Ray got a little smile and his steel-blue eyes twinkled behind his woeful countenance. "Still trying," he said.

Amy laughed involuntarily and almost spit out her drink. "Well, keep trying. I'm sure it's meant to be."

Amy didn't hesitate to phone this new information to Sergeant Scouten. Getting Ray's name right was probably enough to solve the puzzle, but the information about age and spouse might reveal something else. She wasn't disappointed.

A couple days later, Scouten called back. "I got the info on Dudley Raymond," he said. "He did six years for manslaughter. It was so long ago that I can't really find any other records. I don't know the details, but I know he's a convicted felon."

That revelation took Amy's breath away. She had been alternately amused and unnerved by Ray, but the knowledge that he had killed someone pushed her opinion decidedly to the negative. It was bad enough working around people who didn't respect her, but having to deal with a convicted killer made it that much worse. "Is there any way we can find out more about it?" she asked.

"I'll try, but a lot of records from before there were computers were not put in the database. I can go to the courthouse where it happened, but don't count on me finding anything."

"How about the other issue we talked about, the buy-out? Have you found any information about that?"

"I don't know anything about any offers, but I've got a good idea of who would benefit from it. As far as I can tell, the company was set up with the kids being part owners to avoid taxes. Unfortunately, the kids, and in particular the in-laws, are most interested in what the business can be sold for."

"Are you talking about the sons-in-law?"

"Yes. They don't seem too interested in running a barge business. In fact, one of them isn't even with the company anymore because I think there was a divorce."

"Thanks," she said. "Call me if you find anything else."

CHAPTER TWELVE

AMY GOT TO THE OFFICE shortly before the weekly litigation meeting started, so she went straight to the conference room and took a seat. Blowing her own horn was not her style, so she waited for Schreiber to convene the meeting and sing her praises regarding the temporary injunction. In the interim, she just made the usual small talk with the other lawyers. The Tom-Tom twins were laughing boisterously on the other end of the conference table, but she ignored them.

Schreiber called the meeting to order. "I have some big news," he announced to the group. "As some of you know, our colleagues Tom Bethany and Tom Jackson have been actively marketing our services to the General Counsel at Interstate National Bank. This past weekend, Tom Bethany brought him as a guest to the Invitational at Medinah Country Club, and they won the tournament. For those of you who don't golf, Medinah will be hosting the PGA Championship in a couple years. As a result, winning the Invitational is a big thrill. I think we can count on seeing a little of Interstate's work flowing our way. Let's give him a big hand."

Amy clapped along with the rest. She wasn't sure Bethany knew the difference between a mortgage and a movie ticket, but he apparently had skills where they mattered the most.

Schreiber made a few other announcements and then proceeded around the table to have each lawyer discuss their workload and needs. When Amy had helped land work from Minnesota Marine, it had been worth mentioning. Her big victory in court apparently didn't meet the criteria.

When it was her turn, she didn't hesitate to talk about her victory in Paducah. The other lawyers smiled and nodded in congratulation. Jim Schreiber said, "I remember when you were trying to get out of this assignment. It seems like you're taking a liking to it all of a sudden."

She shrugged her shoulders. "Going to court can be an exhilarating experience. I guess that's why we do what we do. Getting a win just adds to that."

"Well," Schreiber said, "I'm glad you're warming up to it because I have another assignment for you with respect to that client."

The temporary injunction had been dropped on her like a bomb, so she held her breath wondering what was to come.

"Minnesota Marine had another loss down in Mississippi. The insurance company said it was going to cancel coverage. Tony Drabeck and I were on the phone with the insurance people all day yesterday. It took a lot of persuading, but we got them to postpone the cancellation based on certain promises."

Amy had a feeling of dread as she pondered how she figured into those promises.

"We told them we'd put a safety inspector on board one of the boats to observe all of the practices and procedures and to recommend ways to make the operations safer."

Amy breathed a sigh of relief. "Good idea. Where did you find a safety inspector?"

Schreiber smiled, but it was not infectious as far as Amy was concerned. "The problem is that the insurance company has already sent people and that didn't help. We told them we needed someone from outside the industry. We decided that you would be the best person to go onboard to observe and evaluate. You'll start in St. Paul and travel down the Upper Mississippi to St. Louis. It will only take a little more than a week."

"Excuse me," she said. "Are you talking to me?"

The rest of the people in the meeting let out a chuckle. "Of course I'm talking to you," Schreiber said. "This is your client, and I don't want anyone else horning in on you."

Amy was not moved by the claimed deference to her relationship with the client. "I'm guessing, but I'll let you tell me, that there aren't a lot of women working on these boats."

"That's true," Schreiber said, "but it's not as bad as you might think. The boats have separate quarters for the cook, and the regular cook is still recovering from her injuries from the boat fire."

"So, I'm going as the cook?"

"No, no," he said. "I guess the crew has been doing their own cooking while she's been out. But you will have separate quarters, so you don't have to worry about your privacy."

"But I will be the only woman?"

"Yes. And I will admit that the women who usually cook on the boats tend to look more like Aunt Bea on Andy Griffith than you do, but you'll be fine."

Amy was shaking her head in quiet protest. "Assuming I agree to this, what is it you want me to find?"

Schreiber stiffened a little at her response. "The partners at Schreiber, Marko & Meath don't really consider this to be a negotiation. You're being given this assignment. If you want to decline, you're basically resigning from the firm."

His comment momentarily paralyzed her. "Okay," she finally said. "Just what is it you want me to find?"

"Just look at it with fresh eyes. These guys might be used to doing things in a certain way and may not even recognize the risks. We want you to spend a week observing and prepare a report about how to improve safety. For the benefit of the insurance company, we need to convince them that we're actively researching the problem to find a solution. That's your job. Don't do anything dangerous. Just stay inside the towboat out of the way and watch the process."

"Aye, aye," she said upon realizing that she had no choice. "When do I set sail?"

CHAPTER THIRTEEN

AMY SPENT MOST OF FRIDAY with a feeling of dread. As bad as her impending assignment seemed, it didn't match the anxiety that she felt about her trip home. This was to be the first meeting between her family and her boyfriend. She had been dating Chadwick for almost a year, but had done what she could to keep this day from coming. She knew her family would not be enamored with the high-society nature of her boyfriend, and was even more terrified of his reaction to her rural roots.

Chadwick Pemberton was everything Amy left Prairie du Chien to find. His family was rich, but it wasn't necessarily the money that attracted her to him. Chadwick was refined -- he could taste the difference between a Syrah and a Shiraz, and he could explain the reasons. He was polite – as their dating led to increased degrees of intimacy, he always asked permission. He was sophisticated – as he'd sooner watch the symphony than football. The hardscrabble life in rural Wisconsin did not produce many men of that type.

He picked her up in his BMW after work. As she exited her building, he jumped from the car to assist her.

"What are those on your feet?" she said with surprise.

"Those are my new cowboy boots. I thought I should try to look the part. Do you like them?"

She smiled, but it was because of amusement and not joy. "Do you really think they go with that V-neck tennis sweater you've got tied around your shoulders?"

"Hey, I'm just hoping to fit in. I don't want to be mistaken for a local."

"Trust me," she said. "The fact that you don't get your hair cut by a relative while sitting in someone's kitchen is probably enough for people to know that you're not a local."

Chadwick was amused. "You make it sound as though we're going to the Smokey Mountains to visit your six-fingered, coal-mining kin. I've never been to Prairie du Chien, but I can't believe it's as bad as you make it sound. I mean, it has kind of a cool name."

Amy laughed involuntarily. "It means 'prairie of the dog.' Look, I never meant to suggest that Prairie du Chien is bad, per se. What I want you to realize is that my family is not the most sophisticated. Before there were wine coolers, nobody in my family had ever drunk wine. The closest they ever came was whatever that beer is that calls itself the 'Champagne of Beers.' I think it's fair to say that my genealogy includes at least a Camaro or two."

"That's it!" Chadwick said. "The "C" in C. Amanda Prescott stands for 'Camaro.' You don't want anyone to know because you were probably conceived in the back seat of one."

She smiled, but not because she thought it was funny. "If that's what you want to think, have at it."

He was staring at her looking for more of a reaction. "What's the big secret about your first name? Don't you think you should tell me what it is?"

"Chadwick," she said, "if we ever get to the point where we're filling out an application for a marriage license, I'll put my full name on it. Until then, can't you just be happy dating someone named Amy?"

"Yes, I can be happy, but I'd be happier if I was dating someone who felt strongly enough about me to share her most embarrassing things."

"I didn't say I was embarrassed about my first name. I just don't use it and I don't want anyone else to be tempted to use it for any reason."

"You didn't say that you were embarrassed about it, but it's pretty clear that you are."

She let out a deep breath. "Is there anything else we can talk about?"

He hesitated and then shrugged his shoulders. "I suppose." He thought some more and then said, "So tell me, are you the only one who escaped from the farm, or were there others?"

"Well, since I never knew who my real father was, I guess he might have escaped. Believe me, though, my family thinks that I'm the one who's odd. When I told them I'd saved my money from selling eggs and I wanted to go to boarding school, they were only too happy to let me go.

The idea of college was a complete shock to them, which was probably good because their lack of financial preparation helped me get a scholarship. When they found out I wanted to spend another three years and go to law school, they knew I was lost to them forever."

"Well, I'm glad I found you."

"Fate's funny," she said. "Just think. If we hadn't both gone to that fine arts fundraiser, we would've never met."

"Oh!" Chadwick said with a start. "There's a Starbucks. Let's stop."

"I don't think I need caffeine at this time of day, but we can get you something."

Chadwick pulled the car into the lot and they went in. Given the time of day, the crowd was minimal. "Half caf, extra hot, double latte with a vanilla shot," he said.

Amy closed her eyes and shook her head at the production involved with ordering a cup of coffee. The woman behind the counter looked at her for her order. "Nothing for me," she said. "I want to be able to sleep tonight."

"You should get what I got," Chadwick said. "It won't keep you up."

"I'm afraid that the day that it takes me a whole sentence to order a cup of coffee is the day I quit the human race."

Chadwick rolled his eyes as if she was the one with the snobbish attitude.

Amy just smiled and waited. "Do you want me to drive?" she asked.

"Well, I think I can drive and drink coffee, but it might be easier since you know where we're going."

Chadwick's drink was delivered and the pair restarted their journey. "This car's got a lot of power," he said. "Do you think you can handle it?"

"Gee, I'll try," she said sarcastically. They got in the car and she started the engine. She had one foot firmly on the brake, but put her other foot on the accelerator. She put the car in drive and it lurched and stopped in an awkward fashion. It was her way of getting even with him for patronizing her.

They drove on the Interstate for as long as they could. Darkness came about the same time that they had to switch to two lane roads. Amy was familiar with the area and glad that she was behind the wheel.

Chadwick had nodded off, but he was now awake and ready to chat. "Tell me again who I'm going to be meeting."

"Did you see the *Beverly Hillbillies* movie?"

"They can't be *that* bad," Chadwick said.

"Don't get me wrong," she said. "I don't think that they're bad people, but they have a lifestyle that isn't for me."

"So, what makes you different?"

"Mostly the fact that I give a shit."

"And you're the only one?"

Amy paused to formulate her answer. "I think my Mom gave a shit and wanted something better in life. She fell in love with a stranger who came to town and she thought all of her prayers had been answered. She got pregnant with me and he never came back. I think she thought that was her punishment for having a dream and decided to basically give up."

"Well, your stepfather must be a pretty good guy if he was willing to raise a child that wasn't his."

Amy was subconsciously shaking her head. "I think that was just the price he was willing to pay. He got to marry someone that was completely out of his league. Before I was in the picture, my mother could date pretty much anyone she wanted, but having a kid changed her options."

"She must have seen something in him?"

Amy had been sharing most of her secrets and didn't see much reason to stop. "I think she would have stayed single, but she didn't have much of a choice. When I was little we lived in a part of town called 'the Fourth Ward.' It was actually an island in the river where the town was first founded. Over the years, the town grew, but the Fourth Ward never got a sewer system or other modern conveniences. It was like living on the wrong side of the tracks, except it was the wrong side of the channel. We had a big flood when I was about five and the government decided to move everybody out. They bought everyone's property, but we were renting. We didn't really have anywhere to go, so my Mom married a farmer and we moved in with him."

"So, you don't like your step-father?"

"We don't really care for each other."

"I guess that's because you're literally the red-headed stepchild."

Amy was quiet for a moment and then said, "It's auburn. My hair is auburn."

"Whatever you say," Chadwick nodded.

She was quiet for another moment. Then, almost under her breath, she said, "Y'know, if you paid more attention during oral sex you'd know that my natural hair color isn't auburn."

"What?" he said with shock. "Did you just say what I think you said?"

She smiled, almost as shocked at what she had said as he was. "I didn't say anything," she giggled.

"I don't think I imagined it, because I don't think I could have imagined something like that."

She gave him a sideways glance and shrugged her shoulders. She was still amused with herself, but said, "Maybe we should find a new topic."

"I think we should go back to the topic we were on," he said. "Did you resent your step-father because you had to share your mother with him or did he resent you for it?"

She looked straight ahead as she responded. "I think he didn't like me because I was a reminder that my mother had been in love with someone else before him."

"That might explain why he didn't like you, but it doesn't explain why you didn't like him. Did he do something to you?"

She exhaled audibly. "Not exactly. Maybe we just got off on the wrong foot and never recovered."

Chadwick was looking at her waiting for more. Finally, she obliged. "My first summer at the farm, we had a heat wave. We had this big sow, and she looked like she was suffering something awful. I went and got a bucket of cold water and threw it on her. I guess she went into some kind of shock or something, and she died. My stepfather went ballistic. I may have made a mistake, but I was only trying to help." Amy was quiet for a moment. "After that, I tried to avoid him as much as possible."

That seemed to satisfy Chadwick. He reclined his seatback and they drove on in silence. There was no moon out, and the night took on a dark blue color that seemed to envelop them. Oncoming traffic was intermittent, so the high beams were going on and off with regularity. Fortunately, there wasn't a lot of traffic going their direction.

After a while, they entered bluff country and the road began to wind up, down, and around. Passing on the two-lane road became more of an issue, but the real concern was people passing who were going the opposite direction. Before long, a semi-truck was behind them and its headlights filled the cabin of the BMW. It wasn't necessarily tailgating, but it felt close. "Boy, this guy's really up our ass," Chadwick said.

An opening came and the truck moved across the dashed yellow line to pass. Given its size, it didn't accelerate particularly fast. Once it was in front of the car, Amy flashed her high beams. Chadwick looked at her with surprise. After the trucker had moved back into the right lane, he turned his lights off and then back on.

"What the hell did you do that for?" Chadwick asked. "I mean, I know he was tailgating, but flashing him was basically the same as giving him the finger. Now he's pissed at us and we're out here in the middle of nowhere."

Amy turned her head to see a somewhat frightened Chadwick. "You don't get out of the city much do you?"

"What does that mean?" he said.

She paused as she thought how to be as delicate as possible. "Flashing my high beams was just my way of signaling him that he could move back into the right lane. People don't drive like that anymore, but there was a time when drivers communicated without their horns and middle finger. His light flash was just his way of saying 'Thanks.'"

Chadwick was a little embarrassed by his lack of savvy, but the embarrassment was outweighed by the relief that he wouldn't have to fight a truck driver on a lonely road in rural Wisconsin.

Before long, they turned off the state highway onto a county road. Soon, they were driving on what was less than a country road. Finally, they came to a gravel driveway and Amy pulled in. There was a house and some other buildings, but it was too dark to see much. Only one window of the house was illuminated.

The night air was cool, and it seemed to amplify the noise from closing the car doors. Chadwick stood by the trunk, but he was looking at the sky. "Look at all the stars," he said. "I've never seen anything like it."

The porch light came on and the screen door creaked open. "I was starting to wonder about you," a woman said.

"You didn't have to wait up for us," Amy said as she and Chadwick removed their bags from the trunk. "Mom, this is Chadwick. Chadwick, this is my mom, Judy Prescott."

Mrs. Prescott was a striking woman. She did not have Amy's refined looks, but the two of them otherwise looked like they could have been sisters. "Nice to meet you," she said. "My husband would've waited up, but the morning milking comes pretty early."

Chadwick shook her hand, and Mrs. Prescott led them into the house. They quietly followed her through the kitchen, through the living room, and up the stairs. "I found your old comforter," she said to Amy. "And I moved my sewing out of the other bedroom so that Chadwick would have a place to sleep."

"Mother, we've been dating for more than a year. I hate to tell you, but we've slept together before."

"Good," the older woman answered. "Then you won't feel compelled to do it when you're under my roof."

"Mother," Amy protested.

Mrs. Prescott guided Chadwick into his room. Pointing to a porcelain pail with a lid on it she said, "There's the pot in case you have to get up at night."

"The what?" he said.

"The chamber pot. There's no bathroom up here, and I don't think you want to be stumbling around if you have to go."

Chadwick nodded his understanding and everyone said good night.

CHAPTER FOURTEEN

THE ROOSTER CROWED AT DAWN. Amy wasn't expected to milk any cows, however, so she rolled over and went back to sleep. Her featherbed provided a sanctuary like nothing she had experienced since leaving the farm. It wasn't that she liked the farm or thought she'd had a particularly great childhood. Instead, it was probably because being at home reminded her of a time when she had few responsibilities and people expected little from her.

By the time she got up, the milking was done and the breakfast had been eaten. She had managed to avoid seeing her stepfather, and that was okay with her. A pot of coffee had been left on, so she filled her cup and went outside.

Little had changed at the farm since she was a child. The gravel driveway ran in a circle in front of the house and then down to the barn before heading back out to the road. There were a variety of other buildings, and none of them looked like they had seen fresh paint in years. Her mother had decorated the area with a variety of tasteless lawn ornaments. Amy had persuaded her to remove the black stable boy and the girl who looked like Aunt Jemima's daughter, but the pink flamingos and a few other choice items remained.

The area circumscribed by the driveway was sort of a play area when she was little. The rope swing that she had used as a child was still there, although it appeared to have been updated for her sister's kids. She sat on the swing and began pumping her legs, albeit with considerably less zeal than a twelve-year-old. She had spent a lot of time on the swing as a child, and it was bringing back memories.

Along with the cacophony from the chicken coop, the pump in the barn ran in a regular rhythm as the motor worked to bring water up, followed by the noise of a release. Every so often, she could hear the sound of vehicles out on the county highway. It wasn't the sound of the engines, however. Instead, the rubber on the road made a gentle whir that carried through the morning air. If it weren't for the condition of the buildings, the setting would be downright bucolic.

She heard the screen door squeak behind her and soon Chadwick joined her. "Sleep okay?" she asked.

"Not bad. Fortunately, I didn't feel the need to pee, so I didn't have to negotiate the chamber pot."

"Be thankful you didn't have to go to the Joneses."

"The what?" he asked.

"The Joneses. That's what we call the outhouse. Whenever anyone goes there they say something like, 'I'm going over to the Joneses to see if they need help with their new fence.'"

Chadwick chuckled at the explanation. "Are you saying you didn't have indoor plumbing when you were growing up?"

"No. We had indoor plumbing, but that didn't mean we didn't use the outhouse. If you were out working in the fields, it was easier to use the outhouse than to clean your feet to go into the house."

"I think I'd go to the trouble of taking off my shoes."

"That wasn't always an option," she said. "Because I was the oldest, I didn't get hand-me-down shoes. So, until I wore out a pair of good shoes, I pretty much went barefoot until the snow came."

"I guess that made it pretty important to watch your step."

She shook her head wondering whether she should continue. "Actually, it was the opposite of what you think. In the spring and fall, it could be pretty cold rounding up the cows. I'd look for a fresh cow pie and stand in it to warm my feet."

"You're kidding?" he chuckled.

"I'm afraid not."

Chadwick took a seat in an Adirondack chair. He took in a deep breath as though the country air actually was some sort of magic elixir. As he looked around to take it all in, he said, "So, this is where you grew up."

Amy suddenly saw things through his eyes and became self-conscious about the condition of things. "Pretty fancy, huh?" she joked. "Kind of easy to see why someone would move to the big city."

"Oh, I don't know. There's something to be said for the country."

"Well, I'm afraid this farm is a little rundown."

Chadwick shrugged and looked around. He stopped and focused on the silo, or at least what looked like a facsimile thereof. "What's the deal with the silo? Isn't it supposed to have a dome on top? Did a storm blow it off, or didn't your stepfather have the money to finish it?"

"Neither. If the crops in the silo get wet, they start to ferment."

"That sounds like a reason to have a dome."

"That's true, but the dome also holds in the fumes. When I was little, a farmer in the next county was overcome by the fumes and died. After that, a lot of farmers removed the tops. The crops got wet, but at least the fumes had someplace to go."

Chadwick shook his head in disbelief.

"See what I mean about wanting to get away from this lifestyle," she said.

Chadwick nodded. "Well, if you're the oldest and you wanted to get out of here, why didn't your siblings want to follow in your footsteps?"

She took a deep breath, as though she'd wondered the same thing before. "I really don't know. Trust me, I love my brother and sister, but they just never seemed to have much curiosity about the world outside this county, much less outside the state or the country."

"How about the friends and neighbors you grew up with? There must be other people who've moved to the big city."

"Only if you count Davenport, Iowa as a big city. Just about everyone I grew up with is likely to die within one hundred miles of where they were born."

"Are you telling me that nobody you knew growing up was ever outside of the country, much less the Midwest?"

"If you put it that way, I can give you the exception that proves the rule. When I was little, we usually had a hired hand for the summer. The Farmers Co-op had a program where it brought in guys from South America. One year we had a guy from Ecuador, and another year a guy from either Uruguay or Paraguay, I can never remember which. So, those guys were better traveled than any of the locals."

"So, what do you suppose accounts for your drive?"

"I don't really know. Some people think it's because I felt rejected because my real father didn't want me, so now I'm trying to prove what a mistake he made. Others think I'm expecting him to show up some day and that I want to make him proud."

"And, what do you think?"

"I guess I used to think about him a lot when I was younger, but I kind of gave that up. I always dreamed he'd come back or I'd meet him somewhere, but every little girl has fantasies." She pumped her legs a little harder and the arc of the swing increased. "The thing is, I always felt out of place with my family."

"What do you mean?"

She stopped pumping and let the swing wind down. "When I was about seven or eight, some neighbors came by to buy some eggs. They wanted six dozen. My mom said, 'They're thirty-eight cents a dozen, so how much is that?' She went to get a pencil and paper, but, without really thinking about it, I said, 'It's $2.28.' One of the neighbors said something like, 'That's pretty close,' and I gave him a dirty look. When my mom finished doing it by hand, she said I was exactly right. Everyone looked at me like I was some kind of a savant. That's about the time that I realized that I probably didn't belong here."

Chadwick seemed genuinely interested. "Well, I, for one, am pretty happy about the fact that you're smart, ambitious, and left here to come to Chicago."

"Thank you," she said with a mild blush. She took the last drink from her cup. "Do you want some coffee?" she asked. "I can make another pot. I can't make you a 'half caf, extra hot, soy latte,' but I can get you some coffee."

He wrinkled his nose and made a face to show her how much he disliked being the butt of her joke, but accepted the offer.

She was gone for quite a while, as the drip coffee maker was deliberate in its purpose. She could see Chadwick out the kitchen window, and watched him to see if he looked like he was planning an escape. He suddenly stood up, and appeared to be looking at something near the corner of the barn. Amy leaned close to the window and saw what he was looking at – a raccoon had come through the garden and was walking along the gravel road. Chadwick was slowly walking toward it with a hand extended as though he was holding a treat for the animal.

Amy rushed to a closet and then burst out the kitchen door. She held the barrel of a shotgun in her left hand. "Get away!" she yelled. As Chadwick turned, she hoisted the gun in the air and pulled back down on the pump handle to cock it one-handed. She aimed and shot and the raccoon lay dead on the ground.

"What did you do that for?" Chadwick snapped. It wasn't an angry voice, however. It was a voice of fear, and it was clear that he had been frightened by the shooting.

"That raccoon had rabies."

Chadwick's voice was still trembling. "How the hell could you know that? I didn't see any foam around its mouth."

She put a hand on his shoulder in an attempt to comfort him. "Raccoons are nocturnal. And I'm not using that word the way you use it. I don't mean that they like to go clubbing on Rush Street until all hours of the night before going to The Lodge at four in the morning for beer and peanuts. When I say nocturnal I mean that raccoons *only* come out at night, so if you see one in the day it's clearly suffering from some kind of dementia, and that almost always means rabies."

Chadwick was starting to regain his composure. Amy smiled and said, "Look, I told you that you might have a little problem getting to know the girl behind the woman."

"Yeah, I know," he said, "but I never realized I was dating Annie Oakley."

She was quiet for a long time. Finally, she apologized for frightening him, but assured him that she was acting for his protection.

THEY SPENT MOST OF THE DAY seeing the sights in the area. That consisted primarily of the boarding school that had been converted to a correctional facility, the park that had once been the Fourth Ward, and the location on Blackhawk Avenue where the locals dropped a carp from a crane every New Year's Eve, *a la* Times Square. Neither regretted not having brought a camera, but it was better duty than helping with the chores.

In the Prescott house, the noon meal was usually the big one. Because they were there to celebrate Mrs. Prescott's birthday, however, it was moved to the evening. Somehow, even though it was her birthday, Judy Prescott still found herself doing the cooking. Amy offered to help, but Mrs. Prescott dismissed the suggestion because Amy had never shown much aptitude in the kitchen.

There were nine for dinner. Amy's brother was a bachelor, so he came alone. Amy's younger sister brought her husband and two kids. The basketball-sized lump under her sweatshirt made it clear that another one was on the way. Amy sensed Chadwick was a little overwhelmed and tried not to leave his side.

Eventually, dinner was served. As she put the platters of food on the table, Mrs. Prescott remarked, "Chadwick, I'm sure you're used to eating much fancier things in all those restaurants in Chicago."

Before he could answer, Amy jumped in. "I'll bet this is the first *home-killed* meal you've ever had."

"What?" he said quizzically.

"This is a farm," Amy said. "This is where food comes from. The eggs this morning were from mom's chicken coop. This beef used to be free rangin' around the fields before they had it slaughtered."

"Amy," her mother barked. "Why do you have to try and ruin his appetite? It's not like we're eating a cow that you raised and entered into the 4H contest."

Amy had an impish grin. "Just thought he'd like to know."

The group quieted down and Mrs. Prescott said grace. As soon as it was done, Amy's stepfather looked at her and said, "Char, could you pass the potatoes?"

Amy held the potatoes, but gave the old man a penetrating look. "My name is Amy. I've gone by that since I was eight. You know it and everyone here knows it, so please show me some respect and use it."

Her stepfather made a gesture of resignation, followed by a gesture to pass the potatoes. The table was quiet for an uncomfortable moment, but the children soon started carrying on and silence could not be found again. Nonetheless, the evening did not get much more comfortable.

Mrs. Prescott did what she could to keep the conversation going. Sometimes that was questions directed to Chadwick, and sometimes it was commentary on what her daughters should wear to make themselves look prettier. It was a tie as to which discussion made Amy most uneasy.

Chadwick was polite and finally initiated discussion on his own. "I'll bet you don't have much crime here," he said.

"That is one of the benefits," Amy replied.

"Have you ever had any crime at all?" he asked.

Everyone at the table seemed to go into search mode. Finally, Judy Prescott spoke. "We had the cattle rustling caper about twenty years ago."

"That hardly counts," Amy said.

"Well, it must have been something," Chadwick said.

"It did make the news at the time," Amy said. "The thing of it was, the cattle always turned up. Someone was opening the gates and driving cattle out. Everyone figured it was PETA or some other animal rights organization. All the farmers started staking out their properties. I doubt they would have hesitated to shoot 'em."

"What happened?" Chadwick asked.

"Everyone was looking for strangers," Amy said, "on account of nobody from here would do something like that. It went on for a couple months and nobody could figure it out. The problem was the cattle sometimes went onto the roadway, and that could cause a pretty bad car accident."

"So," Chadwick said, "what happened?"

"Everyone was so focused on some sort of animal rights plot, that they didn't stop to think that maybe it was just the unintended consequences of something else. It turned out it was just high school kids going into the fields to drink and party late at night. Most of them were from in town and didn't think about what would happen if they left the gates open."

"So, it wasn't even a crime?" Chadwick asked.

"Well, I guess it was still trespassing," Amy said, "but the mystery was solved before anyone got hurt. So, in the end, it turned out to be nothing."

Everyone else tried to think of other exciting events from the past, but they were mostly humorous farm anecdotes. After several hours, the other guests went home and Chadwick and Amy went upstairs to go to bed.

Chadwick stopped outside her door to give her a kiss. "Goodnight sweet Charlotte," he said.

She pulled back and gave him an angry look.

"That is what the "C" stands for, isn't it? So it's okay if I call you that from now on, right?"

Now she gave him a look of mild exasperation. "I still have your keys. Feel free to call me whatever you want if you don't want a ride home."

"Did I get it wrong?" he said. "Is it Charlene?"

"It's whatever you want it to be. Just remember: Call me Amy or don't bother to call me."

"Aye aye, C'Amanda Prescott," he said. He kissed her goodnight and then went to bed.

CHAPTER FIFTEEN

A MY ARRIVED IN ST. PAUL on Monday morning. Because she was going to the river, she didn't have a street address. As a result, the cab driver was at a loss to find Pig's Eye Lake. She had allowed a lot of time to spare, however, as she didn't want to get left at the dock. Actually, she secretly would have been happy to be left at the dock, but only under circumstances where it wasn't her fault.

As she stood on the bank, she saw a switch boat pushing barges into formation. As a barge was pushed into place, crewmembers would throw lines around the cleats in order to tie the barges together. Each barge was about two hundred feet long and forty feet wide. The "raft" that they were assembling was currently three barges wide and three barges long. A half dozen more barges were moored nearby, waiting to join.

Amy spotted the M/V Kay Drabeck at the dock. Crewmembers were wheeling loads of supplies down the dock and onto the boat. Amy threw her pack over her shoulder and headed for the boat. She hadn't been given directions about whom she was to report to, but she was confident that someone would notice her and take care of it.

She was standing onshore next to the dock when she heard a familiar voice behind her. "There's our new safety inspector." The voice belonged to Tucker Sheridan.

She was happy to see a familiar face. "I don't know why I'm the safety inspector," she said. "Shouldn't you be doing it? You know a lot more about what's going on then I do."

"I don't think so. *Some people* think I take unnecessary risks. Who would want that in a safety inspector? The whole idea is to get somebody new. We've all been doing it for years, but apparently we're doing it wrong."

She hadn't expected to talk her way out of the assignment, but still wanted to make her point. "Are you coming along?" she asked.

"Nope. I just came down to show you around and get you situated."

He led her onto the boat. Sitting by itself, the towboat was an awkward structure that appeared to be too tall for its base. When pushed against a load of barges, it had support to provide it with stability. Standing on its own, it looked like it could tip over at any minute.

He led her up two flights of stairs until they came to the cook's quarters. He put her pack in the room and explained that she would have all the security and privacy that she needed.

"Did anyone tell you about the electricity?" he said.

"No."

"It's all direct current, so if you brought a curling iron or anything, don't use it."

"Well, I didn't think I'd be getting dolled up for anything, so I guess it doesn't matter."

He then led her to the bridge where she was reintroduced to Captain Murphy. On the far side of the bridge was Dudley Raymond, and he was eyeing her with a sly smile. *Just what I need,* she thought to herself.

Sheridan was being somewhat attentive. "I don't know how much you understand this process, so I'll give you a once-over. Each barge holds about sixteen hundred tons of grain. That's as much as eighty semi-trailer trucks per barge. From here to St. Louis, we'll push fifteen barges at once and more than twice that amount on the lower river. In other words, we transport a hell of a lot of product for just the cost of running one towboat."

She nodded with interest. It sounded like a speech he had given to a chamber of commerce or a Congressional appropriations committee, but it helped her understand the magnitude of the operation.

"Between here and St. Louis, you'll go through twenty-four sets of locks. When that happens, they have to break the tow apart because the locks are only large enough to handle so many barges at once. That's what takes the most time."

She continued nodding, but was careful not to interrupt.

"There are three things that are dangerous about this process, and you should be able to avoid at least two of them. First, walking out on the barges is always risky. The wrong wave or gust of wind and you could fall overboard, or worse, you could fall between a gap in the barges. Those gaps usually aren't large, but they may be enough to catch a hand or a foot and, trust me, when the gap closes, what used to be your hand or foot becomes food for the catfish."

Amy was a little disturbed by the thought, but stayed quiet.

"Second, stay out of the way when they're tying and untying the tow. Lines snap, barges smash into each other, and the chance of going in the water or getting hit by something is pretty significant."

Amy decided maybe she'd be fine watching the action from the bridge. "What's the risk that I can't avoid?" she asked.

Sheridan looked at Captain Murphy. "Pilot error" he said with a hint of sarcasm. "You could do everything right, but if the captain decides to hit a bridge or another tow, you could be in trouble. Fortunately, Murphy knows the river like the back of his hand. Just make sure he doesn't get into the Irish whiskey before he takes the wheel."

"Very funny," Murphy said. "Before my boat caught on fire, I had a perfect safety record."

At that moment, two more men appeared on the bridge. Neither looked to be much older than Amy. Tucker held a hand toward them to signal an introduction was coming. "This is Sean, the pilot," he said while pointing at the one with the reddish-brown hair and the rosy cheeks that didn't look like they needed to be shaved very often. "And this is Peanut. He's the engineer."

"I'm sorry," Amy said. "Did you say 'Peter'?"

The young man stepped forward. "No ma'am. He said 'Peanut.' It's my nickname and there isn't much way around it."

There also wasn't much question how he got the nickname. He was small. He wasn't short, per se, but he was proportionately smaller in every respect. He reminded her of news anchors that she had seen in person. They looked normal on TV, but tiny in person.

"Nice to meet you both," she said.

Peanut returned the pleasantry, but Sean wasn't so sure. "I can't believe we're going to have a broad riding along on the boat with us," he said.

Amy took a deep breath.

"Sean," Tucker scolded, "that term went out quite a while ago. Women don't really like being called 'broads' anymore."

Amy appreciated the way he came to her aid.

"What am I s'pose to call 'em?" Sean said with a hint of annoyance in his voice.

Tucker paused and then said, "I think now they prefer to be called, 'boxes.'"

Sean and Peanut both busted out laughing. Amy was not amused. Apparently chivalry was dead on this boat – or at least it had been thrown overboard. Amy was never one to suffer in silence, however. "If it's any consolation," she said, "I'm not really looking forward to spending a week with a bunch of guys who probably still think farts are funny."

That seemed to reestablish her position of authority. Tucker decided to have the last word. "All right. You're all going to be spending a week together, so see if you can do your best to work and play well with each other."

"Fair enough," Amy said.

"One other thing," Tucker said. "Try to avoid the rest of the crew. The men who work the river are a different breed. Sean and Peanut are officers and I don't think you have to worry about them, but some of the other guys are not really pillars of society."

"Thanks for that compliment," Peanut said sarcastically. "Maybe you'd like us to start dating your sister."

Sheridan ignored the comment. "If there's a problem, have Captain Murphy radio it in. I doubt you'll get much cell phone coverage other than when you're going through towns."

Amy was still undecided about Tucker Sheridan. He certainly could be a sexist. On the other hand, he seemed to be showing a genuine interest in looking out for her. Only time would tell.

A︎MY FOUND A SEAT ON THE BRIDGE and watched the crew work. She had a lot of questions, but decided to wait until they were underway. The rest of the raft had been assembled and Captain Murphy guided the tow-boat up against the middle barge in the back. Despite the name, towboats pushed rather than pulled – at least on the river.

After the tow and the boat were attached, Murphy put the engines in reverse and pulled the raft out from shore. He then turned the wheel sharply to the left and went forward. The effect was to push the back of the tow to the left – or port side – which, in turn, caused the front of the tow to swing to the starboard. Steering from the back was never easy, and the sheer size and weight had to make it that much more difficult.

Soon, the tow was in the channel and they were on their way. She noticed red and green buoys, and also noticed that they tended to stay between them. She also saw red and green reflective markers on shore, and wondered what good it would do to stay inside of a marker when going close to it would ground the tow.

"Can you explain the buoys and shore markers?" she asked the captain.

"Sure," he said as he turned to face her. "It's known as 'red, right, re-turn.' When you're returning to port – or going upstream in the case of a river – you keep the red marker on your right. Going downstream, it's the opposite. Right now, we need to keep the red markers on our left and the green markers on our right."

"What about the markers on shore? You can't just keep to the left or right of those?"

"They're just for navigation. We spot one and we head for it. Going downstream, if it's green we know we'll be turning left before we get to it and if it's red we'll be going right. So, we head for the marker until we see the next marker and then we turn the tow and head for it."

"What if you come upon a tow heading the other direction? How do you handle that?"

"It's like the normal rules of the road. Everybody's supposed to stay to the right. It's called 'port-to-port.' It means you pass with your port side adjacent to the other tow's port side."

"Don't you have some way of tracking where the other tows are?"

Captain Murphy let out a chuckle. "This isn't like air traffic control. We have radios and everything, but we don't have someone directing traffic on the river."

"Is that a problem?" she asked.

"It can be. If we know we're coming to a bridge or a lock, we can get on the radio to find out where everyone else is. On the other hand, if we come around a bend in the river and there's someone coming the other way, everyone better hope that everyone is on their side of the channel."

This was a system that didn't sound like it had been updated or improved in decades. "What about other vessels?" she asked. "I mean, how do you avoid pleasure boats and guys who are just out fishing?"

"There are a variety of protocols," Murphy said, "but the ultimate law of the river is this: 'when all else fails, the rule of gross tonnage prevails.' We have the right of way because we have the hardest thing to control. As a practical matter, the rule works because of the consequences. Yield the right of way to us or prepare to be crushed. I've never hit a pleasure boat, but, for guys who have, it's not really their fault."

Amy made mental notes and then sat back to observe. After a few hours, they were at the Hastings Lock and Dam. Captain Murphy had radioed the lockmaster and slowed his speed in an attempt to time it right. Ultimately, they arrived a little too soon and Murphy had to try and hold the tow in place while the upstream traffic cleared the lock. Once that happened, he guided the tow past two giant doors in the water and into the lock. The crew jumped off the tow and lashed it to an engine on shore. Other crewmembers unhooked the first nine barges from the back six. Murphy then backed the towboat and half the tow out and the lock gates closed.

"What exactly is happening?" Amy asked.

"First, they'll lower the water level in the lock," Murphy said. "After the water level is lowered, there's an engine and a winch onshore that'll pull those barges forward. Next, they'll probably let some pleasure boats in and they'll raise the water level back up. Finally, we'll go into the lock, they'll drop the water level again, and, when we pull out, we'll hook the other barges back on."

Amy shook her head. "And we have to do this twenty-some times before we get to St. Louis?"

"That's right."

"That doesn't seem very efficient or very safe."

"Well, you're the safety expert, but the alternative is to split the tow and have two towboats and two crews. I think they had some college boys look at it and they decided this was more efficient."

Amy shrugged her acceptance. She decided to go to her cabin and unpack. She'd brought some other work from the office, so she spent some time on it. She'd have plenty of time to talk to the crew and watch them work, so she wasn't going to forsake her other obligations.

After several more hours, she heard the engines roar to slow the tow. She looked out her window and saw that they were coming into another lock. She opened her Upper Mississippi River map and determined that they must be in Red Wing. She had watched the tow go through one lock already, so she didn't feel compelled to race up on deck to watch the process again.

To this point, the cruise had been pleasant but unremarkable. South of Red Wing, they hit Lake Pepin and the scenery took on a whole new aura. The river widened, and the shore rose to greater heights. For the first time, the water was blue instead of brown. The river reminded her of a vacation to the Rhine valley in college. The high bluffs were majestic and surprisingly free of condo developments. The rest of the river might have been "brown water," but Lake Pepin had the feel of something nobler. Contrary to all of her misgivings, Amy was finding this stretch of the river to be quite captivating. She leaned out a window and let the wind blow some of the stress out of her.

CHAPTER SIXTEEN

A T 6 P.M., THE CREW ON DUTY CHANGED. In general, they rotated six-hour shifts. When they weren't going through locks, there wasn't a lot for the deckhands to do other than general cleaning and painting. There was, however, a rotation for who was to be on watch. With the people responsible for steering, it was basically the same. The Captain and Pilot rotated those duties, but they would navigate with the help of someone else.

Sean and Peanut went off duty, so she decided to join them and some of the other crewmen for dinner. Sean was browning hamburger in the galley. "Can I do anything to help?" Amy asked.

"You can, but maybe you'd rather join the rotation."

"What do you mean?" she asked.

"A bunch of us are taking turns cooking until our regular cook is back. Some guys want to just fend for themselves, but it seems easier to rotate. As long as you're riding along, you may as well take a turn."

"I guess that's fair. Anything special I need to know?"

"Obviously, you need to know how to cook. In addition, we have one rule. Anyone who complains about the food has to cook every meal for the rest of the trip."

She smiled. "Sounds like a good rule. As long as I'm here, I'm happy to help you."

Sean accepted her offer and instructed her to open cans and get water boiling. He was making spaghetti. By the looks of the provisions in the cupboards, that was typical of the meals. There were some fresh ingredients on board, but a lot of prepackaged things like Tuna Helper. At least it was better than prepackaged frozen dinners.

Dinner was mostly small talk. Amy asked a lot of questions that might help her safety analysis. At a minimum, she wanted to be able to speak intelligently about the operations. Sean and Peanut subtly tried to get Amy to talk about her personal life, but she wasn't biting. They'd say stuff like, "I'll bet your boyfriend doesn't cook this good," in an apparent attempt to get her to say something that would indicate if she even had a boyfriend. Amy would respond with things like, "Nobody could make spaghetti this good," and thereby respond to the question without answering their real question.

After dinner, a deckhand with a big silver cap on one of his front teeth came in waving a deck of cards. "We playin' tonight?" he asked.

Peanut spoke first. "Skeeter, I'll play, but only if we play small stakes. Euchre is supposed to be a social game, not a way to win or lose a paycheck."

Skeeter looked heartbroken. "Come on, you guys. Do I have to wait until I can get to a casino to have any action?"

Peanut and Sean looked at each other. Peanut spoke again. "Skeeter, we can't be having high stakes games on the boat. We're all together for thirty days at a time. If someone loses too much money, there's no telling what will happen to someone in the middle of the night. The captain only tolerates the gambling because it's friendly."

Skeeter decided that a low stakes game of Euchre was better than no game at all. Ray was enticed into the game, and the four of them cut for partners. Amy gave up her seat at the table, but found a stool nearby in order to watch.

As Sean was shuffling the deck, he caught Amy's attention. "Ever play this game?" he asked.

"What did you call it?" she asked. "Yukon?"

"Not quite. It's not even spelled like that. It's Euchre."

"By any name, I haven't played it. I know how to play cards, but this is one I've never heard of."

"It's pretty simple, really. We just use twenty-four cards, the nines through the aces. We deal each player five cards. One card gets flipped up and that's the trump suit. We play partners and the idea is to bid if you think your team can take more tricks than the other side."

"I learned to play bridge in boarding school. It sounds similar."

"Could be," Sean said with a smile that indicated he had no idea how to play bridge. "It's probably a little different, though, because the high card is not the ace. The high card is the Jack of the trump suit, and the second highest card is the Jack of the suit that is the same color."

She decided to watch and learn. It didn't have the high drama of watching Texas Hold 'em on TV, but it seemed to involve a little more strategy. Starting to the left of the dealer, the first player was given the opportunity to declare. As soon as a player said he was going to go for it, the dealer picked up the card that was lying face-up and discarded something else from his hand. Regardless of who made the bid, the player to the dealer's left played first. If the bidding team got all five tricks, they got more points. And so it went.

Amy wasn't following everything, but she could tell that Skeeter was getting more and more annoyed. It started with slapping cards down when the play didn't meet his liking. It proceeded to profanity expressed at a significant decibel level. Peanut's request that Skeeter "use his inside voice" provided levity for the others, but it seemed to agitate Skeeter even more. After two games, Sean announced that he had other things to do. Deprived of his opportunity to win his money back, Skeeter's vitriol continued. Nobody jumped in to take Sean's place, so the game ended.

Amy went back up to the bridge. It was nearly dark, and that changed the navigation. There was a big searchlight on the bow of the towboat. When it was on, it could illuminate buoys and shore markers that looked to be a mile or more away and thousands of insects that were much closer. For its part, the tow was illuminated with red and green lights showing the perimeter. That way, an upbound boat would be sure to keep clear.

She went outside to stand on the deck. Even though the day had been hot, night was cool on the river. She saw Skeeter down below talking to Dudley Raymond. He still seemed to be agitated, but she couldn't tell what he was saying. She decided, however, that Skeeter was the type of guy Tucker had warned her to stay away from, and she was going to follow that advice.

CHAPTER SEVENTEEN

AMY WAS SURPRISED BY HOW WELL SHE SLEPT. The constant hum of the engines provided a white noise, and the gentle rock of the tow was somewhat calming. The deadbolt and door chain didn't hurt either.

She dressed and went up to the bridge. Captain Murphy was sitting behind the wheel. "Where are we?" she asked.

"We just passed Trempeleau," he said. "Traffic was apparently a little backed up last night. It took us a long time to get through the locks at Alma and Fountain City."

"When do you think we'll get to Prairie du Chien?"

"Probably this afternoon. Why?"

She tipped her head, as though trying to see something in the past. "It's where I grew up. I used to watch the barges from the shore, so I thought it'd be interesting to do the reverse." She had another reason as well.

Amy went out on the deck and pulled out her cell phone. She had a signal, so she called her mother with a special request.

That afternoon, Amy met her mother at the Prairie du Chien lock. While the tow was locking through, Amy managed to get off the boat for a few minutes. Her mother was having trouble believing Amy was riding a towboat down the Mississippi River, and Amy was having a hard time explaining it to her. Mrs. Prescott handed Amy two brown grocery bags, which she then carried back onto the boat and into the galley.

She had volunteered to take that evening's dinner as her turn in the rotation. The delays had not left her much time, so she rushed to get started. Among other things, she didn't want anyone disturbing her while she was cooking.

At a little after six, some of the crew started to show up. Sean offered to return the favor and give her a hand, but she assured him that she had everything under control. She directed them to take seats at the table and told them she'd bring dinner out when it was ready. After just enough anticipation, she walked out with a platter of boiled dinner – except it wasn't New England boiled dinner. The men stared at the food with shock. At the top of the tray was a large beef heart that looked like it could have been stolen from a biology class. Next to it were two beef kidneys. Next to those were --

"Are those what I think they are?" Peanut said while pointing at two orbs sitting beneath the kidneys.

Amy was struggling to keep a straight face. "If you mean bull's testicles, then yes, they are what you think they are."

Nobody was grabbing for the food. Yet, miraculously, nobody made an audible complaint. Only Ray seemed to recognize her ploy. He plunged a fork into the beef heart. He sliced off a big piece, held it up with the utensils for all to see, and then deposited it on Amy's plate. "Is that a big enough piece for you?" he asked.

She couldn't contain her amusement any longer. "I can't believe nobody complained. I was sure someone would say something and have to cook the rest of the trip. You guys are really disciplined or something."

"We're also really hungry," Sean said. "And it looks like we're going to stay that way."

She was entertained by her practical joke even if nobody else seemed to appreciate it. "Don't worry," she said, "this isn't the real dinner." She walked back into the kitchen and came out with a platter of T-bone steaks. She followed that up with a platter of corn on the cob and a big dish of hash browns. "I had my Mom bring some steaks and fresh vegetables from the farm. As long as she was making the trip, I thought I'd put the internal organs to some use."

Seeing the new food changed the crew's collective disposition and they started to laugh and make jokes about the organs. "You should have seen the look on your face when she set the platter down," and "Hey Peanut, you're supposed to eat the testicles, not lick them." And so on.

During dessert, Sean asked Amy if she'd play Euchre with them after dinner. When she declined, Sean pleaded. "If we say you wanted to learn how to play, we can tell Skeeter that we already have four. Nobody likes playing with him, but nobody wants to tell him that. If you'll play, we've got an easy answer." After a little cajoling from the others, she agreed to give it a shot.

By the time Skeeter showed up, they were playing the third hand. Everyone acted nonchalant about Amy's interest in playing. Skeeter didn't appear happy, but there wasn't much he could do about it. "I knew you guys were pussies," he said, "but this really takes the cake. I s'pose you'll be drinkin' tea and eatin' crumpets pretty soon too." He slammed the door as he left.

"Is he always that way?" Amy asked.

"Do you mean, 'is he always stupid?' or 'is he always in a bad mood?'" Peanut said.

"Both, I guess."

"I think he's gotten worse lately," Sean said. "I don't think he was ever smart, but he wasn't always crabby."

Amy waited for Ray to say something. She had, after all, seen him talking to him the night before. Ray just studied his cards.

Amy seemed to grasp the nuances of the game with relative ease. Furthermore, keeping track of twenty-four cards was substantially less demanding than keeping track of fifty-two while playing bridge.

Compared to the night before, Sean and Peanut were more direct, but less personal, with their inquiries. They asked her about where she grew up, where she went to school, and things like that. Amy was less interested in their personal histories, but asked the appropriate questions out of courtesy.

They had agreed to play best of three, and each side managed to win a game. Amy was dealing, and she and Peanut were in reach – which meant they could go out if they made the bid and succeeded. The trump card that was flipped up was a club. Sean passed, and Peanut ordered it up. In other words, he bid and he and Amy would have a chance to win the game and the match.

Sean studied his hand. "I guess I'll try the sure thing," he said as he led the Ace of Hearts. Peanut promptly trumped it. When the play came around to Amy, she threw the King of Diamonds. "Neither of you have hearts?" Ray said with dismay.

As Amy collected the trick, Sean said, "What the hell is she doing throwing away a King?"

Peanut smiled so wide it caused him to squint. "I don't know much, but I'm pretty sure she's trying to tell me to lead Diamonds."

Peanut threw the Queen of Diamonds and Ray pounced on it with the Ace. Amy had a big smile as she played a trump and took the trick. Between Peanut and Amy, they had the rest of the trump and took all five tricks to win the game.

Amy was smiling in satisfaction. "In Bridge, that's called a sluff and a ruff."

"What the hell is that?" Sean asked.

"A sluff is when you manage to discard a losing card on a trick that you've already taken or that doesn't matter. That's what happened when I was able to play the King of Diamonds. A ruff is when you trump a trick. So, a sluff and a ruff is when you basically solve two problems at the same time."

"Like killing two birds with one stone?" Peanut asked.

Amy thought for a moment. "I don't really want to ride down the river arguing metaphors with you boys, but not exactly. Killing two birds with one stone involves one act with dual consequences. A sluff and a ruff is two basically simultaneous acts that solve two problems."

"Thanks for not trying to argue metaphors with us dumb shits," Peanut said. "We'd do okay arguing similes, analogies, or even allegories, but we're out of our league when it comes to metaphors."

Amy couldn't help but laugh. "I'm sorry that I underestimated you," she said.

"I think we underestimated you," Peanut said. "You're a regular card shark."

"In school, they called me a 'card sharp.' I guess it's about the same thing."

Sean tried to persuade everyone to play some more. "Now that we know about the sluff and a ruff stuff, we'll have a better chance," he said.

The others declined. Ray got up and moved to a recliner on the far side of the room. Amy was starting to take a more genuine interest in her new friends, however, so the three of them stayed and talked. "How can you guys have a social life when you work on a boat?" she asked.

"Seamen work thirty days on and thirty days off," Sean explained. "And for guys who don't have a side job or some other hobby, I think they're usually more eager to get back to work than to get home to their wives." Sean turned to Ray. "You've been married the longest. What do you think?"

The old man shook his head. "Sometimes you wonder why you even take the time off."

Sean smiled with the sense that something more was coming. "Do you want to elaborate on that?"

Ray sat up. "It's like the night before this shift started, I was at home with the wife and I said, 'what would you think about going to bed a little early and seeing what happens?' She says, 'Oh, Ray, I have to wash clothes in the morning and then make something for the church bake sale.' So I said, 'hell, if we're not done by then we'll just quit.'"

That got a big laugh from the rest of the crew. Having held court for a moment, Ray sat back with a look of satisfaction.

"What about you guys?" she asked the others. "Are you married? Do you have girlfriends?"

"I'm married," Peanut said. "Sean apparently knows how to use birth control better than I do, 'cause he's got a girlfriend but he's still single."

They waited until they had answered plenty of personal questions before turning the tables on her. "So," Peanut said, "tell us about the guy you're spending a week away from. I'll bet he's a banker. What do you think, Sean?"

"I'm sure he wears a suit and tie to work," Sean said. "Maybe he's an options trader at the Grain Exchange."

Amy looked at one and then the other. "Neither of you are right, but I'm not sure I could tell you exactly what he does because he works for a family business that invests in real estate."

Peanut was smiling in triumph. "At least we finally got you to admit that you have a boyfriend. You were so evasive that we were going to take bets on whether you were going into a convent or mostly interested in watching women's golf."

"Is that how you rationalize it every time a woman doesn't instantly succumb to your charms?" she asked. "She's either a nun or a lesbian."

Peanut nodded his head with enthusiasm. "It spares my self esteem to rationalize it any way I can," he said with a hint of sarcasm. "If I reacted to rejection by thinking I must be ugly, stupid, lazy, or all of the above, I'd probably develop a low self-image."

Amy smiled again upon realizing she had met a worthy adversary.

"Somehow we got off the topic," Peanut said. "I thought we were finally talking about your love life. Is it serious? Do you think you'll get married?"

"We've dated for about a year. I can't really say if we'll get married. If it wasn't at least possible, I wouldn't have hung in there this long."

"Have you been married before?" Peanut persisted.

"No."

"What were your other boyfriends like? Were they all suits too?"

The questions were personal, but Amy didn't mind the discussion. "It's hard to call a college student or a law student a 'suit,' but I guess they pretty much all ended up in white collar type jobs."

"So, they were pretty much all pussies?" Sean asked.

Amy glared at him for a moment. Then she thought about it and said, "From your perspective, the answer is probably 'yes.' I didn't date too many bad boys."

Now it was Peanut's turn, as they double-teamed her. "So, have you ever loved a real man? In fact, do you even know any real men?"

She found that question particularly amusing. "How are you defining 'real men'?"

"Someone who does at least a little manual labor and whose job involves some physical risk."

She looked up as she recalled something in her past. "I grew up on a farm in a farming community. Does that count? Farming is manual labor with physical risk."

"So, why didn't you fall for a farmer?" Sean asked.

"Ya mean, other than the smell?" she quipped.

Sean looked back and forth and then sniffed his own armpits. "Yeah. Other than the smell."

"Those 'real men,' as you put it, were usually brutes," she said. "I think I wanted something more."

"Do you mean they were wife beaters?" Peanut asked.

"Not necessarily," she said, "but they weren't that much better. I mean, my stepfather never hit my Mom, but I don't remember him ever being particularly nice to her either. If things didn't go his way, he'd either yell or pout. If that's a real man, I think I'll pass."

Peanut wasn't going to let her off so easy. "I don't think a girl can go through her teens without ever being in love. There must have been someone who was at least close."

She thought for a long moment. She was warming up to the crew, so she decided to share. "I guess just once I loved someone that you'd consider a real man, and that was really just puppy love."

"Okay," Peanut said with a big smile. "Let's hear about it."

She again hesitated, but it was so long ago that it didn't seem personal. "When I was growing up, we always had a hired hand during the summer. Usually they came from South America, but when I was about twelve, we hired a boy from a nearby town and he was probably eighteen or nineteen. He was gorgeous in a James Dean kind of way. The rest of rural America had long hair and wore Led Zeppelin Tee shirts, but he had short curly hair that he slicked back a little. I realize that twelve-year-old girls are not the most rational beings, but I just thought he was to die for."

"So, was he a beefcake, or was he smart like you?" Peanut asked.

"He wasn't smart, but he thought it was great that I was. I always felt kind of out of place in my family and on the farm, but he treated me like I was something special. I don't think he ever thought about me being his girlfriend when I was old enough, but he must have thought about me being somebody's girlfriend someday, and he always told me to just be who I was and that real men weren't intimidated by smart women."

"That sounds like he was pretty smart," Peanut said.

Amy was quiet for a moment. As she thought about it, her emotions started to catch up with her. "It may have been puppy love, but what I felt for him was definitely love." Her eyes were starting to well up, but she didn't want anyone to see her cry. "The spring after he worked for us, he tried to ride his motorcycle home from a bar after he'd been drinking. They never figured out whether he was run off the road or just crashed, but he got killed. My parents tried to keep me from finding out, but it's a small community. I cried for a year."

Sean and Peanut were quiet. It was an awkward silence, however, so Sean said, "So that put you off on dating real men?"

Amy was still watery-eyed, but his statement made her laugh. "I think that put me off of being in love for a while, and then I apparently was attracted to men who were less likely to get themselves killed."

"Maybe it's time to get back on the horse," Peanut said. He had a big smile as he thought about what he was going to say next. "You can't get much more testosterone in one place than Tucker Sheridan. He seemed to be kind of fawning over you and you seemed to like it. I'm not just pimping for him because he's my boss, but maybe the two of you should hook up."

Amy made an exaggerated shudder to show how cool she was to the idea. "He can be charming when he wants to be, but he's insufferable the rest of the time."

"What do you think your boyfriend's – what did you say his name was?"

"I didn't. His name's Chadwick."

Peanut and Sean both busted out laughing at that. They were enjoying the moment, but then Peanut said, "Well, I don't want to screw things up between you and *Chadwick,* but if you ever get tired of having to be on top, perhaps you should try something else."

"And you think I should try what you call 'a real man.'"

"Look, I don't have anything against guys in suits," Peanut said, "but try having sex with someone who knows that they might not make it home from work the next day or after the next shift on the river. They take it a little more seriously because they know it might be their last time."

She was shaking her head and smiling at how ridiculous she thought he was. "I know," she said sarcastically, "I'll date a terrorist. I don't think you could get more courageous than a suicide bomber. The only bad part is that, according to you, I'd have the best sex ever and he'd never come back. But at least I could say I was with a real man."

Ray had been sitting in the corner reading something, but he apparently overheard the conversation. He set down his magazine and stood up. "That's bullshit," he barked.

The trio turned to look at him. "What's bullshit?" Peanut asked.

"It's bullshit that those suicide bombers had courage." His voice was loud and trembling. "I don't care what those fucking idiots said about the 9/11 hijackers having courage. They don't know the meaning of the word. People who decide that the world would be better if they're dead are not courageous. They're cowards who aren't willing to face life. Courage is someone who loves life, but risks it for others. People with courage don't want to die and hope not to die, but they have the courage to take the risk for something important."

The rest of the group was quiet. Ray was old enough to have been witness to wars where courage was put to the test. He talked about it so forcefully that it suggested he had personal experience witnessing it.

Ray stood looking at the group. "I didn't mean to ruin the party," he finally said. Looking at Amy, he said, "I know you were just joking about dating a suicide bomber, but I have no time for the people I consider to be the biggest pussies in the world."

CHAPTER EIGHTEEN

THE NEXT DAY, AMY DECIDED it was time to explore. Schreiber and Sheridan had both told her to stay off the tow, but what was the point of being a safety inspector if you didn't do any inspecting?

As the engineer, Peanut did not necessarily follow the shift schedule, as there was nobody with whom he could rotate. She found him in the galley reading a book. "Peanut, will you give me a tour of the tow?"

"It's a little dangerous out there," he said. "That's why I have a job that keeps me in here."

Amy was not accustomed to flirting as a means of getting her way, but she did manage to bat her eyes in his direction. "Please. If you don't, I'll probably have to go alone. I don't think Sean is up yet, and I don't really feel comfortable going with Ray or Skeeter or anyone else."

Peanut put a marker in the book and set it down. "I'll probably get in trouble, so you'll have to say you're ordering me."

"Okay," she said. "Consider this an order. But why does it matter?"

"If I'm out there on my own time and I get hurt, I don't know if I'd collect as much. If I'm following an order, then I'm working."

It occurred to Amy that she wasn't a member of the crew and, as a result, had no authority to give anyone an order. She didn't want to bring that up, however, as she was just glad that he agreed to go.

Barges are nothing more than large, flat-bottomed boats. The ones hauling grain or anything else that needs to be protected from the elements have large covers over the top. Around the perimeter of each cover was an area about three-feet wide that served as a walkway. There were no guardrails or safety wires. For the barges on the outside of the tow, the river provided the other border for the walkway, and a missed step meant that a person would be overboard. The walkways between the barges seemed safer because there were two adjacent walkways, albeit potentially separated by the space between the barges. Depending on conditions and how well they were "wired" together, the gap might not present any danger.

Peanut led her down the bow of the towboat. "Regulations require you to put this on," he said as he handed her a life jacket.

"Well," she smiled, "I guess it wouldn't look good for the safety inspector to break the safety rules. Besides, I'm not that strong of a swimmer."

"I probably shouldn't tell you this," Peanut confided, "but the life jacket probably makes it more dangerous. If you fall overboard, you're probably going to get sucked into the draft of the tow. Without a life jacket, you might be able to swim away. With a life jacket, you probably can't move fast enough to avoid the draft."

"How long does it take to stop the boat?"

"Going downstream, we usually figure about a mile. We can shut the engines off, and that should increase the likelihood of survival. Of course, with no engines running we have no control and might float into something."

"What about going upstream?"

"That's a lot better. The tow is a lot easier to navigate going against the current. Most accidents involve downstream vessels."

Amy nodded and pulled the straps to tighten her life jacket. Staying afloat seemed like the best option. Avoiding the outside walkways also seemed like a good plan. She waved to Captain Murphy to let him know where she was going. She wanted him ready to shut off the engines if necessary.

Amy followed Peanut onto a walkway on the interior of the tow. "Before we go any farther," she said, "what would be a reason for deckhands to come out here?"

"Mostly to wire and unwire the barges when they're putting together a tow or taking it apart. Otherwise, they usually check the lines about once a shift just to make sure nothing has worked its way loose."

Amy started walking, but she wasn't doing so naturally. She was so intent on leaning toward the inside away from the gap that she was having trouble keeping her balance.

"Try not to look at your feet," Peanut said. "Just pick a point at the end of the barge and walk toward it."

That advice seemed to help. She focused her line on the edge of the barge cover. She walked with more ease, and kept her head up and level like she was practicing for charm school with a book balanced on her head.

Suddenly her shoe caught something and she lurched forward. She had her hands in front of her, but managed to regain her balance before she hit the deck. "What the hell!" she snapped. She looked to see a manhole cover of sorts that did not lie flush enough to allow her to pass unscathed.

"What the hell is that?" she said.

"That's the entrance to the wing tank," he said. "The cargo hold is surrounded by tanks that are just air. That way, if there's a leak, it will only go into one tank. That keeps the barge from sinking and keeps the cargo from getting wet."

Amy was still a little flustered from nearly falling. "Why do they need entrances?" she asked testily.

"How else would you fix the leak? It's usually easier to get in the wing tank than it is to lift the barge out of the water."

"I guess that makes sense," she conceded.

They continued their walk down the row of barges. Amy decided she wasn't likely to come back on the tow, so she should probably see everything there was to see on this trip. They walked all the way to the front. Amy sat down on the barge cover and wedged her feet against one of the cleats in an effort to make sure she didn't slip. The sun was shining and the breeze was blowing through her hair. "This part is actually pretty nice," she said.

Peanut took a seat nearby. He was considerably more comfortable in the surroundings and didn't need to find something to grab onto. "I should have brought my book," he remarked.

They sat making small talk for quite a while. Amy was waiting until they reached a comfort level before seeking any information. Eventually, she said, "Do you know why you guys don't have a union?"

Peanut had been laying back absorbing the sun, but sat up to answer. "Most of us don't think we need one. Our wages are good, and we don't have to pay union dues."

"Do you think everyone feels that way?"

"I can't really speak for the guys who work on the lower Mississippi, 'cause I don't deal with them as much. As for the guys on this end, just about everyone seems pretty happy."

Amy was trying to keep the discussion conversational, but her cross-examination instincts were finding a way to the surface. "When you say 'just about everyone,' do you mean that there are some people who would like to unionize?"

"A few, I guess," he said. "The only one I can really remember sayin' anything about it was Skeeter. But he's the kind of guy who would go along with anything if someone told him there was money in it." Peanut smiled. "Needless to say, most of us aren't too likely to jump on any bandwagon being driven by someone like Skeeter."

"Do you think Skeeter is the kind of guy who would do something to sabotage the boat or the cargo?"

Peanut turned to face her. "I think he is the kind of guy who would do it, but I don't think he's smart enough to do it. Furthermore, he mostly rides the upper river routes like I do, and most of the losses have been downstream. Before the fire, we'd hardly had anything on our part of the system."

"So, you don't have any idea what's behind the problem?"

"Not really. The thing you have to remember is that it could be just bad timing. I mean, there are losses on the river all the time. We've been experiencing more than usual, but, as far as I know, all of the losses have been typical. I mean, it's not like we've had bombs planted or people murdered."

That statement was enough to lead Amy to a new topic, but she waited a minute before doing so. "What do you know about Dudley Raymond?"

"Ray," Peanut said. "He's one of the great seamen of all time. Instead of *The Old Man and the Sea*, he's like *The Old Man and the River*."

"Isn't he kind of old to be a mate? Why isn't he a captain or a pilot? For that matter, why isn't he working in an office somewhere?"

"River navigating isn't that easy, and it takes some schooling. Besides, I think he probably liked the action too much to sit behind the wheel. Now that he's older, he might wish he'd done otherwise, but it's probably too late."

Amy shrugged her shoulders to signal that she was waiting for an answer to the second part of her question.

"As for why he's still workin' the boats," Peanut obliged, "I think it's just sort of in his blood. He's a bright enough guy, but I can't see him doing much else at this point in his life."

Amy had laid the groundwork, but decided to get to the heart of the matter. "Do you have any idea why he's so tight with Tony Drabeck? I mean, Ray's just a deckhand, but Drabeck claimed he was the most trusted employee in the company."

Peanut seemed to appreciate that he was getting some information from this conversation as well as providing it. "I don't exactly know, but I know there's something to it. Old man Drabeck had a son who got killed. The rumor is that Ray was somehow involved. I don't have any idea what happened. I just know that I've heard some things, but if anyone tries to ask him about it he won't say anything."

"Really?" she said. "Drabeck had a son who died. Maybe that explains why he wants his company to live forever."

Peanut didn't say anything.

While Amy wanted as much scoop and gossip as she could get, she didn't want to be the source of any. Consequently, she decided not to mention the manslaughter conviction for which Dudley Raymond had done time in prison. Peanut had proved to be a good source of information, so she decided to terminate the interrogation before Peanut perceived it as such. The pieces were, however, starting to come together.

Amy had gotten a little more comfortable with her surroundings. She realized that the only way she could get thrown off the front of the tow was if it stopped suddenly – and a stop that took a mile wouldn't likely qualify. As a result, she slid down off the cover and sat on the deck. She hadn't developed enough courage to dangle her legs over the edge, but she had moved closer to the water.

Peanut seemed to be enjoying the pleasure cruise, but announced that he needed to get back to check the engines. Amy thanked him for being her guide, but said she thought that she'd stay a little longer.

She leaned back on her elbows and closed her eyes. The reflection from the water magnified the intensity of the sun's rays. She felt as though the heat was transforming the cells in her exposed skin as she sat there.

She thought about the fact that she wasn't wearing sunscreen and that, growing up, her mother had harped on her more about using sunscreen than she had about using birth control. Fortunately, she had found a way to escape the "pregnant-in-high-school" route to marriage that was common in rural America. Now, she needed to avoid the skin cancer common to sun worshipers.

She was just getting comfortable when a horn boomed from the superstructure above the bridge. Amy turned to look behind her, then turned back to the front and saw a tow heading toward them that had come around the bend and edged over to the wrong side of the channel. The horn boomed again. The oncoming tow was several hundred yards away, but that didn't mean that either could stop.

"Amy!" Peanut yelled. "Come on!"

He had only made it about halfway back when the horn sounded. That meant he was more than a hundred yards away, but at least he was within earshot.

Amy tried her level-headed best to get back to the towboat. She walked along the inside walkway, but she wasn't walking with the zeal of someone who felt comfortable with the task. As a result, she wasn't moving that fast.

Now, she heard a horn being blown by the oncoming tow. She wondered whether the horn blowing was meant to be a signal of sorts, or whether they were being employed merely in the "get-out-of-the-way-asshole" manner used by New York cab drivers. There was no rhythm or cadence that Samuel Morse would have fancied, so she decided they were just sending warning bellows from each side.

"Come on!" Peanut implored.

She felt a jerk and almost lost her balance as the glide of the tow was interrupted. Captain Murphy must have put the engines in reverse. She looked over her shoulder and saw the other tow rapidly approaching. The front of the oncoming tow was slowly moving to its side of the channel, but that was because the other captain was apparently pushing the back end in the opposite direction in order to manipulate the front.

"Hit the deck!" Peanut yelled. With that, he climbed on top of a cargo cover and lay flat on his stomach. "Get down!" he yelled again.

Amy climbed onto the cover of a barge in the middle of the tow and lay down. "Why are we doing this?" she yelled.

"Just do it!" Peanut screamed.

She lay on her stomach and watched the impending collision. The roar of the engines was deafening, and Captain Murphy was apparently pulling out all the stops in order to back up, turn, or otherwise avoid the other tow. Unfortunately, the starboard barges in front were now nearing the shore. The oncoming tow completed its turn and accelerated. It avoided a collision by a matter of yards.

Amy let out a sigh of relief. She propped herself up on her elbows to compose herself. At that moment, the front of the tow ran aground. Despite running the engines in reverse, the current and momentum continued to pull the barges downriver. As one barge caught the shore, the rest of the tow kept moving. Something had to give.

There was a loud creaking noise and suddenly a huge bang that took Amy's breath away. In a panic, she looked around for an explanation. The front starboard barge had been yanked loose, and the line holding it had apparently recoiled and snapped under the pressure. The cover on the barge in front of her had a big dent in the middle where the line hit it. Had she been on that barge, she might now be dead.

She lay there stunned. The tow was moving again and seemed to be back in the channel. The barge that had grounded was still wired to the tow in one spot and floated alongside like a partially clipped fingernail waiting to be severed altogether. She heard a lot of commotion and turned to see the entire crew running toward her.

"I'm okay," she said, a little surprised at the way they were rushing to her aid. As she said it, everyone ran past her to the front of the tow.

Peanut had a laugh at her misinterpretation. "I'm sure they care about your well-being, but they're paid to look out for the well-being of the tow."

Amy collected herself. "I'm getting used to the absence of chivalry onboard this vessel. With all the commotion, I guess I momentarily lost my head and expected more."

Peanut put his arm around her shoulder. It was decidedly not a sexual advance. It was just his way of comforting her. At least he seemed to understand what the word "chivalry" meant.

CHAPTER NINETEEN

THE WEATHER CHANGED FOR THE WORSE. It started innocently enough, as it merely clouded over and started to sprinkle. That progressed into a steady downpour. The lightning and thunder were a little more reserved. The sky occasionally flickered and rumbled, but produced none of the booming bolts that tend to show up when you are far from shelter.

The weather was ultimately more of a blessing than a curse. Visibility was slightly decreased, so the Captain slowed the speed a little. On the other hand, pleasure boaters and all but the most devoted fishermen vacated the waters. All things considered, they were making better time.

Amy watched the crew work in the rain. The potential for accidents seemed to be magnified, and she hoped she could find something to make her time onboard appear to have been useful. The raingear, in particular, seemed clumsy and likely to catch on something. She realized she'd probably be in trouble, however, if a fashion report was the best she could do.

She went to her quarters and studied some existing safety manuals. She read Coast Guard regulations that pertained to the river, and some that didn't. She decided that hundreds of years of shipping must have honed the process. The only thing she could think of was whether there was a way to harness technology to improve safety. Unfortunately, she didn't have much of a technology background.

She had not been excited about the assignment. On the other hand, there was something exhilarating about being on the open water and part of actual commerce instead of cyber-this or giga-that. It gave her an appreciation for Tony Drabeck's comments about being part of what drives the American economy.

Evening came and it was Peanut's turn to man the galley. With no entrails to be found, he opted for ham steaks and macaroni and cheese. Before they were done eating, Skeeter and his big silver tooth showed up.

"I'm not going to be dealt out tonight," he said as he slapped a deck of cards on a nearby table.

Sean and Peanut looked at each other and tried to make facial expressions that nobody else would see. Actually, they always seemed to know what each other was thinking, so a quick glance was probably all that was needed.

Skeeter started to shuffle the cards. "I don't care if sweetheart here wants to play, but I ain't bein' left out again."

"Trust me," Amy said, "I'll yield my chair." The truth is she didn't want to play with Skeeter. She had enjoyed the game the night before, but the company had been different.

Skeeter was getting agitated. "So, what's it gonna be, pussies? Are ya playin' or what?"

Peanut rose and carried some dishes to the sink. "Ray. Are you in?"

"I s'pose," he said.

Sean, Peanut, and Ray all took seats with Skeeter. They cut the cards and Sean and Skeeter ended up as partners. Then they started to debate the stakes. Skeeter wanted to play for more money than any of the rest. They finally struck a compromise. It was more than the normal friendly game, but it was way less than Skeeter was proposing.

Amy got a book and positioned herself on a chair on the other side of the room. She wasn't as interested in the game as she had been before, but she had enough interest that she didn't want to leave the room.

The cards seemed to favor Skeeter that night, and he wasn't shy about letting that be known. Any card game involves a certain amount of randomness, but Skeeter strutted around as though it was only his playing prowess that allowed him to rack up points. The only one who wasn't completely put off was Sean, because, as Skeeter's partner, he was benefiting from the same luck. He was not, however, relishing it.

As the night went on, the tide never seemed to turn. Skeeter wasn't going to be able to retire to Arizona on his winnings, but he did what he could to magnify the significance of what was happening. Ray and Peanut quietly suffered the abuse, but something seemed to have lit a fire in Ray. He wasn't saying much, but his displeasure showed in the veins in his neck. He had apparently already killed a man, and he had the look of someone who'd like to know that feeling again.

Finally, the game broke up. "Let me know when you losers want to give me some more of your money," Skeeter said as he departed.

"You'll be the first person I call," Peanut said. Then, under his breath, he said, "If I need to take target practice."

"What?" Skeeter barked.

Sean answered for him. "He said you'd be the first person he'd call if he needed more practice."

Skeeter sneered, but headed out the door. "You're just lucky I got some things to do before my next shift. Otherwise, I'd have to stay and really give you a lesson."

CHAPTER TWENTY

AMY WAS SOUND ASLEEP when an alarm went off. It wasn't an alarm clock. It sounded more like a fire drill. As she opened her eyes, she heard a lot of scrambling and yelling. She silently cursed Schreiber for having sentenced her to this duty, but wasted no time getting dressed and out on deck.

She looked around expecting to see smoke, fire, or an impending collision. There was nothing. On the other hand, everyone was up and about. She sidled over to Captain Murphy and asked what was going on.

"Skeeter's missing. When the deckhands report for their shift, they always confer with the ones going off-duty in case there's anything they need to be aware of. When the shift changed this morning, nobody could find Skeeter. We've been all through the boat. We think he must have fallen overboard."

"Did you check the wing tanks?" she asked. "Maybe he just crawled down in one to take a nap and is still asleep."

Murphy gave her a patronizing smile. "Actually, that is part of the process. If Skeeter wanted to nap, though, he'd find someplace better."

Amy closed her eyes to consider the situation. She had been put onboard as the "safety inspector," and now someone apparently fell overboard and drowned on her watch. "When was he last seen?" she asked.

"Middle of the night. Sean remembers him going to make rounds on the tow, but doesn't remember seeing him after that."

Amy felt a little awkward interrogating Murphy, but this was her purpose onboard. "Did we find his life jacket?"

"No. That's why we think he must have gone over. Skeeter doesn't always like to follow the safety regulations, but wearing a life jacket when on the tow is pretty basic."

"I'm guessing we don't go back upriver and look for him."

Captain Murphy had a grim smile. "We've reported it and the authorities will look for him. It's really just a recovery at this point. If he did go over, he's either dead or made it to shore somewhere. There isn't much any of us can do."

Amy decided to interview the rest of the crew. She didn't learn much. Nobody had seen or heard anything out of the ordinary. Nobody seemed particularly upset that he was gone, but the most that could be found as a possible motive was the fact that Peanut had not paid his Euchre debt and now wouldn't have to – unless he wanted to send the widow the twenty bucks as a gesture of goodwill.

Amy decided she'd seen enough of the river. She tried to call Schreiber, but got his voicemail. She was glad for that, because that meant he couldn't overrule her decision. She could tell him that she called to confer, and, when she couldn't reach him, she made the decision that she'd be needed to help with filing the report and otherwise dealing with the Coast Guard and the insurance company. As a result, she made arrangements to disembark in Moline and rent a car to get back to Chicago. She said her goodbyes to the crew and left with confidence that she'd never see any of them again.

CHAPTER TWENTY-ONE

NEARLY A WEEK AMONG THE MARINERS made her long for her version of civilization. Between Skeeter, Dudley Raymond, and her near-death experience, her time on the river wasn't likely to make her life's highlight reel. Yet, there were moments that she would remember. In many ways, Peanut and Sean had backgrounds that seemed similar to hers, but spending time with them seemed like meeting people from a completely different world.

After a while, she called in for her voicemail messages. Her greeting had made it pretty clear that she would be out of the office and unable to return calls, but that didn't always stop people from droning on. In fact, when her greeting said she wouldn't be able to return calls, callers seemed to use that as an excuse to filibuster.

Thankfully, the mechanical voice announced that she had only one message waiting. Unfortunately, it proved to be a message she wished had been prevented by a filibuster.

"Amy, what the hell happened?" The voice was Schreiber's, and his anger was clear. "The client is hanging by a string. I send you on an assignment to find some answers to help prevent losses and you lose a crewman overboard! If we can't prevent losses under our noses, how are we going to convince anyone we can prevent losses in the future!"

The words hurt. If she were dressed down in person, it would be hard for her to hold her composure. She wasn't having much better luck even though she was on her cell phone listening to a message. She couldn't fathom how this could be her fault, but it was apparently a situation that required that someone be blamed. Regardless of fault, it looked like the end for Minnesota Marine and all that it could have meant to her career.

"Call me immediately," the message continued. "I'm heading to O'Hare to get on a plane, but you should be able to reach me before I get there."

There was no way for Schreiber to ever determine if or when she got his message. She decided, therefore, to pretend that she didn't get it for several hours. If she timed it right, she could call when he was in the air and leave a message and then spend the weekend staying away from the phone. Her plan worked.

W ITH AMY TRAVELLING AND CHADWICK entertaining clients, they had not spent much time together. They finally found time for a dinner date. Chadwick picked the most recent French restaurant to descend upon the Windy City.

As far as Amy could tell, the weekend at the farm had not caused him to start pursuing other options. It wasn't as if they had a bad time. Furthermore, Chadwick already had a social status, so it shouldn't be required that she have one too. Amy was, after all, accomplished in her own right. Just the same, she dreaded the day when Chadwick's parents would meet her family.

Amy flailed through her closet looking for the right thing to wear. She was lamenting her work situation and decided she needed to do something to change her mood. She wanted elegant, but it had to be sexy. Given the sleeping arrangements at the farm, it had been several weeks since they had been intimate. She wanted her clothes to make a statement. In fact, she wanted clothes that were both stimulating and easy to remove. If Chadwick had the urge, she wanted to be prepared to have sex the minute he walked in the door. Unfortunately, little in her wardrobe fit the bill.

Jasmine's wardrobe was another story. The two of them were about the same size, so Amy called her to get both permission and a suggestion for what to wear. A black Versace cocktail dress was the ultimate choice.

"What about shoes?" Jasmine asked. "I bet you don't have anything that would look right."

"I have some black sandals," Amy suggested.

"You can't wear flat sandals with that dress. Look in my closet. There's a couple pair of CFM shoes near the back."

Amy pondered that for a moment. "I'm guessing 'CFM' isn't a brand name."

"You got that right. It stands for something like 'come fly with me,' but I wouldn't want your virgin ears to hear what it really stands for."

With that, Amy put on the black, spaghetti-strap dress with the plunging neckline and the high-heeled CFM shoes. As she got dressed, she thought about Jasmine's red-thong-panty strategy, and the fact that it would make a good match for her red toenail polish. She didn't own any thong panties, however, and she wasn't about to borrow Jasmine's intimate apparel. After a moment of reflection, she had the answer. She wouldn't wear any panties at all.

She was not normally one to wear a lot of make-up, but she knew how to use it. Her hair required virtually no maintenance when she was going to work, but she spent some time with the curling iron. Finally, she helped herself to some of Jasmine's perfume. When she was done, she barely recognized herself in the mirror.

Chadwick called on the security phone and she asked him to come up. She opened the apartment door and left it slightly ajar so that he could let himself in and she could make an entrance from across the room. She waited in the bedroom listening for him. Finally, she heard two knocks on the door and Chadwick's voice announcing his arrival. She smiled at herself in the mirror and sashayed into the living room. "Hello, darling," she said.

Chadwick looked at her wide eyed and smiled. "Wow, you look great."

She smiled and cocked her head with a "this old thing" kind of look. She stood for a moment, wondering whether he would take off his own clothes first or start with the easy-to-remove cocktail dress. As it happened, he didn't do either. He just smiled and waited. He certainly noticed her and provided the appropriate compliment, so she decided his lust deficiency was probably for the best because it would have taken too long to redo her hair and make-up. In fact, she convinced herself that if he had made a move, she probably would have stopped him anyway. Still, she thought it would have been nice if he had tried.

As they exited her building, a breeze blew through and she felt her nakedness under the dress. There was a stirring inside her to which she wasn't accustomed. She felt like she was walking around nude and, as a result, felt completely sexual.

She sat close to him in the cab on the way to the restaurant. She held his arm, the way a woman would clutch the inside of a bicep if she were being escorted. She took his hand and put it on her bare leg, leaving it to him to explore further. That amount of public affection was not typical for her, and Chadwick seemed to notice.

When they arrived, they were asked to take a seat in the bar until their table was ready. The available spot had a bench seat against the wall and two chairs facing it. Chadwick opted for the bench, but Amy pushed in beside him so that they were sitting close together. It should have been clear to everyone that this was not a business dinner.

Amy was all questions. "How did the big meeting go?" "Are you playing golf tomorrow?" Whatever he said, she laughed or acted concerned, or effected whatever other emotion seemed appropriate.

They were eventually seated in the restaurant. Amy was all smiles, and she was attracting attention. She was aware of that fact, but kept her entire focus on Chadwick. She was doing her deferential best, with one exception.

When the waiter came to take their order, she was still making up her mind. Chadwick had pieced together his order as follows: "I want the salmon, except I don't want it medium rare, I want it well done. And then I don't want the champagne cream sauce that ordinarily goes with it. Could I get the red pepper aioli that normally goes with the squab, but can I get it on the side? And instead of the couscous, could I just get some steamed vegetables."

The waiter took detailed notes running down the side of his pad. Amy opted for the duck breast. "How would you like that done?" the waiter asked.

"What does the chef recommend?"

""Medium rare."

"Fine," she said.

"Sauce on it or on the side?" the waiter asked.

"Whatever is normal," she said with a slight smile. "Unlike some people, I don't see much point in going to an expensive restaurant and asking the chef to cook you a meal the way you'd cook it at home if you were inclined to stay home and cook. At a place like this, I expect the chef to show me a thing or two." The waiter gave her an appreciative smile as he walked away.

Amy suddenly realized that she had strayed from her plan. She shrunk down in her seat with a hint of regret for having mocked Chadwick. "Sorry if that sounded kind of mean."

He smiled broadly. "Actually, it was a little bit of a relief. I was starting to wonder if you were really Amy Prescott. The way you're dressed and the way you've been acting, I thought maybe aliens kidnapped the real Amy and put you here as a stand-in."

She wasn't sure how to respond, so she subtly stuck out the tip of her tongue in a way that only he could see it. Chadwick chuckled at the sight.

He gave her an amused look for a long time. "Please don't think that I don't like the way you're dressed or the way you've been acting, but I'm wondering if something's going on."

She tried to avoid the subject. "What do you mean?"

"You're usually Amy Prescott, professional woman in charge. Tonight, you're Chadwick's arm piece and eye candy. I'm not objecting, I'm just curious."

She was looking down, but raised her eyes to look at him. "I guess I was starting to think that it would be easier to just be Chadwick's girl instead of Amy Prescott, professional woman in charge. Being your arm piece is a little easier than fighting the battles I have to fight day in and day out."

"Something bad happen at work?"

"No, nothing in particular." After a moment, she said, "Or maybe, yes, everything." She shook her head and frowned. "I don't feel like anyone takes me seriously. I went out to that towboat fire and they basically ignored me. I go to interview the crew, and I get hit on by some fossil and leered at by the rest of the lowlifes. Even when I went to the owner of

Minnesota Marine Transport to tell him about my investigation plans he scolded me and told me not to do the things I think are the most important. Now, someone fell overboard and I'm getting blamed."

"Is it just this assignment? Maybe you just need to put it in perspective."

"That's the thing. It's not just this. I'm working my butt off to make partner, and I feel like I'm being shut out by the old boys' club. Mr. Schreiber acts like he's my supporter, but I think he would be just as happy having me as his mistress."

"Has it ever occurred to you that you seem to have a problem with male authority figures?"

"I don't think that's the issue. I'll admit that I haven't had much respect for most of the male authority figures in my life, but I think that's just a matter of circumstance."

He put his hand on top of hers. "I didn't know you were so unhappy."

"I'm not saying I'm unhappy. I'm just tired of not feeling like I'm respected. Hell, even the guys in the mailroom make fun of me with that C'Amanda Prescott crap. I never ask for special treatment. I just want credit for what I do. Or, at least I thought I did. If I change my focus to just being Chadwick's girl, the criteria for success are a little clearer. I need to look pretty, and I need to make you happy. Somehow, I think there'd be a lot less pressure."

Chadwick was nodding his head slowly as if to indicate he was weighing the options. "Amy, you're good enough looking to be anyone's trophy, but that's not your style. Don't get mad at me for saying this, but you're just not a girly girl. And I'm not saying that just because of the way you handled that shotgun when we were at the farm. The real Amy Prescott is the woman who mocks guys who make too much of a production ordering dinner. I'm not saying I like being the butt of your barbs, but that's the Amy Prescott that everyone knows and loves."

"So, you don't think I'm a bitch?"

He hesitated a little too long, and she spoke up again. "You think I'm a bitch?"

"No, I don't think you're a bitch. I think you're someone who always speaks her mind, and that's one of the qualities that makes you stand out.

You have a strong personality and a strong presence. I don't think there's any way around that. You can't try to be something you're not."

"Are you okay with that?"

Well, as long as you've brought it up, I have been giving our relationship a lot of thought."

Amy didn't like where she thought this was heading. "And?"

"Maybe it's time we think about seeing other people."

Those were the most dreaded words in the history of relationships. "Is it because of my family? Is that what this is about?"

"No, it has nothing to do with that."

Amy doubted his words. "This seems kind of out of the blue."

"I'm not saying it's over. I just think we should slow down." That was the second worst sentence in the history of relationships.

"What's the point? If you're no longer interested, slowing down will just be a slow death."

"I didn't say I was no longer interested. I just have my doubts."

Amy had doubts as well, but she figured that was part of the equation. She wasn't certain Chadwick was the one, but he was closer to it than anyone else she'd ever met.

CHAPTER TWENTY-TWO

A MY COULDN'T FIND A REASON to get out of bed Saturday morning. She drifted in and out of sleep, but mostly just lay there devoid of an urge to do anything else. When she heard Jasmine get up, she knew she'd been in bed too long. For her part, Jasmine apparently assumed Amy was up and gone, as she turned the stereo on at a level that would wake anyone in the apartment. Amy wasn't prepared to explain to Jasmine why she was still in bed, so she stayed in her room until she heard Jasmine leave.

She finally got up and walked to the bathroom. She turned on a light and looked at herself in the mirror. She was always comfortable with her physical appearance, but there was something that troubled her that the mirror didn't really show. If she looked close, it might be revealed by the emptiness in her eyes. She had never really found her place in life, and that void seemed to keep her from ever being truly content.

She felt out of place on the farm, but she felt equally out of place among Chadwick's friends. She was confident about her skills as a lawyer, but felt unappreciated and isolated as a woman in a firm dominated by men. She liked to joke about Jasmine's promiscuity, but at least Jasmine seemed to know what she wanted and was comfortable in her own skin. Amy's life seemed to be a constant journey, with the eternal hope that the next day she'd reach her destination. While that unending quest was a struggle, today it looked farther from reach than ever before.

For all of her resistance to taking the Minnesota Marine case, she now wanted more than anything to stay on it. Based on the tone of Schreiber's voice, she wasn't sure that would be an option. Being taken off the case would deprive her of more than just an opportunity for vindication. Minnesota Marine was looking like her best chance to make partner, and that hope was fading fast.

As if her professional dilemma were not enough, her personal life had a newfound problem as well. She had invested a lot of time with Chadwick and not having him as a boyfriend was going to leave a void. She tried to convince herself it was for the best. Chadwick was sweet, and she'd had no trouble telling him that she loved him. Being *in love* with him was, however, a different story. She never doodled his name on the side of a notepad during a boring meeting. She never fantasized about their life together five months down the road, much less five years. Still, she never expected to get dumped.

Amy could not coax herself to even smile at her reflection. She decided to take a picture of herself. *This is the most depressed I can ever remember being in my life,* she thought. *I'll take a picture to remind myself and hope that I never feel this bad again.* Unfortunately, she hadn't made a plan for how she was going to improve things. She just assumed that things couldn't get any worse.

She put on jeans and a sweatshirt. She didn't bother to shower, so she tucked her hair into a baseball cap. She wasn't sure what she would do, but she was determined not to stay at home all day. She caught a taxi that dropped her off by Lake Michigan.

She walked along Lakeshore Drive, and then decided to walk out on Navy Pier. Walking the pier always reminded her of what she liked about Chicago. It was the strong, silent type. Chicago didn't argue like New York or scream for attention like Los Angeles. Chicago was a big, muscular place that didn't need to tell anyone it was there. New York was money made on investments, and Los Angeles was money for being pretty. Chicago had the feeling of a city that worked for a living.

As with most summer weekends, the crowd was mostly tourists. She walked by families with small children and couples holding hands. The thing she didn't see was anyone else walking alone. Being around so many people made her feel even more isolated.

She walked up to Grant Park and sat by the fountain. She stared at it long and hard, as though it would hold the answers. It didn't. Still, the sun was warm and the mist felt good. She didn't have any place else to be. Her office was nearby, but she didn't think that would help her mood.

She got up and started to walk around the perimeter of the fountain. As she strolled, an old man in a tattered sport coat and some semblance of a bowler hat rushed toward her. If he had a kerchief on a stick, he could have been the poster boy for a hobo convention. "Excuse me," he said, trying to undo the startled look on Amy's face. "I don't want to bother you, but I desperately need a quarter. Please. It's a matter of monumental importance, and if you could just give me a quarter it would take care of everything."

Amy paused and was momentarily overcome by his chicken-soup body odor. She was never one to encourage panhandlers and usually had to restrain herself from actively insulting them or otherwise trying to discourage them. This one had a genuine look of earnestness that suggested that the money wouldn't be used for liquor or cigarettes. Of course, it's probably a short distance between "earnestness" and mental illness. Nonetheless, Amy reached in her pocket and produced a quarter.

"Thank you ma'am," he said with an appreciation that would have been more appropriate if she had just pushed him out of the way of a speeding truck. "This will take care of everything. My entire life is going to change because of you."

Amy smiled, but wasn't eager to have a discussion or otherwise do anything that would prolong his presence. "I'm glad," was all she said.

The old man was clutching the quarter in his hand. She watched him walk over next to the fountain. He held his fist in front of him and started saying something to himself. He opened his hand and kissed the quarter. Then he threw it in the fountain.

As she walked toward home, she couldn't stop thinking about the old man. At least he had a plan for how he was going to make his life better.

CHAPTER TWENTY-THREE

S HE MANAGED TO AVOID SCHREIBER all weekend, but on Monday it was time to face the music. She was having difficulty understanding how she could be at fault and was trying to prepare a defense. Something about the whole thing just didn't seem right. Her depression was starting to combine with anger. When the elevator didn't arrive quickly enough, she punched the button over and over again as if that would get it there quicker.

When she got to the office, some of the lights were on. Valiant was working on something in the mailroom. He noticed her and let out a jovial, "Good morning, Ms. C. Amanda Prescott."

Amy started to say something, but then walked by in silence. She had bigger problems.

She turned on her computer and checked her voicemail. There was another message from Schreiber complaining about not being able to reach her. When the computer finished warming up, there was more of the same in her emails. It was a mystery to her what could have needed doing over the weekend, and she was not regretting her plan to avoid work and everything related to it.

She didn't really have anything to work on, and wasn't in a mood to work anyway. She looked out the window, and then surveyed her office. Most of her legal career was encapsulated on her wall and bookcase. She had her diplomas and bar admissions framed on the wall behind her. She had a variety of trinkets and mementos from cases that she'd handled and places that she'd been. There was a toy bus from a transportation company that she'd represented in front of the Interstate Commerce Commission. There was a replica of the Eiffel Tower with a pencil sharpener in the base, which she had bought as a joke when she had to go to Paris in connection with a licensing dispute. Her favorite was a pencil with a two-headed eraser that made it look like a gavel. She bought it in the gift shop at the United States Supreme Court when she was there to watch arguments related to a case she was handling.

She put her head on her arms and rested them on her desk. She wasn't crying, but she was certainly maudlin. Things seemed like they were changing, and she wasn't sure she liked the direction.

After several minutes, she heard a soft knock on the door. She looked up to see Valiant with a somber look on his face. "Ms. Prescott, are you okay?"

She looked at him while she considered the best response. Finally, in an angry voice she said, "Don't you mean, 'Are you okay, *C'Amanda Prescott?*'"

That seemed to catch him by surprise.

"That's right," she said, "I know about your little nickname for me."

Valiant had a sheepish smile. "Is that what's bothering you?"

She let out a deep breath. "I have bigger problems than that. It's just that, once in a while, it'd be nice not to have to deal with all the little problems as well."

Valiant was shaking his head. "I know that name sounds bad, but it's not meant to be."

She let out an involuntary "Hah!" She looked away from him. "Of course. Calling me C'Amanda Prescott is probably an honor compared to calling me 'Bitch Prescott.'"

He didn't respond right away. He moved from the doorway to a chair across from Amy's desk. "It actually is a compliment, but we didn't think it would be taken that way."

"I can see why," she said. "How can it be a compliment?"

Valiant was choosing his words carefully. "It's on account of Martin Luther King's dream going both ways."

Amy could tell he was being sincere, but that didn't mean she could tell what he was talking about. "I don't follow," she said in a voice that had some of the grit taken out of it.

"Dr. King dreamed of a world where black people would be judged not by the color of their skin, but by the content of their character. I think that should go both ways. If a black person screws up or does something illegal, that shows bad character and that person should be judged accordingly."

"Valiant, I'm still not following you."

"You're the only one in this firm who treats the African-Americans like they should be held accountable. If one of my guys lies about being sick or screws something up, the old white guys act like it's just the way we are and that we can't be expected to do any better. And if we're ever asked to do something that's not part of the regular routine, they explain it in painful detail like we couldn't figure it out."

He looked at her as if trying to see if she was following him now. "You, on the other hand, give orders like we're in the army and everyone knows what to do. If someone screws something up, you're not shy about letting them know. You treat us like you treat everyone: direct and to the point. We never wonder what you're secretly saying behind our backs because you say everything in front of us."

"Okay," she said, "but wouldn't you rather have the kid-glove treatment?"

"Look," he said, "if I have to choose between someone who's gonna treat me bad just 'cause I'm black and someone who's gonna treat me good just 'cause I'm black, I'll take being treated good. What I really want, though, is someone who doesn't do either."

Amy was dumbstruck. She had been ready to lay into him, but now couldn't think of a thing to say.

Valiant wasn't having that problem. "With the old white guys, they act like we're doing a good job if we don't do drugs on our lunch break. But when Amy Prescott stops by the mailroom to thank someone for doing a good job, it actually means something. So, I'm really sorry if we upset you with that name, but it really wasn't meant to be mean."

Amy wasn't sure whether to laugh or cry. "I have to admit," she said, "it was kind of clever."

"Well, I'll tell the boys to stop saying it." As he spoke, he rose from the chair and started for the door.

"Valiant," she said. "You don't have to say anything to them. They can keep calling me whatever they want." She paused until she caught his eye. "But I'd appreciate it if you'd start calling me Amy."

CHAPTER TWENTY-FOUR

SCHREIBER DIDN'T COME INTO THE OFFICE at all on Monday. In the afternoon, Amy got a message that she needed to go back to Minnesota Marine's headquarters in St. Paul. She wasn't told the reason, but the situation seemed grave. She wasn't sure whether she was being called because she was still working on the file or because Schreiber wanted to yell at her in front of the client.

When she arrived the next day, Schreiber was already there. He gave her a look like a doctor about to tell a person his relative was not going to survive. Drabeck was hunched over the conference table studying some documents. He looked up and greeted her with a weak smile. "Thanks for coming," he said.

"Mr. Drabeck, I'm sorry about what happened," she said. "I don't know what I could have done differently, but I'm sorry about what happened and I'll do whatever I can to help."

"I think my little world may be coming to an end," he said with resignation. "Minnesota Marine has become the target of a hostile takeover."

Amy wrinkled her face to show her disbelief. "Sir, I'm not a mergers and acquisitions lawyer, but hostile takeovers generally involve companies that have publicly traded stock. You're the majority owner of Minnesota Marine, so how can there be a hostile takeover?"

"Do you remember those Rube Goldberg cartoons?" he asked. "You know, the ones where the toaster pops and the toast knocks loose a marble, and the marble rolls down a ramp, and so on? That's basically what happened."

"I'm listening," she said.

"For starters, we lost our insurance. We're covered for everything that's already happened, but we have no coverage going forward. Next, we have a line of credit at the bank, and one of the conditions of the loan is that we have insurance in place. It's just like a mortgage company requiring you to have homeowner's insurance. Anyway, because we don't have insurance, we're in default on the terms of the bank loan."

"So, the bank is trying to take you over?"

"No. I'm not done with the Rube Goldberg part. I own the majority of the stock, but, for everyone's protection, we have a buy-sell agreement in place. If I'm running the business and it goes into default, the other shareholders have the right to buy me out. The idea was that if I ran into problems they could still save the company."

"That makes sense," she said. "So, what's the problem?"

"My youngest daughter and her husband got divorced several years ago. As part of the settlement, they split the stock. The son of a bitch didn't deserve any of it, but my daughter's lawyer thought it would be a good idea because a minority stake in a private company isn't really worth anything unless we sell the company. There's no public market for it like a regular stock, and nobody outside of the company is likely to buy it. The problem is that he's getting impatient waiting for me to die or sell the company."

"So, you're ex-son-in-law – what's his name?" she asked.

"Frank Bogardus."

"So, Frank Bogardus is conducting a hostile takeover?" she asked.

"Not really. I think he's being backed by Amalgamated Grain. If I'm right, they'll pay for his attorneys, and he'll sell the company to them if he's successful." As he spoke, he smiled at her. "How's that for a predicament?"

"That's a doozy," she said. "Let me make sure I'm following this. If we can find insurance, will we be okay?"

"If we find it soon enough," he said.

"And if we can get the bank to waive the default or if we can get a new bank that doesn't require insurance, will we be okay?"

"That's true, but much easier said than done."

"Last, if we can prove that Bogardus isn't entitled to exercise the buy-sell because of misconduct, fraud, or something else, will we be okay?"

Drabeck's eyebrows arched to show that he hadn't thought of that. "I guess that's right," he said.

"So, we have at least three avenues to pursue. Get insurance, make a deal with the bank or another bank, or find a way to invalidate the buy-sell agreement."

Drabeck had a smile for the first time in the meeting. "When you put it like that, you make it sound like we have lots of options."

"Well, there may be more, but you haven't really given me time to analyze the situation." She smiled back. "Where should we start?"

Schreiber had been on the sidelines, but stepped forward and dropped a stack of papers in front of Amy. "Right here," he said. "It's a motion to evict Tony from the premises immediately. It's scheduled for next week."

"Next week!" Amy said with shock. "How can they do that?"

"Simple," Schreiber said. "They called it an eviction action, and evictions are handled in a special housing court. They're done on short notice because most of the cases involve landlords who aren't getting paid rent. We already tried to talk to the clerk's office to tell them that this wasn't a simple eviction, but they said we'd have to tell it to the judge."

"All right," she said. "Give me the paperwork and I'll start to analyze it."

"Anything else?" Drabeck asked.

She thought for a moment. "Has anyone talked to Skeeter's next of kin? Maybe we can work something out before the personal injury lawyers get involved."

"Not to my knowledge," Drabeck replied. "I think he has a common-law wife in Missouri who would be the beneficiary."

"Why don't you get me the name and address and I'll try to make contact," Amy said. "If we can avoid having to pay an injury lawyer, we can pay less and she actually gets more. If we can work the right deal, maybe the insurance company will reconsider."

"Anything I can do to help?" Schreiber asked.

"Maybe you can work the business end. See if you can find another insurance company. Or talk to the bank and see if something can be worked out."

"Aye, aye," Schreiber said.

CHAPTER TWENTY-FIVE

THE EVICTION MOTION WAS OF PARAMOUNT importance, but there was enough time to prepare. Contacting Skeeter's wife was, however, something that couldn't wait. Amy got the information from the company and booked a flight to St. Louis. Skeeter actually had lived downstate aways, but she preferred to avoid the regional airports when possible.

She rented a car and pointed it toward Arkansas. As the scenery became more rural, she found it both familiar and frightening. The landscape and the buildings were similar to the rural part of Wisconsin from which she hailed. On the other hand, there was something decidedly southern about it, and she'd seen enough movies with unflattering depictions of southerners to make her uneasy about the prospect of the car breaking down.

Skeeter's real name turned out to be Peter Willard. Amy had thought the reason he got his nickname was because he was as annoying as a mosquito. Instead, when he'd first become a deckhand, he was paired with another guy named Peter. Skeeter was first called "skinny Peter," before it was shortened to Skeeter. His personality may have helped the nickname stick after the other Peter moved on.

Skeeter's wife had the somewhat unfortunate first name of Estrus. Amy's mission was to find Estrus Willard and ask her to consider a quick and easy settlement. Amy had no intention of cheating Mrs. Willard. Indeed, a settlement signed by a widow under pressure would probably not hold up anyway. She did, however, want to reach her before a personal injury lawyer pressured her into signing away a third or more of the money to which she was entitled.

The Willards lived in an area that apparently didn't rely on signs to mark the roads. Amy was sure she was close, but wasn't making progress.

She finally stopped at a dilapidated Texaco station for directions. Asking about the address didn't seem to help, but, when she said she was looking for the Willard place, the attendant was able to direct her.

The Willard house turned out to be a trailer home set back from the road in the woods. As she pulled onto the gravel driveway, two barking dogs ran out to greet her. She slowed out of concern that she would run them over, but then realized that they must have been through the drill before. Still, her general reluctance about the meeting was enough to keep her from hurrying.

The Willard place was a menagerie of half-completed projects. A 1950's vintage Thunderbird sat to one side of the house with its hood open like it was in mid-repair, but with weeds growing so high around it that nobody could have been near it for at least a season. Nearby was a wooden trailer with one side propped up on blocks waiting for a new wheel. Toward the back were the beginnings of some type of project and a stack of graying boards ready to be assembled. Somebody at the Willard place was apparently a lot better at concepts than execution.

Amy spotted a woman hanging clothes on a clothesline. She had a head full of curlers and a cigarette cocked in the corner of her mouth. The woman finished pinning a sheet and walked toward the car. Her expression was not necessarily hostile, but she did have the look of someone who regarded every stranger as possibly a "revenuer."

"Can I help you?" the woman said.

Amy had opened the window, but hadn't yet turned off the engine. "Are you Estrus?" she asked.

The woman nodded. "Yeah, but I go by Esty."

Amy shut off the car and got out. "I'm Amy Prescott," she said while extending her hand for a shake. "I've come here on behalf of Minnesota Marine Transport."

Esty shook her hand, but gave her a suspicious once over. "Someone already came and told me about Skeeter. What do you want?"

Amy hadn't really rehearsed what to say because she didn't want anything she said to sound rehearsed. Unfortunately, she now found herself a little at a loss for words. "First, I want to say how sorry I am about your loss. And I don't mean just on behalf of the company. I met your husband briefly, and, even though I didn't really know him, I want to express my sympathies."

Esty Willard was nodding as Amy spoke, but not becoming any more welcoming. Amy continued, "I want to talk to you about your financial needs now that Peter is gone."

"His bills are all gone," Esty snapped. "Peter told me if he was dead that I didn't have to pay any of it."

"That may be," Amy said. "I don't really know much about family law in Missouri or anywhere else for that matter. If he had debts and you weren't part of those debts, then you probably aren't responsible for them. You'd have to ask a local lawyer and you'd probably have to provide a lot more specific information."

Mrs. Willard's hostile expression was still not abating. Amy decided to switch gears. "Have you talked to anyone about a funeral?"

"No," she said. "There's nothin' to bury. They haven't recovered his body."

"I s'pose," Amy said, "but what about a memorial service or something?"

Esty shrugged her shoulders. "Then I'd just have to do it all over again when they did recover the body." Her tone and behavior did not suggest much grief at his passing.

"Mrs. Willard," Amy said, "your last name is Willard, isn't it?"

"I guess so," she said. "We never got a license that said so, but the people at the county say we got a common-law marriage."

"Well, whether you're a common-law wife or a regular wife, you're entitled to something when your husband dies. Once a coroner officially rules that your husband is dead, the insurance company will pay you something for your loss."

"What if they don't find his body?" she asked. "Can they still say he's dead?"

"I think so," Amy said, "but there's probably some sort of waiting period." Esty seemed to drop a little of the hostility. "That's why I've come," Amy said. "I'm pretty sure that the insurance company will pay you something for your loss, and I want to give you some advice. Do you know any lawyers?"

"Not really. I mean, I know the names of the lawyers in town, but I don't know 'em."

"Okay. I'm going to give you a check for $5,000. It's a down payment on what the insurance company will pay. Do you know what a contingent fee lawyer is?"

"Not really."

"It's a lawyer who agrees that he'll take your case but won't charge you anything unless he recovers something. Sometimes that's a great deal, but sometimes you end up giving the lawyer part of the money that you could have had anyway. I'm giving you the $5,000 because I want you to hire a lawyer and pay him by the hour to advise you. I think the insurance company will offer you a couple hundred thousand dollars. Instead of giving a third of that to a lawyer, I want you to hire a lawyer and I'm giving you the money to do it. That way, you'll get everything the insurance company pays. If the lawyer says the insurance company isn't offering enough, you can go ahead and hire him to sue the company, but you should tell him you're only giving him a percentage of the amount above what is offered."

The magnitude of the recovery was changing her mood. "Would the check just be made out to me?" she asked.

"Of course," Amy said. "Who else would be on it?"

Esty looked a little startled by that response. "Well, other times we got checks, they was made out to the bank too."

"Well, I don't know the details of your financial situation, but it would ordinarily just go to you. However, if you have debts, the bank might make a claim."

Amy was a little surprised that southern hospitality hadn't warranted an invitation into the house or the offer of a cold drink. She didn't want to prolong her stay, but she wanted to feel like she'd gained some trust or, at a minimum, got Esty to understand. Unfortunately, that was probably not the case.

After an awkward moment, Amy said, "It was a long trip down here, so I think I'll go into town and look for a room. If I have other questions, will you be home tonight or are you going out?"

Esty let out an involuntary laugh. "No ma'am. I'll be right here where I am every night. I'll be thinkin' and prayin' about Skeeter. Woman like me don't got nowhere to go, 'specially with my man bein' gone."

"Yes," Amy said. "Again, I'm sorry for your loss."

BACK ON THE HIGHWAY, Amy clicked on her cell phone and called her investigator. "Have you found anything else about the Dudley Raymond conviction?"

"Absolutely nothing," Scouten said. "I'm not sure if there are no records, or if it was just an accident I found the first one."

"What do you mean?"

"Well, maybe his record has been expunged. You know, wiped off the books. Maybe I just found the conviction because someone forgot to seal all of the records."

"Okay," Amy said, "but I might have some more information for you. Drabeck had a son who died, and Ray might have had something to do with it. Maybe that will help."

"What was the son's name?"

Amy paused. "I don't know."

"Where did it happen?"

Amy paused again. "I don't know that either."

"How long ago did it happen?"

"I'm getting your point," she snapped.

"Hey, I'm just telling you. The internet is nice, but older records are a different story. Besides, even if I find an obituary, it probably won't be tied to Ray."

"Okay," she said, "don't worry about that right now. I've got something else for you. If I need some surveillance in southern Missouri, do you have someone you can network with or will you have to come down here yourself?"

"Depends. What do ya got?"

"I came down to visit with the widow of a crewman who went overboard and is presumed drowned. Something doesn't seem quite right."

"Hey, she's probably a little distraught. Cut her some slack."

"That's the problem. She doesn't seem too distraught. I think she might have been getting a little side action when her husband was away. At best, she's a common-law wife, and her claim for loss of comfort, care, and consortium may be undermined a bit if she's spending a lot of time in bed with someone else."

Scouten was quiet for a moment. "I haven't done that kind of stake-out for quite a while. What are you basing your conclusion on?"

"Isn't woman's intuition enough?"

"If you're paying me by the day no matter what I find, I guess it could be."

"You apparently don't think I have any instinct for your line of work."

"Maybe," he said. "Or maybe I do think you have an instinct and I want in on it. What's your basis for thinking she's horsing around with someone else?"

Amy wondered whether she should wait to see if her hunch played out before revealing more, but decided to share. "In part, because she didn't seem distraught and seemed pretty interested in the money. The real thing, though, was that she was wearing curlers even though she told me she didn't have any plans to go anywhere. I specifically asked her whether she was going out, and she insisted she was just going to stay home. If that's the case, the only reason she'd have curlers in her hair was if she was expecting company."

"Clever," he said. "She probably didn't think to lie because she probably forgot she was even wearin' 'em."

"My thought exactly."

"Well, I can get there tomorrow," he said, "but it sounds like you need someone there tonight."

Amy was quiet as the rational part of her brain tried to negotiate with the adventurous side. Finally, she said, "I'll stick around tonight and see what I can find. Make sure you get here by tomorrow, though, 'cause I've got to get ready for a hearing."

She gave him detailed information on how to find the house. She hung up and drove to the nearest town. Actually calling it a town might have been an overstatement. It was an intersection that had some type of commercial establishment on each corner. One was a small grocery store.

Amy walked the aisles until she found cheese, fruit, and various other items appropriate for a picnic. She went to a small meat case to browse. An old man who had been sitting by the cash register came over to ask if she needed help.

"Yes," she said. "Do you have any beef shanks? You know, the bones with the marrow still in them."

The man looked at the rest of her picnic lunch with curiosity. "They're in the freezer section," he said.

Amy bought two frozen shanks to go with her lunch and then drove around until she found a suitable place to eat. The only picnic table she could find was at a rest stop, and it was not a particularly nice one. She was alone, and that made her uneasy. The sound of cars approaching only heightened her anxiety. Finally, she decided to eat in the car.

She sat, ready to pull out if someone else pulled in. That never happened, but she finally grew tired of the whole situation. She pulled out and drove around aimlessly until dark. She then headed back to the Willard residence.

She wanted to stake out the driveway, but there wasn't an inconspicuous place from which to do so. She parked on a side road a quarter mile up from the Willard driveway. She turned off the car and waited. Over the course of an hour, two cars went by and neither pulled into the Willard residence. Amy was not content to wait all night. Furthermore, she decided the visitor might have shown up earlier. For that matter, he could have been in the house when Amy was there earlier in the day.

She started the car and pulled it further onto the shoulder. She had originally positioned herself for a quick exit, but now she wanted to move the car out of the way in case someone came along the road. She turned off the engine and got out of the car. She did her best to close the car door without making much noise.

The woods were dark and she didn't have a flashlight. As a result, she walked along the side of the road until she was near the Willard driveway. As soon as she stepped onto the Willard property, two barking dogs were upon her. She crossed her arms and stood motionless while they stopped to conduct their olfactory-based investigation. While the dogs were sniffing, Amy reached into her purse and pulled out the beef shanks. She handed one to each dog, and they no longer had any interest in her whatsoever.

She stood motionless in case the dogs had aroused interest from the house. She didn't see any lights come on. After a minute, she decided it was okay to get closer. Walking in the woods was ordinarily a difficult task in the dark, but the Willard obstacle course made it even worse. Her steps were slow and short, as she fully expected to stub her toe.

As she approached, she could hear music. She also heard a woman occasionally giggling over the music. When she got within twenty feet, she recognized the song as "Free Bird," also known as the "Redneck Bolero" because it was a favored accompaniment for coitus among the bumpkin class. The slow melody at the beginning basically enforced a minimum foreplay requirement, while the hard pounding finish suited the sexual technique most in vogue.

Now she could hear murmurs from a man and a woman. She couldn't make out anything that was being said, and she couldn't recognize the voices. She could, however, tell by the giggling that it was a romantic interlude. That wasn't necessarily what she wanted to hear, but she took some comfort knowing that the occupants of the house would be too engaged to notice someone creeping around in the brush.

She moved next to an open window. There was a screen, and the curtain was fluttering in the breeze. From the sounds coming out, she determined that it was the bedroom, or at least the room where the occupants had decided to have relations.

Amy strained to decipher any of the words being spoken. Perhaps Estrus would shout her partner's name in a fit of passion and end the mystery. The voices inside remained low, however, and she was unable to recognize anything.

The band was in the upswing, and Amy was expecting something to happen soon. At the very least, perhaps they would finish and turn on a light so that Amy could confirm her suspicions. She was so focused on the sounds coming from the house that she didn't hear a car coming in the driveway. Instead, she saw parts of the yard suddenly illuminated by the headlights.

She ran to the back of the house and stood silent. Her heart was pounding out a rhythm worthy of Sousa. The engine of the car was turned off, and Amy noticed that the music had been turned off as well. A car door slammed and was followed by loud knocking on the Willards' door.

"Who is it?" she heard Esty yell.

"Where is he?" the visitor barked.

"Who are you talking about?"

"You know who I'm here for."

"There's nobody here but me."

"I ain't leavin' until I've searched every inch of this property."

That was all Amy needed to hear. She walked as quickly as she could away from the house. When she got far enough into the woods, she cut back toward the road. When she got to her car, she paused and wondered if she should try to observe from a distance. The rational part of her brain quickly disabused her of that notion. She started the car and headed home.

CHAPTER TWENTY-SIX

AMY SPENT SEVERAL DAYS RESEARCHING the eviction motion. Real estate has two basic components – ownership and possession. The person who owned property didn't necessarily have the right to possession if, for example, someone else was leasing the property. Similarly, the person in possession might not have any claim to ownership. Depending on the component involved, the relevant legal proceedings might vary.

Possession issues usually involved apartment dwellers that failed to pay their rent. Because there was not an ownership issue involved, expedited hearings were held in order to allow evictions. Deciding who owned property was another matter. The common law called that procedure "ejectment," and it was designed as a means to seek a change in the title to the property. The concepts were obviously similar, but the lawyers for Bogardus had apparently decided to ignore the distinction in order to push the matter forward as quickly as possible.

The hearing was scheduled as part of the regular housing court calendar. The attorneys for Bogardus filed a cursory Complaint, but not a detailed brief. Amy decided that she did not want to prepare a brief anticipating possible arguments because she might inadvertently raise an argument that hadn't occurred to the other side. She did, however, try to prepare for every possibility.

Amy met Drabeck early in the morning in order to prepare. "Are you ready?" he asked.

"I think so."

After a pause, he said, "Look I don't want to tell you how to do your job, but I think it's just a matter of telling the judge what a bum Bogardus is. He's lazy, he cheated on my daughter, and he can't hold his liquor." It wasn't clear which of those traits Tony found most objectionable.

She smiled. "Nothing I've learned about him made me think he was an overachiever."

"Well, let's tell the judge and maybe we can be done with this."

Arguing the facts was not what she anticipated would happen on this day. Explaining that to Drabeck was not likely to be easy. "Tony, do you play cards at all?"

"Some. Why?"

"I think we need to handle this with a little finesse. By that, I mean we don't put all our cards -- or even our best cards -- on the table yet. We have some good procedural arguments for today, so I want to save our other weapons until later."

Drabeck looked disappointed.

Amy tried to reassure him. "Whatever happens today is just the first round. We'll be back. If we tip our hand too much, it'll give him a chance to prepare for the testimony."

That seemed to satisfy him.

Amy grabbed her briefcase and led Drabeck to the Ramsey County Courthouse. The classic elegance of the building was somewhat subverted by the imposition of metal detectors. It wasn't just the chrome and glass contrasting with the wood and marble. The building had not been designed for a screening area, and traffic flows were completely snarled as a result. Some doors were now designated only as entrances, while others were now only exits. Unlike airline passengers, attorneys couldn't avoid the hassles of the machinery by wearing flip-flops instead of dress shoes.

Amy and Drabeck found the housing court. Normally, out-of-state lawyers have to associate with a lawyer in the state in order to appear in court. Because of the informal nature of the proceedings, Amy managed to get permission to appear, at least initially, without local counsel. That was good from a cost standpoint, although the presence of an ally with local knowledge was frequently worth the cost.

The courtroom and the lobby outside of it were crowded with people waiting for their hearings. The tenants did not always show up, and sometimes they showed up because they thought they had to, even if they didn't have a defense. Still, it would be a cattle call, and Amy could only hope that they wouldn't have to sit through a morning of other hearings. That hope would not become a reality.

They found seats in the gallery. The judge had not taken the bench, but the clerk and court reporter were in their places. Like most courtrooms, the judge sat above the rest of the proceedings, while the clerk and court reporter were lower than the judge, but still elevated above the rest of the courtroom.

A middle-aged man with a dark tan and a blue pinstripe suit was leaning an elbow on the clerk's desk. He was telling a story of some sort, and otherwise acting chummy with her. He did not spare his attention on the court reporter, however, making a point to bring him into the story as well. When the bailiff entered, the man greeted him by name. This was, apparently, the courthouse schmoozer.

After a while, he seemed to notice Amy. He excused himself from the conversation and walked over to her. "Excuse me," he said, "are you the attorney for Minnesota Marine?"

She was a little taken aback. "Yes. I'm Amy Prescott." She stood and extended her hand.

The man took her hand, but not in a shake. Instead, he held her hand as if he might kiss it or at least declare *enchanté* as a greeting. He smiled as if he expected that they would soon be lovers. "I'm Mark Cavanaugh," he said. "I represent Frank Bogardus."

Amy managed a suitable greeting. She wasn't sure how to react to him. There's a fine line between charming and smarmy, and she hadn't decided which side he fell on. He certainly had the ability to attract attention, however. She was trying to decide on appropriate small talk when the judge entered and court was in session.

The clerk began calling cases. The first several were defaults, which meant one or both parties didn't show. Provided the landlord was there, an order allowing them to recover the property was generally issued.

The court then began hearing contested matters. The stories provided by the tenants tended to run the gamut. Some claimed that they had deliberately withheld rent because the property had not been properly maintained. Some had sob stories. One man's defense was that he didn't pay when the rent was due because he was in jail at the time. While the process gave tenants a chance to speak, few had explanations that changed the outcome.

As cases were called and heard, the courtroom slowly emptied. Before long, the only people left were the people then arguing their case and the lawyers and clients in the Minnesota Marine matter. The Court had apparently saved the best for last.

Judge Elizabeth Pendens looked to be in her mid- to late thirties. When Mark Cavanaugh made his appearance for the record, he greeted the judge like an old friend. If home field could be considered an advantage in the courtroom, Cavanaugh was doing everything he could to maximize it. Amy wondered whether she should have found some equally engaging local attorney to sit at counsel table with her.

The judge nodded without much expression as the rest of the participants introduced themselves for the record. When that was done, she advised that their case had been kept until the end because it was likely to take the longest and that it seemed the fairest thing to do. Whether they agreed or not, the participants were not going to take issue with the procedure chosen.

Cavanaugh was first to argue. He said he had witnesses that were prepared to take the stand, but first he wanted to explain his case. "I represent Frank Bogardus, and he is a minority shareholder in Minnesota Marine. As a minority shareholder, he has virtually no rights to make decisions for the company. Furthermore, he has no real rights to sell his stock because it's not a publicly traded stock. To protect him and his rights, there is a buy-sell agreement that gives him the right to buy a controlling interest in the company if there is ever a default. More importantly, the real estate is set up to automatically transfer to the other owners in the event of a default. That's what happened here."

Cavanaugh spoke with force, but with a calm voice devoid of rough edges. He spoke quickly, but the words flowed so smoothly that he didn't seem rushed or remotely uncomfortable. He explained the underlying transaction in detail, but then focused on the default and the likelihood of losing everything. He wanted the Court to know that, if his client did not receive immediate relief, the damages could be monumental.

Amy had given a lot of thought to what she wanted to say, but she wasn't sure whether she would actually say it or take a more conventional approach. She still had not decided at the time she began her response.

"Your Honor," she said, "there are a lot of facts in dispute and a lot of other reasons why you can't order the relief sought here today, but above all else is a question of procedure. With barely a week's notice, Plaintiff is in here asking you to award an entire shipping empire to him. We've had no discovery, no pretrial proceedings, and nothing else that even hints at Due Process of Law. We are in here today on an eviction action, but this case clearly involves much more. This is not a simple case of a delinquent tenant."

Amy was sometimes a little tentative when she started, but she always developed momentum as the argument consumed her. "As this Court knows, real estate rights are divided into ownership rights and possession rights. Terminating possession rights is a much less significant event and, as a result, in some circumstances is done through eviction procedures like the ones that preceded us here today. Terminating ownership is a completely different story. A party cannot be deprived of ownership on a few days notice. The proper procedure for trying to take an ownership interest from someone is known in the common law as 'ejectment.' In a properly pled ejectment action, the owner of the property is given the opportunity to raise defenses, take discovery, and otherwise dispute the claims during a trial. It is not meant to be an expedited procedure."

Amy paused to decide whether to follow her instinct or to follow the normal path. Instinct won out. "Your Honor," she said, "this procedure is all wrong. What Mr. Cavanaugh has brought is not a proper eviction claim. He is trying to change title and improperly trying to do it on an expedited basis. Ultimately, this can only be characterized as a *premature ejectment*."

The court reporter started to laugh immediately. Judge Pendens took a moment before the double entendre took hold, but began chuckling as well. That appeared to be the signal that allowed everyone else in the room to laugh. Mark Cavanaugh wasn't laughing or smiling, and his face was turning from bronze god to ripe peach. Amy was glowing, but she was trying to keep from breaking a smile.

Judge Pendens turned to Cavanaugh and said, "Mr. Cavanaugh, I think I see you in the society pages now and then. I wonder what everyone would think if they found out someone thinks you have a premature ejectment problem?"

Cavanaugh tried to maintain his composure, but he wasn't going to maintain his seat. "Your Honor," he barked. "That was a bad joke and an affront to the dignity of this Court. I request that it be stricken from the record and that Ms. Prescott be sanctioned for her unprofessional conduct."

When he finished, Judge Pendens gave him a patronizing look. "Mr. Cavanaugh, I'll decide what is an affront to the dignity of this Court. You sat through the morning from hell along with me, but you had the luxury of being on the sidelines. I had to listen to pathetic story after pathetic story. Sometimes they're pathetic because I have no choice but to evict someone who seems like a good person who just can't make the payment. Sometimes they're pathetic because the excuses for nonpayment are so stupid. Personally, it makes me happy when someone comes into my Court and can inject a little levity. I'm sorry if you think it was an attack on you, but I can assure you that it will have nothing to do with my ruling."

Cavanaugh couldn't have expected anything different. After all, the judge was laughing as hard as anyone. It did, however, give him a chance to raise his voice and otherwise attack an opponent.

Amy had made her most important point and was tempted to quit while she appeared to be ahead. She could not know how the judge would ultimately rule, however, so she felt compelled to get all of her arguments into the record in case she needed to take an appeal. Her second most salient point was that expedited proceedings – other than evictions – are premised on the idea of preserving the status quo until the issues can be tried. Changing ownership would not preserve the status quo, it would be changing it.

Cavanaugh's rebuttal focused on the same argument, but with a different twist. He argued that the default had triggered events that might lead to foreclosure by the bank and that preserving the status quo meant allowing his client to take control in order to preserve the company and keep it from foreclosure. His argument might have had more force if a bank foreclosure could move that quickly. The fact of the matter, however, was that a bank foreclosure required notice and an opportunity to cure. In other words, there would still be time to grant the relief in the future and prevent the bank foreclosure.

Judge Pendens opted for the typical Solomonic compromise. "I agree that an eviction proceeding is not the way to resolve this issue. I also agree that putting this case in the normal scheduling cycle may not be appropriate because the foreclosure might occur before it's decided." Turning to Amy, she asked, "Would you have any objections to some sort of expedited proceeding?"

"It depends on what you have in mind."

The judge continued, "I cannot grant Plaintiff's motion without giving you a better chance to prepare. On the other hand, we could have a motion for a temporary injunction in a couple weeks and everyone can call witnesses, but then we'd still have to have a trial several months after that. The rules allow me to combine those proceedings, and I think it might be easier to just hold an expedited trial and do it in one step. Otherwise, the ownership is in limbo for too long."

The proposal presented Amy with a dilemma. The longer the case was delayed, the more likely the bank default could be cured. On the other hand, if she acted like delay was her objective, it might suggest that she felt she had a weak case. She leaned over to confer with Drabeck. After a moment she turned to the judge and said, "We're happy to get this matter resolved sooner rather than later, provided we get appropriate cooperation from the other side."

Turning now to Cavanaugh, the judge said, "How much time do you need for the trial?"

"I would estimate three days, but we may be able to do it in less."

Turning back to Amy, the judge said, "Counsel, what do you think?"

"If Mr. Cavanaugh is proposing three days total, I think that's fine. I really haven't had time to look at the issues, but I can't imagine either side taking more than a day."

The judge asked her clerk to review the calendar for available dates. While that was going on, the judge turned back to the litigants. "You're in luck. We had blocked four weeks for a securities fraud lawsuit, but it settled unexpectedly. We've been moving up other cases, but I think we still have some time available."

After another moment, the clerk advised that there was an open week starting two weeks from the following Monday. The lawyers checked their calendars and announced that they'd be available.

"Okay," the judge said. "For the record, I'm going to treat today's proceeding as, in essence, a motion for a temporary injunction that was denied without prejudice. We're going to have a trial in a few weeks, but with a little more preparation and formality. If either party fails to cooperate, I'll have to rethink the scheduling. Otherwise, I want you to work out pretrial details. We'll hold a pretrial conference the preceding Friday. If anybody plans to request a jury, the instructions and other pretrial materials will be due by the pretrial. Ms. Prescott, by rule you'll have to associate with a local attorney. I'll understand if you can't get someone up to speed, but I'd like you to have someone with a local address. They don't have to participate in the pretrial proceedings, but you should have someone with you during the trial." The judge looked at the parties to see if anything was left to cover. Finally she said, "If nobody has anything else, we stand adjourned."

CHAPTER TWENTY-SEVEN

THE NEXT TWO WEEKS were a flurry of activity. Most civil cases don't go to trial for more than a year after they are commenced. The lawyers don't spend all of their time getting ready for just one case, but they usually have considerably more time to prepare. On the other hand, Amy thought that most lawyers used the extra time to find excuses to do things for which they could bill clients. If your case was a winner, it shouldn't take long to prepare it. Even if it's a loser, extra time rarely made any difference in dreaming up arguments.

Amy had spent time prosecuting criminal matters, and criminal law was almost all from the hip. Thus, the expedited procedure was likely to create more of a problem for Cavanaugh, who probably used jury consultants, held mock trials, and otherwise overprepared cases in an effort to fight until the client's last dollar was gone. Amy also had an advantage because her investigator had already been researching Bogardus for weeks.

For the most part, the case was just a question of contract law. Drabeck had originally given shares to his children and their spouses as a way of avoiding inheritance taxes. That was not remarkable, as it was standard estate planning for business owners. Furthermore, Buy-Sell Agreements are typical as well. The idea is that a small company is more like a partnership and the owners want to have some say over the identity of their partners. Thus, Buy-Sell Agreements provide for an automatic buyout under certain conditions. For example, if one of the owners dies, the remaining partners don't want to be in business with the spouse of the deceased shareholder, so the agreement provides a buy-out of the shares from the deceased partner's estate. Similarly, if a shareholder has financial trouble, they don't want a bank suddenly owning those shares. Provided there is a reasonable basis for valuing what is paid for the stock, such agreements are generally upheld.

This Buy-Sell Agreement had a little twist, however. Drabeck was a widower. He so hated being alone that he remarried in haste and, as the saying goes, repented at leisure. He remarried so fast that his financial advisors were unable to persuade him of the benefits of a prenuptial agreement. It did not take long for Drabeck to realize his second wife was the reason that people have prenuptial agreements. His financial advisors then concocted the Buy-Sell Agreement as a means of keeping the company stock out of her hands. Under certain circumstances – like a divorce decree awarding all or part of the stock to a spouse – the Buy-Sell Agreement allowed the other shareholders to buy the shares in question for a relatively modest amount, with the payments made over several years. When the divorce occurred, the second wife still got a healthy financial payout, but she didn't even try to get the company.

Ultimately, the reasons for the Buy-Sell weren't really relevant, but Cavanaugh would certainly argue to the contrary. By portraying the Agreement as motivated by greed, Cavanaugh would be giving the jury a reason to punish Mr. Drabeck. Amy had already envisioned Cavanaugh calling it ironic, or poetic justice, or a case of someone being hoisted by his own petard.

Amy met with Tony Drabeck a week before trial. "How do things look?" he asked.

"I think I understand their arguments. I haven't figured out all of our defenses yet. I think we might have a basis to claim that he shouldn't be allowed to invoke the contract for a variety of reasons. Unfortunately, I'm not sure what all of them are."

"If he's allowed to invoke it, are we in trouble?"

"Well, the language of the contract isn't great, but we may be able to find some other things. That's part of why I wanted to meet with you today."

He smiled with the look of someone trying to have a positive outlook of his time on death row. "I've got nothing else going on," he said. "I can spend all week helping you."

"Good," she said. "Before we get to our defenses, let's talk about their case. Did you know your ex-wife has been listed as a witness?"

Drabeck's face went white. "Oh shit. That's going to be a killer."

"Why do you say that?"

He shook his head in disbelief. "Lots of reasons. First, she's an evil . . ." he hesitated.

"Were you going to use the "B" word?" Amy asked.

He thought for a moment. "Actually, I was going to skip right to the next letter of the alphabet."

Amy laughed. Neither the "B" word nor the "C" word seemed like they were part of Drabeck's regular vocabulary, so his distaste for his ex-wife must have been substantial.

Drabeck smiled at his own quip, but the look of dread was lingering. "Not only is she bitter and evil, she's a terrific con artist. You are going to have to dismantle her on the stand. I mean, this will take cross-examination like you've never done before."

"Really?" she said. "What if I can't?"

"Then we'll lose. We settled the divorce because we knew on the stand she'd tear us up. Is there any way we can keep her from testifying?"

"I don't think her testimony is really relevant, but I don't want to make too big of a deal out of it. To get it excluded, we'd have to argue that the evidentiary value was far outweighed by the fact that it might prejudice the jury against you. The problem is that I'd have to explain to the judge that the jury would have an adverse reaction because they might think less of you because you came up with the Buy-Sell Agreement in order to gain an advantage in your divorce. Thus, we might keep it from the jury, but we'd be laying it in the judge's lap and, to the extent she has to make rulings, it might affect her opinion of you."

Drabeck's expression grew even more sullen. "So, I guess I'm screwed."

Amy looked at him. She did not think less of him because he tried to protect his company from a gold digger. "Let me spend some time on it," she said.

♣ ♦ ♥ ♠

Amy sat down with the Rules of Evidence in an effort to find arguments to keep the testimony out. Nothing was coming together. The ex-wife's expected testimony would probably be biased, which was a basis to discount it but not to exclude it. In legal parlance, it went to the weight of the evidence, but not the admissibility.

Amy and Drabeck met again the morning of the pretrial. "I've barely been able to sleep," he said. "I thought that witch was finally done ruining my life, and now she's right back in the thick of it."

"Don't you think you might be exaggerating a little?" Amy asked.

"I wish that were the case. I'm afraid you're underestimating her."

Amy studied his pain. Finally, she said, "I have an idea that you might want to consider."

"I'm all ears," he said.

"Do you know how you always read about guys on death row who claim that they got ineffective assistance of counsel because their lawyer slept through parts of the trial?"

"Sure. I've seen that before."

"Well, there may be some instances where their lawyers really did fall asleep, but it's actually a deliberate trial tactic."

"You mean they have a losing case, so the lawyer deliberately pretends to be sleeping so that the defendant can claim to have had a crummy attorney and get a new trial?"

"Actually, that's just a side benefit. They do it for several reasons. You see, any trial, even a murder trial, is long and at times boring. It's hard to get a jury to pay attention. Think about it. If you were a juror and noticed a lawyer sleeping, what would you do? For one, you might become so focused on watching him to see if he drools or snores or falls out of his chair that you won't hear a thing coming out of the witness's mouth. Alternatively, you'll figure that the testimony must not be very important if the defendant's lawyer can't even stay awake for it, and, as a result, you will either not pay attention or will discount the testimony."

Drabeck's demeanor was improving. "That makes sense."

"There's also another reason," Amy continued, "although it's more relevant in a criminal trial. If the jurors are paying attention, they start to wonder what a good lawyer would be doing instead of sleeping. They start thinking up their own questions and then filling in the blanks. In a capital murder case, having a bad defense lawyer, in itself, may create reasonable doubt. I mean, think about it. All of the jurors go into the jury room and all they can think about is whether the defendant might have had a defense if he had a better lawyer. As a result, the defendant doesn't even need to go to the Supreme Court to claim ineffective assistance of counsel. The jury acquits the defendant because they witnessed the ineffective assistance of counsel and that created the reasonable doubt. The idea is to make the jurors believe there's something there that a good lawyer would bring out, and I think we can apply that strategy in a civil case as well."

"Now that you say that it makes perfect sense. How come I never heard that in any of the articles about the death penalty?"

"Probably because trial strategy is privileged information," she said.

"So, is our plan for you to fall asleep during the wicked witch's testimony?"

Amy smirked. "I'm afraid that would seem pretty suspicious. I was thinking that I'd pretend to have a conflict and wouldn't be there for her testimony. I'd have our local counsel handle it. That way, the jury would think we didn't think the testimony was very important. Furthermore, with someone inexperienced in my place, they'd start to wonder about how I would have cross-examined the witness if I had been there."

Drabeck was taking to the strategy in a big way. "Isn't it going to look odd if they call her as a witness and suddenly you leave?"

"I'll arrange to be gone in advance."

"How will you know when she'll be testifying?"

Amy had a devious smile. "I won't. But I think Mark Cavanaugh will take care of that for us. I'll tell the judge I have a conflict Tuesday afternoon. Cavanaugh will be adamant that we can't delay the proceedings. I'll agree to have local counsel handle it, and Cavanaugh will time his case so as to present his big witness when I'm not there."

"Are you sure he'll fall for that?"

"He's a man, isn't he? Whatever hand he's dealt, all he'll focus on is playing his winners. Strength versus strength. If you want to be good at this, you have to figure out how to play your losing cards as well, and most male litigators haven't learned that art. Besides, after that 'premature ejectment' comment, I'm sure he's just dying to get back at me."

Drabeck stared at her for a long time. Finally, he said, "I'll bet your family's proud of you." If only he knew.

CHAPTER TWENTY-EIGHT

Amy DECIDED TO STAY IN ST. PAUL to prepare for the trial. The travel to and from Chicago would eat up too much preparation time. Furthermore, she would be less distracted working in her hotel room. The only consolation was that Tucker Sheridan had offered to take her to dinner. She was glad for the company and, under the circumstances, might have even accepted an invitation from Mark Cavanaugh.

She met Tucker in the lobby at six o'clock. He looked out of place among the well-heeled crowd at the St. Paul Hotel. On the other hand, he had an air about him that made him look comfortable in any setting. The unconstructed sport coat look from the "Miami Vice" era had apparently only recently made it to the Midwest and it suited him fine.

Amy had packed mostly business suits in anticipation of trial. She did, however, bring a pair of black slacks and a Donna Karan top that accentuated her femininity while avoiding the conclusion that she was slutty.

Tucker's eyes opened wide. "Wow," he said. "You don't look like the buttoned-down lawyer that's been representing the company. You look outstanding."

Amy was taken aback by the flattery. She reasoned that Tucker couldn't possibly have any hope or expectation of bedding her, so his comments must be more than the programmed response of the typical lustful male. Either way, the compliment made her very happy.

"Thank you," she said. "And I must say you clean up pretty well yourself." She regretted those words from the moment they left her lips. It wasn't because she didn't want to compliment him. It was more because it seemed almost demeaning.

Tucker seemed to take it in stride. "I even shaved," he said facetiously. "Not that you were worried about razor burn."

She smiled, but decided to quit while she was ahead – or at least not behind.

They walked out to the car. Tucker drove a late model Corvette. That was the Holy Grail among the young men where she grew up. On the other hand, Jasmine had always said that guys with fast cars were compensating for a small something else.

When they reached the car, the bellman rushed over and opened her door. She wondered whether Tucker would have done it otherwise.

"I hope you don't mind," he said as they pulled out. "I bought this car as an investment, and I haven't driven it all year. I know that Corvettes are a little pretentious, but I thought it would be good for where we're going."

Tucker was suddenly showing a lot more savvy than Amy would have expected, and she liked that fact. "Really," she said. "And where are we going?"

"Stillwater," he said.

She shrugged her shoulders. "I guess that doesn't mean much to me, but there probably aren't too many places you could have named that I would have recognized."

Tucker drove deliberately. He wasn't necessarily speeding, but he made a point of accelerating through every curve in order to display the car's handling ability. He carried on a normal conversation, but his eyes and hands never strayed from the mission.

They exited the freeway and drove on a state highway. Amy lay back in her seat to enjoy the late-autumn colors. Then she watched him as he drove. He was in his element and he was in control. She found his calm confidence to be enticing.

Stillwater, as it turned out, was a small town on the St. Croix River. The downtown sat on a few blocks between the bluffs and the water. They parked the car and went to one of the restaurants near the shore. There was a large deck for outdoor dining in the summer, but it was now too cool to sit outside.

The hostess seated them by a window and they could see the river. "Why is the St. Croix so blue, when the Mississippi is so brown?" Amy asked.

"Mostly because it's deeper."

"So, when they were searching for the headwaters of the Mississippi, why didn't they go up the fork that was deeper. I mean, shouldn't this river be the Mississippi?"

"I s'pose the explorers thought it didn't look like the Mississippi. If you were paddling up a brown river and got to a point where one fork was brown and one was blue, you'd follow the brown because that's what you think the Mississippi is."

That satisfied her. "This is a nicer view. Maybe it's just as well that barge traffic is on the Mississippi instead of here."

After more small talk, Tucker asked her how she felt about the impending trial. "Nervous," she said. "But I always feel that way."

"Do you think we'll win?" he asked.

"I never make predictions," she said. "It's bad luck." She was responding to his questions, but not advancing the discussion on the subject. She smiled at him. "I was hoping to use this time as a mental break from trial preparation."

Tucker nodded. "Sorry. Old man Drabeck thought I should take you to dinner so that you could get a little break, but I'm concerned about the company so I couldn't help but ask."

Amy wasn't sure how to interpret that. "So, this is a work assignment for you?"

Tucker scrambled for a response. "I didn't mean it like that. I don't want you to think that I didn't want to be here. It's just that I said something to Tony about it, and he thought I should offer to take you to dinner."

"Okay," she said, still not really sure how that made her feel.

Tucker half closed his eyes and looked at her. "Did you think we were going on a date?"

She wasn't sure she even knew the answer. "I guess I didn't when you asked me, but I wouldn't think you'd get your fancy car out of storage for a business dinner. We could have just eaten at the hotel."

Tucker was at a loss to refute the point. "I guess you're right," he finally said. "I haven't been out for a nice dinner with a woman in a while, and I guess I wanted it to be something more than just a business dinner. On the other hand, we have a business relationship, and I don't think that should change now when the future of the company is in the balance."

"That's not an issue," she said. "There's a big gulf between calling this a date and the two of us having a romantic relationship. I don't think I would've accepted your invitation if I knew you thought it was a date."

"Wait a minute," he protested. "Just because I wanted to spend a nice evening with you doesn't mean I was expecting anything else. You're right that if you were a guy, I wouldn't have picked you up in my Corvette and requested a window table in a nice restaurant on the river, but that doesn't mean I'm making a play for you."

She found his backpedaling to be rather charming. He apparently wasn't used to not being in control, and his vulnerable side was a nice contrast. "Okay," she said with the smugness of someone who thinks they've already won the point.

"Look," he said, "I felt a little bad about the way I talked to you when we first met. I was hoping that a nice evening out might leave you with a better impression, so you wouldn't keep carrying around the first impression."

Amy felt decidedly in control, and she liked the feeling. Just the same, abusing that power was not her style. "I've put our first meeting behind me. I thought you were a jerk, but when I thought about it I realized that you were under a lot of pressure. I wasn't exactly cordial either, and I think that was because I was uncomfortable in foreign surroundings. Anyway, I've never thought there was much of a point in dwelling on the negative."

Airing their feelings seemed to unlock the evening. The conversation switched from their initial feelings toward each other to just about everything else. Tucker had been in the Navy and then the Merchant Marine before ending up on the river. He was in his mid-thirties and hadn't managed to get married. He blamed that on his travels and his schedule and not on a fear of commitment. He was emphatic that he'd be thrilled to settle down and start a family when the time was right.

As the evening progressed, Amy was feeling the pull from the wine. What had started as a gentle buzz became an imperative. Each sip increased the euphoria she was feeling. Amy was pretty confident that she had the genes of an alcoholic. She had always made it a point to avoid too many drinking situations because she had learned long ago how much she liked it. Tonight, the alcohol was winning. And she was enjoying herself.

Tucker wasn't discouraging her. He didn't go so far as to order Jagermeister shots, but he didn't hesitate to refill her wine glass when it was empty, or even when it wasn't. "Does it take alcohol for you to let your guard down?" he asked.

"Why do you ask?" She wasn't slurring, but she was enunciating a little too much.

"No reason. It's just that you're a lot of fun when you're not all business."

Now she spoke in artificially low tones as if trying to convey a secret, but still talking loud enough to be heard by anyone nearby. "This is the first time you've ever seen me when it wasn't a business setting. I don't need alcohol to be fun. But when you're a woman in a man's world, you have to act business when you're doing business."

"If you say so."

"I do say so," she said. "And don't try to tell me you don't act differently around the crew than you do around the boss or around me."

Tucker decided to steer the conversation back toward the more lighthearted. They carried on through the evening until the crowd in the dining room was thinning out. That didn't mean it was particularly late, however, as they were, after all, in Minnesota.

At about ten, they headed for home. Amy declined his invitation to go to a nearby music bar. The morning was going to come early enough, and she was ready to call it a night.

Tucker was quick to open her door when they reached the car. She sat back in a bit of a stupor and closed her eyes. Tucker did not appear particularly affected by the alcohol. She had overdone it a bit, but Tucker was there to take care of her. She liked that. Even as a child, she had felt compelled to look out for her mother and siblings. Her relationship with Chadwick was not much different, as she often felt like he wouldn't pay close enough attention to what he was doing. For that matter, she had the same protective behavior with Jasmine. Now, for once, she could be irresponsible and let someone take care of her.

They drove largely in silence. Tucker played a CD of a Minnesota singer that Amy had never heard of. He had a jagged voice, and was singing "Into the Mystic." She had listened to the Van Morrison version many times and wondered whether it was a song about a sailor coming home to his love -- "*When that foghorn blows, I will be coming home*" -- or simply a meditative musing -- "*I want to rock your gypsy soul, just like way back in the days of old.*" She liked it either way.

In the darkness, she could look at Tucker without being obvious about it. The light of the dashboard illuminated his profile, and she found it pleasing. She was feeling an urge, but the confines of the sports car made it impractical. She reached over and put her hand behind his head. She ran her fingers through his hair and then rubbed the back of his neck. He leaned forward to give her room.

He made a soft moan as she rubbed. "I'm afraid I might close my eyes and drive off the road," he said.

"Do you want me to stop?" she asked.

"Absolutely not," he said.

If she were Jasmine, she'd probably be undressing by now. While something about that scenario titillated her, she couldn't bring herself to do it. Instead, she eventually lay back and let the alcohol put her to sleep.

The next thing she knew, Tucker was holding her door open and helping her out of the car. She struggled to find her shoes, which she had apparently kicked off during the ride home. She held out her hand and he pulled her up. She immediately noticed that he had parked near her hotel, but not in the driveway in front. He closed her door and clicked the lock. He then guided her into the lobby.

When the elevator came, she turned to face him. "Thanks for a lovely dinner and for walking me in." She leaned forward and up on her toes in order to kiss him on the cheek. "Goodnight."

"What?" he said dumbfounded.

The effects of the alcohol had apparently dissipated somewhat, and her plans changed. "I'm not saying it's out of the question," she said smiling. "I'm just saying that it's a bad idea for tonight." With that, she stepped into the elevator and turned around to face him. His mouth hung open in disbelief as the doors between them closed. Part of her was sure she'd made the right decision. The other part of her was of a decidedly different opinion.

CHAPTER TWENTY-NINE

THE PRETRIAL CONFERENCE was held in open court. Frequently, the proceedings were less formal and took place in chambers. Judge Pendens apparently had a different perspective. Ultimately, it probably helped her establish her position of authority in that she was younger than many of the lawyers who appeared in front of her.

The proceeding followed a typical litany. The judge inquired whether the parties had explored settlement and whether there was anything the Court could do to facilitate an amicable resolution. When that proved fruitless, she inquired about the need for a jury and asked her clerk to notify the Court Administrator when both attorneys expressed a desire for one. The judge then inquired about whether everyone had been able to prepare adequately in the time allotted. Everything was on schedule.

"Ms. Prescott," she asked. "Have you managed to retain a local counsel for the trial?"

"Yes, your honor. Tom Steinman from the Delahanty law firm will sit in." His name was Tom, but, because of his youth, Amy couldn't help but think of him as anything but "Tommy."

"Okay," the judge said. "I hope you both are still planning on being done in three days. I've scheduled another trial to start next Thursday, and the parties are flying people in from around the country."

"That should be fine, your Honor," Cavanaugh said.

Amy rose from her seat. "About that, your Honor, I have a conflict next Tuesday afternoon. There's a deposition in an asbestos case that I'm involved with, and I am planning to participate by phone." The statement wasn't false. The fact of the matter, however, was that Amy had potential conflicts virtually every day of the week. She could have found someone to cover for her, but she didn't want to.

Cavanaugh pounced like a cat. "Your Honor, we can't delay this trial for Ms. Prescott. We only have three days. You said so yourself."

"Your Honor," Amy said, "I don't think it's asking too much for a little change in the schedule. Perhaps we can go a little later on Monday or take shorter recesses."

The judge looked back at Cavanaugh. "Is there something we can do to accommodate Ms. Prescott's schedule?"

"I'm afraid not, your Honor," he said in a voice so artificially grave that it would have made a television evangelist blush. "These are crucial issues that must be resolved promptly. It wouldn't be fair to my client to delay the matter, and it wouldn't be fair to the jury or anyone else if we changed the normal schedule."

Amy normally saw her role as solving judges' problems and not causing them. In this instance, it was part of the plan. "Your Honor," she said, "I'm assuming that Mr. Cavanaugh will still be presenting his witnesses on Tuesday afternoon. If that's the case, I will have Mr. Steinman cover that part of the trial. If Mr. Cavanaugh finishes early, I'd request that you dismiss the jury until Wednesday. I anticipate my case will only take a day."

Before letting the judge respond, Cavanaugh chimed in. "That's what we'll do then. We'll finish our case Tuesday afternoon."

The judge hesitated and it appeared that she might have a different opinion. For her part, Amy wondered why she had not had more success manipulating men in her personal life when it was so easy for her to do so in her professional life. She didn't want the judge ruining her plan, so she quickly acquiesced to Cavanaugh's demand. "All I ask is that the Court explain to the jury that I had to attend to another matter and that I'll be back the following day." Amy's strategy might not work, but she was pleased that Cavanaugh gave her the opportunity to put it to the test.

CHAPTER THIRTY

AFTER THE PRETRIAL CONFERENCE, Amy went back to her hotel to go to work. She looked at the hastily assembled trial notebooks littering her room. She felt like she knew what was there, but didn't know it back and forth, inside and out. This case was going to be an old fashioned lawsuit. Rather than carefully orchestrated presentations that were new to the jury but nobody else, this trial was going to develop on the fly. She knew what arguments and testimony to expect, but she wasn't at all confident that her expectations would prove out.

She decided to make a few calls. She reached Scouten. "Any news?" she asked.

"The stakeout at Skeeter's place hasn't turned up anything. I haven't seen anyone come or go on the main road, and the dogs keep me from getting in close. I'd like to start asking questions around town, but it's too small of a community. It'd get back to the widow in a heartbeat."

"Anything else?"

"Well," he said, "they found Skeeter's life jacket. It washed up on shore down river from where he fell in."

"Anything noteworthy?"

"No, but maybe that in itself is noteworthy. It was pretty much intact, so he must not have had it strapped on all the way. I mean, it looks like he went in the water and it came off and he drowned. I guess that's better than going through the propellers."

"How about Dudley Raymond?"

"Glad you asked. I did manage to find something. I located the transcript from his sentencing."

"That should be helpful."

"Just a minute while I grab it." There was a short pause while Scouten dug it out. "I'll read you the best parts. The judge says: *Mr. Ray-*

mond. You have been found guilty of involuntary manslaughter for your role in causing the death of another human being. The Complaint charges you with, and you have admitted to, drinking alcohol with the victim and, after the victim became intoxicated, coaxing him to race his car to a railroad crossing, at which time the victim collided with the train and died.*

"Wow," Amy said. "That's pretty weird."

"It gets better. The judge asked him if he had anything to say and, listen to this, he said, '*If I'd known I was going to go to jail for it, I'd of killed the son of a bitch with my bare hands.*' Then the judge speaks again, '*Mr. Raymond, the Court acknowledges that the victim had a history of domestic violence, but it is not your place to take such matters into your own hands.*'"

Amy had mixed emotions about that news. She found the apparent motive to be somewhat redeeming, but the callous wish to do it over again barehanded to be chilling. Finally, she realized that he wasn't her concern at the moment. "How about my evidence for this trial?"

"It should arrive today" he said. "I hope it helps."

"Thanks. So do I."

CHAPTER THIRTY-ONE

A MY MET TONY DRABECK IN the hotel coffee shop for breakfast. Tony was looking grim. Entrepreneurs are rarely thrilled about any situation in which they are not in control. The possible consequences made this situation even worse.

"This doesn't seem fair," he said. "I spent a life building something and now this lowlife can try to take it from me. There should be consequences for him if he loses."

"That's the problem with having something. It makes you vulnerable. Bogardus doesn't have that problem."

"That's for sure," Drabeck said. "Anything he does have he already got from me."

"In my business, we say that the most dangerous opponent is the one who has freedom," Amy replied.

Drabeck looked at her quizzically.

"It's from a Janis Joplin song. 'Freedom's just another word for nothing left to lose.' It's hard to reason with someone with nothing left to lose."

"So, what do we do?"

"Try to find something for him to lose. Or just win."

They were both quiet while Drabeck tended to his coffee. "I was tossing and turning all night thinking about this," he finally said. "Do you think we made a mistake by agreeing to this expedited trial?"

"No. We would be having a trial today no matter what. The only difference is that we'd be having a preliminary trial in which the judge would be basically predicting the outcome of the next trial. When you like the status quo, you want to give the other side as few chances to change it as possible. If today was just a preliminary injunction hearing, the other side would get a chance to learn our strategies and arguments and prepare differently for the next trial. By eliminating the extra trial, the other side has one less chance to get someone to rule for them. If this doesn't go well, it will be easy to second guess it later, but I think this is the way to go."

That answer seemed to give Drabeck some comfort. "That makes sense," he said. "And don't worry about me doing any second guessing. I know that the best lawyer in the world can do the best job possible and still not always win."

"Thanks," she said, "but let's not talk about the possibility of losing."

THEY MET TOMMY STEINMAN at 8:15. Court started promptly at 8:30. Judge Pendens again tried to float the idea of a settlement but didn't seem surprised when it didn't get off the ground. Some other preliminary details were reviewed, and then the bailiff brought in a big crop of prospective jurors. When a case involved high profile parties or crimes, it could take days just to find enough people who hadn't already formed opinions. With a basic contract dispute between family members, that was less of a problem. Furthermore, the expedited pretrial schedule eliminated much of an opportunity to develop juror profiles.

Amy's strategy for jury selection was to avoid asking personal questions that might make a prospect feel uncomfortable. She would ask questions like: "Do you have grandchildren?" "Do you like all the lawyer shows on TV?" "Will it be a problem for you to be here this week?" Each question could be defended as relevant if challenged, but she really wasn't looking to do anything other than make a good first impression.

Cavanaugh might have been equally interested in first impressions, but he took a decidedly different approach. He tried to be authoritative and commanding, as if controlling the courtroom would allow him to control the jury's deliberations. He wasn't aggressive or nasty, but putting the jury prospects at ease was not his intention or the result.

As the process continued, Cavanaugh seemed to favor the young women in the pool. He tried to dismiss the professional men for various reasons that didn't make sense, while he fought to retain women who might otherwise be dismissed for knowing someone who had worked for Minnesota Marine. In Amy's mind, his strategy confirmed her belief that he was going to make the ex-wife's testimony the centerpiece of his case. Of course, it was equally likely that, based on his alleged social life, Cavanaugh had a particularly high opinion of his ability to influence or even manipulate women.

Ultimately, Amy didn't really care. If any of them started smiling or winking at Cavanaugh during the trial, it would be an easy ticket to a new trial if necessary. More importantly, however, most women jurors secretly cheer a female lawyer going toe-to-toe with a man. While it was a situation that could backfire, Amy was happy to have women jurors. If they read romance novels or idolized Bridget Jones, so much the better. In the end, there were four women and three men. A civil jury only required six jurors, but a seventh was added as protection against someone not showing up.

The Court took a short recess before continuing. Cavanaugh was first to give his opening statement, and it was brief. He outlined the Buy-Sell Agreement, explained how the loss of insurance had caused a default, and stated that the lawsuit was brought in order to exercise the rights in the agreement. He didn't mention the testimony from the ex-wife. Apparently he wanted to drop it like a bomb.

Opening statements are supposed to be a statement of the facts that the attorney expects will be introduced. It's not a time to argue about which witness is more likely to tell the truth or which evidence is more reliable. It was a subtle distinction, and Cavanaugh didn't hesitate to cross the line. While Amy could have successfully objected to some of the things he said, she didn't want to look like a nagger or a complainer.

When it was her turn, Amy started with the simple maxim that every story has two sides. She spent an inordinate amount of time discussing the efforts of Drabeck to build the company up from next to nothing in order to become a significant player in river transportation. She also made it clear that the evidence would show that the plaintiff was trying to acquire a company for which he had done very little. She was conditioning the jury to favor her client over someone who was seeking something for nothing. If she could establish that mindset, it might carry over to the ex-wife's testimony as well. Ultimately, Amy gave very little detail about the defenses that she would present. She implored the jurors, however, to wait until all of the evidence was in before making up their minds.

Cavanaugh began calling witnesses. Amy had offered to stipulate to most of the underlying facts, but Cavanaugh apparently thought there was value in the testimony. Thus, he called the Plaintiff to explain the reason for the Buy-Sell Agreement, a representative from the insurance company to testify that insurance coverage had been revoked, and an employee of the bank to testify that the loss of insurance caused the loan to go into default.

Amy did little cross-examination. She didn't ask Bogardus any questions, but reserved the right to recall him later. As for the others, they were disinterested witnesses, so there was little reason to challenge their testimony. To the extent she had to get hostile with witnesses, she wanted it to resonate as the exception and not the rule. If the jury thought she didn't get upset easily, they'd give more significance to the times when she did.

Ultimately, the testimony breezed along so quickly that it was unclear how Cavanaugh could delay things enough so that his star witness wasn't on the stand until Amy was gone. Somehow, Amy was sure he'd think of something. Day one ended with few fireworks and little fanfare.

CHAPTER THIRTY-TWO

D AY TWO STARTED WITH A LOT OF technical testimony. Cavanaugh called an expert to explain the barge business. Additional experts testified about the potential risks of operating
without insurance. Finally, witnesses were called to detail all of the things
that needed to be done to take over the company. Ultimately, however,
that testimony may not have had the desired effect. While Cavanaugh was
apparently trying to show how critical it was that the ownership change
immediately, he also demonstrated what a monumental change his client
was seeking.

The testimony dragged on. Amy was pretty sure that she knew why,
but didn't care. In fact, she'd barely prepared for the ex-wife's testimony,
so she wanted the other testimony to take up the entire morning. Ultimately, Cavanaugh's case was pretty cut and dried. Standing on its own,
his position was thus far a winner. While jurors had been asked to reserve
judgment, it would only be natural for them to have decided that Cavanaugh would win unless they heard something to contradict what had
already been presented.

When the lunch break came, Amy pulled Tommy Steinman to the
side. "There's something I forgot to tell you," she said. "I have a conflict
this afternoon. I need you to handle things while I'm gone."

"What!" he said with bulging eyes. "I've just been sitting in to satisfy
the Local Rules. I haven't really even paid much attention."

"I'm sorry. I know you'd like time to prepare, but it's really not a
problem. I don't want you trying to win the case. I just want you to be
here. You can object to the form of the questions, and otherwise protect
our interests, but I don't want you arguing relevance or making motions.
Just let the testimony come in."

He was not warming to the idea. "I don't understand why you didn't tell me sooner."

"Look," she said. "You're in a big firm and you don't really get to go to trial much do you?"

"No."

"In fact, you're so eager to go to trial that you would have prepared hours of cross-examination if you knew you were going to get a shot. Am I right?"

He looked a little sheepish. "Maybe."

"Maybe," she said with a laugh. "You've been salivating at the chance to prove your worth. I'm sure you're a good lawyer, but you're going to have to wait to prove it until later on." Somehow she doubted he would honor her request, and that was fine with her.

AMY SPENT MOST OF THE AFTERNOON preparing for the next day. She did participate in the deposition, but she was too distracted to give it much attention. At four o'clock she went to the hotel lobby for high tea. She was expecting trial to end a little early, so she thought she'd wait for Drabeck and Steinman. Her intuition proved to be correct.

At about 4:15, she spotted the two coming through the lobby. She waved, and Drabeck pointed to indicate that he was going to stop in the men's room. Tommy walked toward her with an angry look. "How did it go?" she asked.

"How do you think it went?" he snapped. "I looked like a fool. Every time I said anything I was shot down."

"That's why I told you not to say anything. I'm guessing that you didn't follow my advice."

"How could I? The ex-wife was a professional con artist. I didn't have a chance."

"What did I tell you?"

"That wasn't the worst of it," he barked. "I was hoping to get a little help from the client, but when I turned to ask him a question he was sleeping."

Amy couldn't help but laugh. Drabeck had apparently decided to do a little improvising. "Don't worry about it," she said.

Tommy had declined a seat, and stood in front of her fuming. "Do you need me anymore today?" he asked. "Because if you don't, I'd like to take off."

She excused him, and Drabeck soon arrived. "Where's Tommy?" he asked.

"He left," Amy said. "He was a little upset."

Drabeck started to laugh. "If you wanted him to look incompetent, it was a success. I think the jury started keeping score just to see if he'd ever win an objection."

"And how about you?" she said. "I heard you had a little drowsiness problem."

He chuckled again. "Watching him was painful. Pretending to be asleep was easier."

"How do you think her testimony went otherwise?" she asked.

"Hard to say. She did come across like a shrew. Tommy did make some objections that her divorce trial was over and that this wasn't the time to rehash it. I think the jury may have seen that as well."

"Well, the real trial starts tomorrow. Today we dealt with our losers. Tomorrow we play our trump cards."

"Are you talking about me?" he asked.

"Not really."

"Didn't you list me as the first witness?"

Amy smiled. "Do you remember when I asked you if you played cards?"

"Yeah."

"Well, what I did with the witness list was basically the same as what's called 'false-carding.' If you're playing Bridge, sometimes you'll play cards in a way to mislead the other side as to what you have. I put you at the top of the witness list, and then put the other side's witnesses on the bottom. It makes it look like I'm listing them only for protective purposes. That, however, is not the case. If things go right, I may not have to call you at all."

CHAPTER THIRTY-THREE

AMY WORE A DRESS TO TRIAL on Wednesday. She owned plenty of business suits, but sometimes resented the fact that women's admission to the professional world seemed to require that they dress like men. Today, she wanted the jury to see a female – not a male wannabe. By dressing like Cavanaugh, it emphasized his seniority. A dress allowed her to distinguish herself as a woman and would hopefully help to influence the intangibles.

Mark Cavanaugh was sitting at counsel table with Frank Bogardus. They had finished putting in their case and were smiling and chatting as though they hadn't a care in the world. "Welcome back," Cavanaugh said with a voice that suggested she'd missed the excitement.

"Thank you," she said.

"You missed a lot of fun yesterday," Bogardus smirked.

Amy smiled politely at him. "Hopefully we can have some fun today as well." *At your expense,* she thought to herself. The key to the case was the testimony of Frank Bogardus. She had always known it, but it wasn't clear that Bogardus realized it.

After a few minutes, the judge entered. "Welcome back, Ms. Prescott," she said. "Are you prepared to present your case?"

"We are ready. Before we bring in the jury, will you entertain a motion for a directed verdict?" A directed verdict was something that happened when the judge had heard all of one side's evidence and determined that there was no possible way it could prevail.

"Do you honestly believe you have a basis for it, or do you just want to preserve the record?" Judge Pendens asked.

The question got right to the point. Amy did not think she was entitled to a directed verdict based on the evidence that had been received thus far, but sometimes you had to make the motion in order to preserve the argument for appeal. "I guess mostly the latter," she said.

"Okay," the judge said, "then I'll deny the motion. Based on what's in the record so far, I believe it is possible for a jury to find in Plaintiff's favor."

Amy nodded her consent and the judge summoned the jury. As the jurors filed in, several smiled at Amy. She wasn't sure if they were happy to see her or amused by what had happened in her absence. Today would be the last day of testimony, however, so it was what counted.

After the jurors were seated, the judge instructed Amy to call her first witness. "Defense calls Frank Bogardus," she said.

That seemed to take Cavanaugh and Bogardus by surprise. They had to have anticipated that Amy would call Bogardus at some point, but apparently expected her to follow a more conventional presentation and start with Tony Drabeck. Convention was never particularly important to Amy Prescott.

After Bogardus was sworn, Amy wasted no time in attacking him. "Mr. Bogardus," she said, "it's true, isn't it, that Minnesota Marine Transport is a company that was started by your ex-wife's family?"

"Yes," he said.

"And the company had been in existence for more than fifty years before you ever worked there?"

"Yes."

"And the company was successful before you ever worked there?"

"It depends on what you mean by successful. Just because it was surviving doesn't mean it couldn't have been more successful."

"Yes," she said with a smile. "We'll get to the concept of relative success in a bit. At this point, I just want to confirm that the business had operated profitably before you ever got involved."

"I guess that's true."

"It's also true, isn't it, that you had no experience in the shipping business prior to going to work for Minnesota Marine?"

"Yes."

"In fact, you didn't really have a business background at all. You were playing in a rock and roll band."

"That's right."

"And then you married Tony Drabeck's daughter."

"Yeah." His tone was turning a little surly as he realized her intent was to minimize him.

"When you went to work for the company, did you apply for that job?"

"Excuse me?"

"Did you apply? I mean, whether or not you answered an ad or something else, did you take the initiative or did Tony Drabeck basically just offer you a job?"

"I don't know if I'd call it an offer. My wife and I were expecting our first child and Tony told me that I couldn't keep playing in the band and that I'd have to take a job with the company in order to support my family." Bogardus apparently thought that fact would make the jury think his father-in-law was overbearing, but Amy was pretty sure that it was having a different effect.

"So, with no experience to speak of, you started with the company at a salary of $75,000 a year?"

"Yes."

"How did that compare with your rock and roll salary?"

"It was higher."

Amy chuckled. "That's a bit of an understatement isn't it?"

"What do you mean?"

"Isn't it true that your reported income during the year before you joined the company was approximately $6,800?"

Bogardus raised his eyes as though looking for the answer. "That sounds about right."

"Did you do any analysis of the company before you joined to see if it was profitable?"

"Not that I remember."

"Would it surprise you if I told you that before you joined the company it was averaging about fifty million dollars a year in revenue and almost ten million dollars a year in profits?"

"I don't really have any idea."

"So, even after you joined the company, you never looked at the financial performance?"

"I wouldn't say that. It's just that it wasn't my area."

"Your area was advertising, wasn't it?"

"Yes."

"In all of your years with the company, how many television ads did it run?"

"None."

"How about radio?"

"None."

"Newspaper?"

"None."

Amy gave him a forlorn look. "For the amount of money you were getting, please tell me that you at least ran one of those ads above the urinals in public restrooms."

Bogardus gave her an angry look, and getting him to lash out would be the best result of all. "I was responsible for placing announcements in trade publications," he said with an attempt at defiance.

Amy's strategy wasn't just to discredit Bogardus. To the extent the ex-wife's testimony from the previous day was on any juror's mind, she wanted to set a theme that negatively portrayed anyone who wanted money for nothing. "The company was already running ads and things in trade publications when you started, isn't that right?"

"I think so."

"As a result, you just had to oversee something that was already in place?"

"I don't know if I'd say that."

"You may not say it, but it's true, isn't it?"

Cavanaugh had been sitting on the edge of his chair itching for an opportunity to object. Now he stood. "Objection. Argumentative."

Judge Pendens pondered it for a moment. "Overruled," she said.

Amy didn't wait for Bogardus to give an answer. "It's true, isn't it, that you didn't have to figure out how to run trade announcements because you took over a job that was already being handled?"

"I guess."

"Who handled it before?"

"Shirley."

"And that was Mr. Drabeck's secretary, was it not?"

"Yes."

"So, you took a job at $75,000 a year, and your responsibilities had previously been handled by a secretary in her spare time?"

Bogardus let out a long sigh. "Apparently someone thought that the job needed more attention and I was asked to fill that role."

"I'm sorry," Amy said. "Remind me again of what qualifications you had for this job?"

Cavanaugh was up again. "Your Honor, that's been asked and answered. Counsel is simply badgering my client."

Judge Pendens had not appeared too impressed with Frank Bogardus, but didn't want it to show. "Sustained," she said.

Amy never liked to lose on an objection, but, if the jury was paying attention, they already knew the answer. "To your knowledge, did you compete against anyone else for this job?"

"I don't know."

"Well, it wasn't advertised in the paper was it?"

"I don't think so."

"As the son-in-law of the owner, isn't it true that you rose through the ranks and you were made Chief Operating Officer for a time?"

"That's right."

"But you didn't have any competition for that job either, did you?"

"I wouldn't know."

"Who would?"

"Tony."

"If I told you that if I call him as a witness he'll testify that there weren't any other candidates considered, would you have any basis to dispute that?"

Bogardus had tried to be obstructive, but that had only made matters worse. "No," was all he could say.

Cavanaugh wasn't used to being a spectator, so he rose to address the Court. "Objection, Your Honor," he said, "what's the point of all of this? Whether my client is an experienced business person has nothing to do with the contract."

"Your Honor," Amy piped in. "Mr. Bogardus has taken the position that the Court needs to grant him relief in order to save the company. I think it's fair for us to explore the fact that the company will probably suffer substantially if Mr. Bogardus is put in control."

"I'll overrule Mr. Cavanaugh's objection," the judge said. "I think Mr. Bogardus has opened the door to this type of inquiry."

Amy let those words sink in with the jury before continuing. "Isn't it true that under your management the company suffered the only losses in its history?"

"I don't really know that," he said. "Who knows what it means by the time the accountants are done with it."

"So, are you saying the company was profitable when you were running it?"

"It's hard to say. I don't really know."

"Don't you think that the Chief Operating Officer of a fifty million dollar company should be able to tell whether the company is making a profit or not?" Amy was still thinking about the smug look on Bogardus's face that morning and was relishing wiping it off.

"What? I'm sorry, could you repeat that?"

"Is it fair to say that you have no accounting background?"

"I've never taken classes for it."

"So, you don't really know whether the company was profitable or not when you were at the helm?"

He shrugged his shoulders. "I know that was the excuse they used when they replaced me."

"So, why do you think they replaced you?" Amy realized that there was a danger in asking open-ended questions, but wasn't too concerned in light of the caliber of the witness.

"They wanted to keep more control for themselves."

"So, they felt they were losing control when you started having an affair with one of the women in the office?"

"Objection!" Cavanaugh shouted as he rose from his seat. "What does this have to do with anything?"

The judge looked at Amy with inquisitive eyes.

"If he doesn't want to give me straight answers, I'm going to get them myself. I wasn't here yesterday afternoon, but I understand that the testimony was nothing more than the rantings of a bitter ex-wife. If that could possibly have any relevance, this is clearly admissible."

Amy noticed that several jurors were smiling. The hope was that they were imagining how much Amy would have discredited the ex-wife the day before. Given the ex-wife's claimed propensity for guile, that might not have actually happened. The fact that the jury believed that it would have was enough.

"Ms. Prescott," Judge Pendens said, "if you had been here yesterday and made objections, some of that testimony might not have come in. For purposes of the objection before me, I need to know whether this is relevant or whether you're just trying to prejudice the jury by portraying the witness as either an unfaithful husband or a sexual harasser."

"Your Honor," Amy replied, "I don't think the witness's past behavior reflects very good judgment. Furthermore, the witness tried to claim that he was replaced as Chief Operating Officer because my client allegedly wanted more control. If he wants to admit that the reason was his poor judgment, we can move on. If he wants to dispute that, I think we should be allowed to challenge that."

The judge nodded as she absorbed the argument. "I guess I'll overrule the objection on the grounds that it's impeachment. I don't really want to spend much more time in this area, however, so I'm encouraging you to move on."

"Thank you, your Honor," Amy said. Turning back to the witness, she said, "It's true, is it not Mr. Bogardus, that you haven't had any special training or experience in the interim that would make you any more likely to succeed if you were put back in charge of the company?"

"Yes, that's true."

"So, if in fact your management was the reason for the past problems, there's every reason to expect the company to suffer the same or similar problems, am I right?"

Bogardus paused. He looked at her defiantly. "No," he said with emphasis.

Amy reacted as if the answer had taken her by surprise. "No?" she said. "Why's that?"

"Because I've made a deal with Amalgamated Grain for them to take over the company." He was smiling with the belief that he'd just played his own trump card.

"Is that so?" she said.

"Yes," he said triumphantly. "Whether or not I'm a good manager is irrelevant. The company will now have the most experienced management in the industry."

Amy didn't immediately respond, and that gave Bogardus the opportunity to gloat. Finally, she said, "So you've sold your shares to Amalgamated?"

"Not exactly," he said. "I've sold them an option for my shares and the rest of the company depending on this lawsuit."

Amy walked to a stack of documents on the corner of the table. She rummaged around for a moment and then pulled one out. "Mr. Bogardus," she said, "on Monday your lawyer put the Buy-Sell Agreement into evidence as Exhibit One. Could you get that document in front of you please?"

Bogardus shuffled through a stack of exhibits piled near the witness stand. "I have it," he finally said.

"Mr. Bogardus, you introduced this document into evidence because you contend that it gives you the right to acquire all of the stock in the event of a bank default, isn't that right?"

"Yes," he said with continued confidence.

"But Mr. Bogardus, if you turn to page eighteen, doesn't it also state that anyone who intends to sell his shares needs to first offer them to the company and the other shareholders?"

The smile went away from his face, but he wasn't giving in. "Tony went into default first. Right now we're just dealing with my right to get the rest of the stock. Once I have it, I can do anything I want with it."

"That may or may not be true," she said, "but you don't have it yet and you have already purported to sell it."

"Just an option. I said they had an option."

"But they've already given you money for it, haven't they?"

"Yes."

"And they're paying your legal costs to be here, aren't they?"

"Objection," Cavanaugh chimed in. "The arrangement regarding attorneys' fees is protected by the attorney-client privilege."

Amy let out a long sigh. "Your Honor, the attorney-client privilege protects communications from a client to an attorney because the client should be able to disclose all relevant information to the attorney without fear that the attorney could be compelled to disclose the information. The payment of fees does not have anything to do with a client communication."

"Overruled," the judge said. "Mr. Bogardus, please answer the question."

"Yes," he said. "Amalgamated is paying the legal fees."

Amy allowed a half smile to cross her face. "So, you've already sold your interests in the company, haven't you?"

"That's what you say."

"Well, can we at least agree that you didn't offer Minnesota Marine or the other shareholders the right to buy an option on your shares?"

"I didn't think they would be interested."

"Whether they would have been or not, it's true that even though the agreement requires it, you did not even make that offer, right?"

"That's right, but I didn't make the deal with Amalgamated until after the default occurred."

"Do you have proof of that?"

"The option agreement wasn't signed until after. I can show you that."

"Well, whether or not the agreement was signed or not, the agreement was already in place, wasn't it."

"No."

"When did you first meet with representatives from Amalgamated?"

"I don't remember the exact date, but it was recently."

"Did you have a prior relationship with Mr. Cavanaugh, or did you meet him as part of this transaction?"

Bogardus was starting to regain his swagger. "Never met him before."

"So, you're telling this Court that the negotiations on your deal didn't even start until what – some time in October?"

"That's right."

Amy went to her briefcase to retrieve the ammunition Scouten had sent her. After requesting and receiving the right to approach the witness, she said, "Mr. Bogardus, I'm showing you a photograph taken at an outdoor restaurant in Minneapolis. Do you recognize yourself in that picture?"

Bogardus was now in unexpected territory. "Yes."

"And that's Mr. Cavanaugh sitting next to you, is it not?"

Bogardus was staring at the picture, but it wasn't providing him with the lie he needed. "Yes."

"And who is the other man in the photo?"

He scrunched up his face as if the photo was not clear. "I'm not sure," he said.

Amy got a big smile on her face. "I'm not sure either, but I am pretty sure that he's sitting in the back of the courtroom and has been sitting in every day watching the trial." She now walked toward the gallery. Pointing at a man in a blue suit, she said, "Isn't it true that the person in that picture is that gentleman right there?"

There wasn't any way around it. Amy could show the picture to the jury and let them decide, or Bogardus could admit the obvious. "Yeah," he finally said.

"And he's with Amalgamated Grain, isn't he?"

Bogardus perked up as he apparently had a new idea. "Yes. And this picture must have been taken in early October like I said."

"So, is it your testimony that people in Minneapolis are still dining outside in October?"

"Sure. Thank God for global warming."

She ignored his attempt at humor. "Let me show you another picture that was taken from inside the restaurant." As she spoke, she glided back up to the witness stand. "Do you see how the three of you are wearing the same clothes as in the first picture?"

"Yes."

"So, you'll agree with me that the pictures were taken at the same meeting?"

"Yeah, I guess."

"Do you notice all of the activity in the background?"

"What do you mean?"

"Well, as I understand it, this particular restaurant is right across the street from Orchestra Hall, and in this picture it looks like there's some kind of concert being held on the plaza."

"I don't remember anything about that."

"Are you aware, Mr. Bogardus, that they have free concerts on the Orchestra Hall plaza during the summer."

Bogardus shrugged. "I guess I've heard of that."

"Are you also aware that those concerts are only held between Memorial Day and Labor Day?"

Now he was shaking his head. "Well, this must have been some other event, then. You have no way of proving that the people in the background were at one of those concerts."

Amy took a deep breath and did what she could to show her disappointment in his approach to the truth. "Actually," she said. "I can." With that she walked back to her briefcase and pulled out her laptop computer. "Mr. Bogardus, as you know, people can now record movies on their cell phones. I have a movie clip from a phone and, with a little technology, I can broadcast it here in the courtroom."

She connected her laptop to a projector. The bailiff dimmed the lights and the show started. The video showed three men talking. The audio, however, was distinct. "Do you recognize the gravelly voice singing in the background?" she asked.

"I don't think so."

"Well, surprisingly, I do. That's a local singer named Mick Sterling."

"Objection," Cavanaugh blurted. "Is Ms. Prescott going to testify now?"

Amy didn't wait for a ruling. "Point taken," she said. "Let me rephrase. Mr. Bogardus, do you see the guy in the back of the courtroom with the long black hair and the earring?"

"Yes."

"If I told you that he's Mick Sterling and that he's prepared to take the stand to confirm that the gravelly voice in the video is his and that he performed on the Orchestra Hall plaza this past August 28, would you have any basis to dispute that testimony?"

Bogardus looked at Cavanaugh for help, but coaching wasn't really allowed. Cavanaugh gave a brief nod, and Bogardus took his cue. "All right," he said. "Maybe we did meet in August, but that doesn't mean we had a deal back then."

"Mr. Bogardus, after what we've just been through, what makes you think any of us would believe another word you say?"

"Objection," Cavanaugh shouted. "Argumentative."

Before the judge could respond, Amy said, "I'll withdraw it. We have no more questions for this witness." In all likelihood, she could have trapped him into more lies if she kept him on the stand. At this point, it didn't really matter. She had demonstrated his willingness to say whatever he thought would help his case, and nothing he ever said again would be given any credence.

CHAPTER THIRTY-FOUR

L ITIGATION GENERALLY INVOLVES TWO THINGS. The first is to tell a story in a way that the judge or jury wants your client to win because it seems fair. The second is to give the judge or jury a legal justification to accomplish that result. The most likable litigant in the world would not necessarily prevail if there were no legal basis for it.

Amy's strategy was to portray Drabeck as a kindly old man who was only trying to keep what was rightfully his. Thus, she called him as a witness to explain how he had built the company up from next to nothing into a thriving business that provided jobs and income to many people. By comparison, the plaintiff's case had consisted primarily of people who wanted what he had, but wanted to achieve it the old fashioned way – by marrying into it.

The legal justification was simple. Bogardus had breached the contract first. He had sold his interest in the company before the bank default occurred. As a result, he should not be able to enforce the contract. More importantly, his sale triggered a right of the company and other shareholders to buy his stock. If that meant he was no longer a stockholder, he wouldn't have any rights to enforce the buy-out when the bank declared a default. All the jury had to do was find that Bogardus effectively sold his stock to Amalgamated before the bank declared the loan to be in default.

Amy took the position that the case was basically over after she demonstrated the lack of respect that Bogardus had for the truth. She had scored big on that point, and didn't want to belabor the matter. If she had spent a lot of time on other things, the jury might think that she needed to do more to win. The problem was that the other testimony might not come off as well.

Because she abbreviated her case, closing arguments were made on Wednesday afternoon. Unfortunately, that meant the jury did not have time to deliberate that day. The waiting game had begun.

Drabeck walked Amy back to her hotel. "What do you think are our chances?" he asked.

"Well, I was one of the combatants. You might have a better idea as a spectator."

Drabeck smiled. "I know this. If it depends on who was the better lawyer, we won it with ease. You were in complete control of the courtroom. In fact, you were in control even the afternoon you weren't there."

Amy couldn't help but blush. For all the uncertainty and anxiety that permeated her personal and professional life, the courtroom was the one place where she felt completely at ease. She was good at it, and felt confident that it was what she was meant to do. "I thought our case went in pretty well. I think the jury wants to rule for us, so they just have to find that Bogardus breached the contract. Then, the Court will enter an order allowing us to buy out his shares."

"Do you think it would have helped if we had been able to show that he was causing the losses that led to the default?"

"There's no question that it would have, but where were we going to get the evidence? That's all speculation."

"Couldn't we have asked him when he was on the stand?"

"Sure, but we didn't have anything to trip him up. Personally, I think he's just an opportunist. I doubt he'd have the savvy to figure out a way to cause all the losses."

The old man paused to think about that. "I suppose, but even if we win we still have to figure that out."

"I realize that," she said. "And that's what's so troubling about all this. A verdict in our favor only solves the current problem."

They reached the St. Paul Hotel. "What's the protocol now?" Drabeck asked. "Do we go to the courthouse tomorrow and wait for the jury to decide?"

"No. The Court will call us when the jury reaches a verdict. We just need to be able to get there in fifteen minutes. I'll call you as soon as I hear."

AT 11:00 THE NEXT MORNING, her cell phone rang. The jury had reached a verdict and everyone was being called back to court. They had probably deliberated less than two hours. Everyone always had a theory on what such short deliberations meant, but the only thing it really meant was that the jurors had all reached pretty much the same conclusion.

Amy met Drabeck in the hallway outside the courtroom. His life's work was at stake, and it showed in his disposition. "Any last thoughts?" he asked.

"You deserve to win," she said. "I can't guarantee anything, but in my opinion you deserve to win."

Drabeck smiled and nodded. "I can't believe it can come down to this. A group of strangers has the power to take away everything that I have."

Amy thought about his predicament. She was an advocate, but the outcome of each case merely affected her won-loss record. For the participants, the outcome could be life changing. "Have faith," was all she could say.

The jury filed in and took their seats. "Have you reached a verdict?" Judge Pendens asked.

A woman, who had apparently been elected foreperson, stood and said that they had. The jury had been given a special verdict, which means they had been asked to answer several specific questions instead of simply making a ruling in favor of a party. At the judge's direction, the foreperson handed a document to the bailiff, who brought it to the judge. She looked it up and down to make sure it was done right.

Judge Pendens then began to recite the results. "The first question was whether plaintiff breached the contract by failing to advise the company and the other shareholders of the sale of plaintiff's stock. The jury answered 'Yes.'"

Amy felt a huge rush of relief. As much as she thought she'd won the case, the celebration never comes until the verdict is in. Cavanaugh apparently thought he would win as well, as his smug smile had turned to a look of disbelief.

The judge continued. "Because the jury found plaintiff violated the contract, there was no reason to answer the rest of the special verdict questions. As a matter of law, the company or the other shareholders have the right to buy out Mr. Bogardus. The terms of that transaction will be set by this Court after further briefing."

The Court then indulged Cavanaugh and his client by allowing them to poll the jury and make whatever motions they thought were appropriate. An appeal by Bogardus was still possible, but the company and Tony Drabeck had dodged a bullet. Unfortunately, the outcome was that Drabeck would continue to operate the business, but would be doing so without insurance.

CHAPTER THIRTY-FIVE

THE SATISFACTION OF A JOB WELL DONE was enough to improve Amy's outlook on life. As a result, she decided to give herself the rest of the week off. She was going to bask in her triumph and not let anything else interfere.

Unfortunately, while her body stayed away from the office, her mind always returned to the dilemma. Bogardus had merely been a manifestation of the larger problem. Minnesota Marine was still in desperate shape. She'd managed to save the company – and her best ticket to partnership – for now, but the problem was far from solved. The loan was still in default, and it was only a matter of time until the bank began its own foreclosure. Furthermore, the lack of insurance made every day of operations a risk of the greatest magnitude.

She laid out the possibilities in her mind. Amalgamated Grain remained a suspect, but it was hard to imagine how it could be causing the losses. The union angle was still on the table, so she needed to rekindle that litigation. She hadn't even ruled out the insurance broker. She had not, however, figured out how to connect Skeeter's demise to any of those theories.

She determined that merely reviewing files from her office in Chicago would not provide the answers. The documents provided the details necessary to process the claims, but there was likely to be other information that wasn't necessary for the reports that might connect the losses. Her first stop would be New Orleans.

Louisiana was the hub connecting the brown water market with the blue water ocean vessels. The quantity of commodities moving through the Mississippi delta was enormous. It stood to reason, then, that it would also be the epicenter for claims and losses. As a result, Minnesota Marine's principal trial lawyer was located there. Amy decided to pay a visit.

She called Tony Drabeck on Monday to get the information and to have him coordinate the meeting. Tony emailed her the address information and the timing. He concluded his email with: "Try to have some fun while you're there. You've earned it."

Amy booked a room on the edge of the French Quarter. That gave her a chance to experience the history and the nightlife of the city, but left her within walking distance of the law firm. She checked in and then walked up Canal Street until she found a building that matched the address she'd been given. She looked again at the name – "G. Garson Graves, Attorney and Proctor" – and wondered how bad his first name could be that he'd go by "Garson" instead.

She took the elevator up to the offices of Graves & Élan, P.A. "I'm here to see Mr. Graves," she told the receptionist. "My name is Amy Prescott."

After several minutes, a silver-haired gentleman appeared. "Ya'll must be Amy," he said as he extended his hand.

The leather sofa in the reception area was a little too plush, and Amy struggled as she tried to get up. "And that must mean that you're Garson Graves," she said after finally reaching her feet.

"Please," he said. "Call me 'G.'"

Now Amy wondered whether the G stood for something or whether his first name was actually just G. She decided to postpone her curiosity for the moment. "Well then, G, it's nice to meet you."

As they shook hands, Amy noticed a large block-lettered, monogrammed G on a shirt that looked to be custom made. Graves was an elegant dresser, almost bordering on flamboyant. The cigarette smell on his clothes seemed more nostalgic than offensive. He looked like he could have spent time with Sinatra, Martin, and the rest of the Rat Pack. He wasn't that old, but he seemed to be from that era.

"How was your flight?" he asked. "Hotel okay?"

"Yes," she nodded. "Everything's great."

"Can we do the business tomorrow?" he asked. "It's been a long day and I think we should unwind a little."

"Fine with me," she said.

Graves retreated to his office for his suit coat and then gave instructions to the receptionist. They were out the door and on the street in no time. Graves asked her if she'd been to New Orleans before, except he didn't pronounce it that way. He said: "Have ya bin ta N'awlins befo'?"

When she admitted that she had not, he suggested that they go to some of the landmarks. "It's not really tourist season yet, so it won't be that bad."

They turned on Bourbon Street and started through the French Quarter. The architectural change was dramatic. It was like walking into a Mark Twain novel, albeit one with a lot of tee shirt shops. The buildings were well preserved, but with designs that had been in style in the 1800s. "This looks like Disneyland," Amy remarked. "I don't know anywhere else in this country where you could see a city that looks so old."

"There aren't many," Graves remarked. "Most of the rest of the South was destroyed at the end of the War Between the States. It wasn't enough for the Union army to win, the sons-a-bitches had to destroy everything in their path."

"So, how did the French Quarter survive?"

"By realizin' that there was no point in fightin'. N'awlins surrendered before the troops arrived and, as a result, the French Quarter was spared."

Amy thought about that for a moment. "G, I don't mean any disrespect, but are you telling me that the French even found a way to surrender during the American Civil War?"

Graves let out a big laugh, and it was clear that he either was not French or not offended if he was. "The folks here were French, but this wasn't a French Colony at the time. That had changed with the Louisiana Purchase."

"I was just kidding," she said.

"It's okay," he said. "The French influence is what makes N'awlins great, and we'll take the good with the bad."

After a few blocks, they turned off Bourbon Street and made their way to an establishment named: "Pat O'Brien's." A maitre de rushed to greet them. "Mr. Graves, so nice to see you. Let me find you a table in the courtyard." As they walked through, Amy noticed several people waving or nodding at her, but then realized that they were acknowledging the person behind her.

When they were seated, a waiter promptly descended upon them. "Have a Hurricane," Graves said. "No point coming here and not having the drink of the house."

Amy agreed. She didn't hear Graves order anything, and assumed he must be having the same thing. When the waiter returned, he set a huge hourglass shaped drink in front of Amy. He then set a lowball glass in front of Graves and said, "Here's your Old Charters and water, Mr. Graves."

Amy's drink was about five times the size of his, and one taste and she realized it wasn't all fruit punch. "I don't think this is going to work so well with me drinking this giant party drink."

"Don't worry," he said, "I think I'll be able to keep up." Graves pulled a silver cigarette case from his coat pocket and then removed a cigarette from it. "Do you mind if I smoke?" he asked.

Amy was not in a good position to refuse. Equally important, she didn't really care. It only added to the nostalgic atmosphere. "Of course not," she said.

The Hurricane went down easily, but she made a deliberate effort to pace herself. Graves never ordered a drink, but new ones kept showing up when the old ones were gone. Each time, Graves would smile and nod his appreciation to the waiter, and it was clearly a ritual that had been followed many times before.

When Amy finally finished her drink, Graves suggested that she return to her hotel and freshen up, as dinner would not be until nine. Amy gladly accepted the offer, but worried about whether her buzz would wear off in the interim. Graves walked her to her hotel, and suggested that she take a cab to the restaurant. He'd meet her at Antoine's.

WHEN SHE ARRIVED AT THE RESTAURANT, there was a long line winding down a porch and around a corner. She walked to the front to look for Graves. There was no sign of him, and he seemed like the last person who would keep a lady waiting. She walked along the line looking for him, but still didn't see him. With no other clear option, she got in the back of the line.

She was feeling a little flustered when she heard his voice behind her. "Please accept my apologies," Graves said. "I had some other business to tend to and it took longer than expected."

He had not gone home to freshen up. In fact, his breath and clothes smelled like he'd gone for more cocktails and cigarettes. "Come with me," he said, and led her around the back of the building. When they got there, he picked up a telephone. There was no dial or buttons -- just a telephone on a cradle. After a moment, he announced his presence. A nearby door swung open and a man wearing a restaurant tuxedo appeared. "Mr. Graves," he fawned. "So nice to see you."

The man proceeded to lead them through a long hallway and into a dining room that was separate from the public dining room in the front. There were several tables of diners, and it was clear that this was an area reserved for the high rollers. Amy and Graves were seated at a table in the corner, and the waiter promptly asked Amy for her drink order.

"Try a Sazerack," Graves suggested.

"Is that a big giant drink with several shots of booze?" she asked.

"No," he assured her. "It's kind of a N'awlins martini. I'm sure you'll like it." She acquiesced.

Within a few minutes, the waiter appeared with the drinks. He set a lowball in front of Graves and said, "Here's your Old Charters and water, Mr. Graves." Again, Amy had no recollection of Graves having placed an order.

They spent the next several hours enjoying the finer things that Antoine's had to offer. Oysters Bienville, shrimp étoufeé, jambalaya, the works. Graves liked to talk, and he went on and on with stories of the history of Antoine's, the French Quarter, and anything else he could think of. Amy found him interesting, although the booze might have made a Jehovah's Witness seem like the life of the party.

Amy excused herself to the ladies room. As she walked, she noticed that some of the tables appeared to be business dinners, while others were occupied by couples. More often than not, the couples had a great age disparity, suggesting that this was a place to take business associates and mistresses.

When she returned, Graves was quickly out of his seat to pull out her chair. He may have been from a different era, but at least he had all of the charm that went with it.

While they were waiting for their dessert, a burly man with a big smile came up behind Graves. "G, you hound dog, you. How've you been?"

Graves turned in his seat and stood to shake hands. "Marcel, how are you, sir?"

"I will be better once we take care of that Hendrickson claim. I need the money for my vacation. What's been taking so long?"

Graves' face went white, and he struggled to remain composed. "Marcel, I would like you to meet Ms. Amy Prescott. She is the new attorney for Minnesota Marine."

Marcel's smile quickly disappeared, and both men wore uncomfortable looks. Amy stood and shook his hand. As she expressed pleasantries, the back of her mind started working for an answer.

Marcel was the first to recover. "My apologies, madam. I thought you were just having a social engagement. I did not mean to intrude on attorney-client communications."

"Not at all," she assured him. As she sat down, the connection hit her. Hendrickson was one of the files she had reviewed at the insurance company. She had not planned to use the evening to discuss cases, but the time now seemed right. After Marcel had left, she asked, "Is he the opposing counsel in the Hendrickson case?"

"I'm afraid he's opposing counsel in almost every injured seaman case."

"So you must deal with him a lot."

"Yes."

"In fact, he's responsible for a lot of your work, isn't he?" Amy asked.

"I suppose that's true, but if it wasn't him it would be someone else."

Amy couldn't dispute that fact, but there was something unsavory about the interaction that had just occurred between Marcel and Graves. It was fine for opposing lawyers to be cordial to each other, but the greeting exchanged in the restaurant seemed to go beyond that.

Graves seemed to notice her concern. "Haven't you ever heard that you should keep your friends close and your enemies closer?"

"I've heard that expression applied to organized crime, but I didn't know it applied to the practice of law," she said.

"It is true that Marcel and I have a symbiotic relationship, but that is the nature of the beast. Better to have the devil you know than the devil you don't."

Amy wondered what other clichés Graves was going to use to justify his relationship with Marcel. In Amy's experience, witnesses who were at a loss for words frequently clamored for the words of others. Grave's continuing efforts to justify the relationship was only increasing her suspicion that Marcel was paying a "commission" to Graves out of settlement proceeds – or something worse. Finally, she decided to change the subject.

After dinner, they strolled through the French Quarter. They stopped in a rundown building to watch the Preservation Jazz band. The band was made up of old African American men playing anything requested – except "When the Saints go Marching in." There was no liquor or food service, and the band subsisted only on tips. After a couple songs – and nearly fifteen minutes without a drink – Graves suggested that they move on.

The next stop was the Blue Nile. On cue, a maitre de greeted them at the door and called Graves by name. As they were seated, the waiter set a drink in front of Graves and asked Amy for her order. She had already had enough varieties of alcohol in her to make her choice irrelevant. She decided to return to her mainstay – martinis.

She slowly lost all concept of time. Before she knew it, her watch read one a.m. She offered to take a cab back, but Graves would have none of it. He paid the bill and escorted her to her hotel. Amy had allowed herself to drink beyond her limit. She was not incapacitated, but she was more impaired than she should have been considering she was in unfamiliar surroundings.

Graves apparently sensed that and used it as an opportunity to instill a warning that he could deny in the light of sobriety. "Ms. Prescott," he said as they neared her hotel. "I have a relationship with Minnesota Marine that goes back many years and I have a reputation in the Maritime

Bar that is second to none. I would do anything to preserve those things. And I do mean anything. So, Ms. Amy Prescott, as the new lawyer for the company, it would be most unwise for you to do anything that might harm my position."

The words were sobering, but Amy didn't want to give them any credence so she let out a drunk giggle. "What are you talkin' about, G? You the man," she slurred. "I wouldn't want anyone else representing Minnesota Marine." For her part, she had played along. Graves presumably was giving her a warning that he hoped would be processed by her subconscious, but not remembered in detail by her conscious mind. By pretending to be drunker than she was, she could pretend like she hadn't heard his threat. It had, however, made an indelible impression.

CHAPTER THIRTY-SIX

T HE VISIT TO GRAVES' OFFICE the next day was a little awkward. She complained about a hangover and feigned an inability to remember much of anything after Antoine's. "I was just relieved I woke up in my hotel room, and that I was alone," she added.

Graves made a sad face as though her comment was directed at him.

"No offense," she said, "but under the circumstances I don't think it would be a good idea for us to be intimately involved." That and having sex with a relic didn't seem that enticing, she thought to herself.

Graves led her to a small conference room. "I've had my assistant bring in all of the current files and everything that's been closed within the last two years. The older files are in storage. We can get them if you need them, but I was told that your concern is the recent wave of losses."

Amy thanked him. "I'll start here and let you know. I don't think I'll need anything else."

"For your convenience, I'll have my assistant sit in with you to answer any questions," he said.

Convenience, my ass, she thought to herself. The assistant was being placed as a spy. That was a tactic ordinarily employed by opposing counsel who wanted to monitor what the other side found significant in a document production. Graves was apparently concerned about something.

After he left, Amy made small talk with the assistant while perusing the files. She started with the pleadings folders. The pleadings represent the documents filed with the Court and the formal documents exchanged with the other side. They told the basic story.

Within each file, she then reviewed the correspondence, the legal research, and the internal memoranda. As she did so, she was struck by the fact that some documents appeared to have been removed. Thus, she was at a loss to understand exactly how some of the cases had been resolved.

She took detailed notes of the cases, the status, and as much settlement information as she could discern. A comparison to the company's records and the insurance records would be in order.

After several hours, she asked the assistant to summon Graves. "G," she said, "some of these files seem to be missing documents. Are there things that haven't been filed yet?" She had no expectation that the missing documents were the result of a slow-moving administrative staff, but she didn't want to be confrontational.

"I don't think so," he said. "Anything that was removed was because of attorney-client privilege."

That didn't make any sense because Amy was an attorney for the client as well and a disclosure to her would not invalidate the privilege. Again, she decided to take the path of least resistance. "Well, I can talk to the company to see if they want to waive the privilege to let me see the documents. Can you give me an idea of how many documents we're talking about?"

"Very few," he said. "But, in Louisiana, if I show you the documents, then they become public documents and I have to show them to anyone who asks for them."

In Amy's estimation, that was about the stupidest rationalization that she had ever heard. Nonetheless, attorney-client privilege seemed to confuse a lot of lawyers, so it was possible that Graves actually believed the crap he was spewing.

"I don't think that's accurate when I'm an attorney for the company as well. Even if it is the case, Minnesota Marine may have no choice but to waive any privilege claim."

"That's fine," he said, "but what about the privilege claim of Graves & Élan?"

Stupid was giving way to stupider, as far as Amy was concerned. "The privilege belongs to the client, not the law firm," she said. "I'll talk to Mr. Drabeck and get back in touch with you."

That answer didn't seem to sit well with Graves, but there wasn't much left for him to say. They exchanged a few more words and Amy left for home. She had come looking for answers and left with even more questions.

CHAPTER THIRTY-SEVEN

AMY WENT STRAIGHT HOME from the airport. Jasmine was preparing for a night on the town. "Come on along," she said to Amy. "You did pretty good last time when you weren't even trying. Now that you and Chadwick aren't an item, you'll do even better."

"I don't think I have the energy," Amy said. "Besides, I have some work that I need to tend to."

"You need a little more fun in your life. You know what they say about all work and no play."

"I have a client that's about to be put out of business. I need to think of something to save it."

Jasmine wasn't persuaded. "It's just a business. It's not like someone's on death row."

Trying to persuade Jasmine that Tony Drabeck's life was at least figuratively on the line seemed like a daunting task, so Amy changed strategies. "I'm still nursing a hangover from last night. New Orleans was everything I thought and more."

"Get any beads?" Jasmine asked.

"I got drunk, but I didn't get that drunk. Besides, it's not the season."

Amy retreated to her room and checked her voicemail. Chadwick had called. They hadn't really dated since he had suggested they see other people. They'd met for lunch and talked a few times on the phone, but nothing else. His tone seemed obligatory, as if he wanted to maintain a connection, but had no burning desire to see her. She decided not to call him back. She wanted to make it clear that she was not available for him anytime he should change his mind.

She did decide to return a call to Scouten from earlier in the day. When he answered, she said, "How's the best investigator in the Midwest?"

He chuckled. "Actually, I'm afraid I might be slipping. Estrus Willard has disappeared."

"What do you mean?"

"She's gone. I thought maybe I had just missed her coming and going, but I finally went up to the house and just about everything has been cleared out. I mean the junk was still in the yard, but the TV and the clothes and stuff were all removed."

"What about the trailer home itself?

"It's there, but I found out the finance company owns most of it and the bank has a mortgage on the land."

"So, do you think she was the victim of foul play or she just took off?"

"Took off," he said. "It wasn't like the place had been ransacked. Furthermore, the dogs are gone."

Amy was perplexed. "Why would a woman who is about to come into money disappear? It doesn't make sense."

"Maybe she had warrants for her arrest and the money was going to draw too much attention to her," Scouten suggested.

"That's a thought, but it wasn't like she won the lottery. I mean, the news media wouldn't be covering it." The line was quiet for a moment before she continued. "I wish I knew who was in Esty's bed the night I was there. Somebody was looking for whomever it was, and I'd like to know why."

"Sorry I can't help. I never saw anyone come or go other than Esty. I went to the post office and asked if she had a forwarding address, and they said they never delivered mail to the old address. I think she used a P.O. Box."

"That wouldn't surprise me. When I was little, my mom used a P.O. Box. She said it was because we moved around a lot, but I think it was because she didn't want creditors to know where we lived. In fact, it was kind of a joke that the mailman for my neighborhood had the easiest route of all, because most of the residents went to the post office to get their mail."

"I'm not sure what we do now," he said. "Any ideas?"

She paused as she thought about it. "Maybe," she said. "I'll make some calls in the morning, but it doesn't seem that promising."

CHAPTER THIRTY-EIGHT

THE NEXT MORNING, she called Ted Hollerback to ask about Esty Willard's insurance claim. It took a moment to refresh his recollection as to who she was, but he recovered quickly. "Did you hear about the attorney who turned down a big contingent fee?" he said. Without waiting long, he blurted out, "Neither did I!" And then he laughed uproariously.

Amy waited for his laughter to subside. "That's very amusing," she said. "I'm sure there are a lot of insurance brokers who have their commission checks sent straight to orphanages."

The line was quiet for a moment. Then he said, "You kind of take the fun out of lawyer jokes."

"I'm sorry," she said. "It's just that I've been under some pressure, and I'm a little confused by some of this insurance stuff and I need your help."

"Fair enough," he said, "but next time you could at least chuckle."

"That's a reasonable request." The truth was that she generally enjoyed lawyer jokes, but she had too much on her mind. Finally, she got to the point. "Do you know anything about the insurance claim relating to Peter Willard?"

"Yeah. It settled. The widow agreed to take $100,000. Normally, the insurance company takes longer to verify the facts and everything, but they wanted to settle it before she changed her mind. $100,000 is a lot of money, but she probably could have gotten a lot more if she waited."

Amy's mind raced in two directions. "Is there a chance that the insurance company will now reinstate Minnesota Marine's coverage?"

"It helps, but the company still has unexplained losses. We're submitting a proposal to Lloyd's of London to try to find coverage. The

British have been in the insurance business a lot longer, and they have fewer government regulations to deal with."

"Okay," Amy said. "How about the payout? Do you know how it was handled? Was she mailed a check? Has she cashed it?"

"It was mailed to a P.O. Box in Missouri. I know because we got a copy for the file. I have yet to receive confirmation that she cashed it."

"Did she have a lawyer? Did she sign a release?

"I don't think she had a lawyer, because the check was just made out to her. As for a release, I'm sure the company required something."

Amy was struggling over what to ask next. "Do you think it's kind of suspicious that she took the money and disappeared?"

"I guess, but what difference does it make?"

Amy raced through a variety of scenarios in her head. "I think it might mean she wasn't entitled to the money. I think it might mean that Skeeter's still alive, so she grabbed the money while she could and took off."

"That's an interesting twist," Hollerback said. "Do you think he's in on it, or do you think that she took the money and is hiding from him?"

"I suppose it could go either way, but I think Skeeter jumped overboard to fake his own death. The weird thing is that I'm not sure he did it for the money. Estrus seemed genuinely surprised that she could collect insurance money, and, believe me, I don't think she's clever enough for it to have been an act. I think Skeeter wanted people to think he was dead for some other reason."

"Like what?"

"Hard to say." Amy replayed the night outside the Willard home. If Skeeter was the guy the visitors were looking for, they were pretty intent on finding him. "Maybe he double-crossed somebody. Maybe he slept with the wrong guy's wife."

Amy hung up the phone and considered her latest dilemma: How to find someone who didn't want to be found. Locating Skeeter was about more than getting the insurance money back. Skeeter had the potential to unlock the mystery. He was running from something, and whatever it was might be tied to the rest of Minnesota Marine's problems. Unfortunately, even Scouten didn't have any ideas on what to do.

Amy called Minnesota Marine to see if there were any records of where Skeeter went to high school or anything else that might help her track down his relatives. There was next to nothing. His next-of-kin was listed as Estrus Willard, and the only address information was the trailer home.

With that much money in hand, neither Estrus nor Skeeter was likely to get a job or do anything else that would result in a public record. The one thing they'd probably need, however, was a bank. The police could subpoena records to see if a person was using an ATM, but there wasn't enough evidence of a crime to cause the police to pursue it. If Skeeter and Esty wanted, they could be basically invisible.

She was focusing on what Skeeter and Esty would do with the money when something dawned on her. It was a long shot, but, at that moment, it was the only shot she had. She walked down the hall to the bookkeeping department.

"I need to look at the bank records for the last month," she told the clerk. "Have we gotten a statement lately?"

"It came in a few days ago," was the response. With that, the clerk walked to a file cabinet and pulled out a file folder. "Anything in particular you're looking for?"

"I gave a check to someone named 'Estrus Willard.' I need to find out if it was cashed and, if so, where."

The clerk handed the file to Amy. She found the cancelled checks and began to review them. Halfway through, she spotted it. She pulled it out and looked on the back. The endorsements indicated it was cashed at an establishment called "On Golden Pawn." There wasn't an address, but there was enough to get started.

Amy searched the internet and found an "On Golden Pawn" in Greenville, Mississippi. There could have been other stores with that name that didn't bother trying to get business through the internet, but it didn't seem likely. After all, the name wasn't particularly clever.

Amy called Scouten again. "I think I've found them," she announced. "Esty cashed a check in Mississippi."

"That's odd," he said. "Why would she wait to do it somewhere else?"

"Maybe because she didn't want anyone in her hometown to know she had come into money. Or maybe she was afraid the check I gave her was a trick so she didn't cash it until she got the bigger one. I grew up on a farm, but I can't really read the minds of hillbillies."

Scouten grunted a laugh. "I guess I should go check it out. The problem is I have to testify in court in Wausau. I don't think I can get to Mississippi until next week. Will that be soon enough?"

She looked at her calendar. There was no specific deadline for Minnesota Marine, but the other shoe could drop at anytime. She weighed the options and then said, "I want you to be prepared to go next week, but I can't just sit and wait. I'll go down there myself and see if I can find anything, and you can relieve me if nothing turns up." Soon, Amy was off to see another part of the country she had never planned nor wanted to see.

CHAPTER THIRTY-NINE

"ON GOLDEN PAWN" PROVED TO BE AS seedy as Amy had expected. A painted sign hung over the door, and the window listed the variety of services offered – check cashing, money orders, loans, pawn, prepaid phone cards. Everything necessary for someone who lives in the modern world but wants to be functionally "off the grid."

Finding the pawnshop was a good start, but that was about as far as it went. The people who used such services tended to favor anonymity, so there wouldn't be much of a paper trail even if Amy could devise a way to uncover it. Furthermore, the community seemed a little too big to simply hope to run into the Willards at the grocery store.

She was sure Scouten knew how to either muscle or cajole people in the pawn business, but she had no such experience. Asking about the Willards wasn't likely to result in a response. She might be able to tell by body language whether the person behind the counter was being truthful in response to questions, but she needed to know more than that the Willards had been there. She needed to know where they were living.

Her only real chance was not to ask anything. Instead, she needed to create a false impression that might lead to the disclosure of the information. She walked inside and pretended to peruse the merchandise. When the other customers left, she walked to the counter. After being greeted by the clerk, she leaned over and spoke in low tones. "I see that y'all cash checks. Can you cash a check for $100,000?"

The clerk's head popped up with surprise. "What the hell's going on in this world? Someone else asked me the same thing last week."

"Does that mean you can?" she asked.

"Yes, but it's a process. We don't give you the money until we've received it from the bank it's drawn on."

"So, how long does that take?"

"A few days for the transfers. Then, if you're crazy enough to want it in cash, we have to make sure our bank has enough on hand."

"I don't understand," Amy said. "What alternative does someone have other than cash?"

"Prepaid debit cards. They're like credit cards, but they're only good for the amount on deposit."

"How long does it take for that?"

"Usually a couple days to get the card."

"So, what are we looking at total?"

"It varies. I think the woman from last week is picking hers up tomorrow."

Amy wondered whether she should ask anything more direct. The clerk asked her if she had the check with her and wanted to proceed, which she deflected by indicating that she did not. She thought about it a little more and then said, "Maybe I'll be back."

CHAPTER FORTY

O N GOLDEN PAWN WAS ADJACENT TO A STRIP MALL, so Amy found a coffee shop within view. Shortly before noon, she moved to her car. With nobody to talk to and nothing else to do, she started to get impatient. She also wondered whether it was possible that she'd missed the Willards or that the clerk at the pawnshop had been wrong about the timing.

Finally, she pulled out her cell phone and called the pawnshop. "I'm calling to see if the money for Estrus Willard is available to be picked up," she said.

"Yes, Mrs. Willard," he said. "I was told you'd be here about two o'clock. Can I still count on that?"

"That should be fine," she said as she hung up. Now that she knew the timing, she felt like she could take a break and get some lunch. Still, she didn't let the pawnshop out of her sight.

At 2:15, an old pick-up truck pulled into the lot and Esty Willard got out. Amy waited until Esty was inside before approaching. To her disappointment, there wasn't anyone else in the truck. Now she had a dilemma. She could confront Esty about Skeeter or she could try to follow her to see if she led her to him. In all likelihood, she wouldn't be able to do both.

Finally, she decided that the risk of tailing her was too great. It was against the longest of odds that she'd located Esty this time. The likelihood of finding her again was not good. Greenville was not necessarily Esty's new domicile. She might have just stopped long enough to cash the check.

Amy waited outside the shop next door. She didn't want Esty to see her and look for a back door, and she wanted to be able to position herself between Esty and her truck. When the door opened, Amy walked toward it. "Mrs. Willard," she said. "I need to talk to you."

Esty stared at her in shock. "How the hell did you find me?"

"That's not important. I need to talk to Skeeter."

"You leave him alone. He's got nothing to say to you."

Amy usually had to work a little harder to get information out of someone. "So, he is alive?"

Esty shriveled as she realized how easily she'd given up such vital information. Her expression was soon replaced by one of fear. "He won't be if you don't leave him alone."

"What do you mean?" Amy asked.

Esty's eyes widened as her anxiety increased. "Look, he didn't want to have nothin' to do with any of that business in the first place. It was the other ones that did it. Just leave Skeeter be!" With that she pushed past Amy into the truck.

"Look." Amy said. "Maybe I can help. Who were the others and what did they do?"

Esty started the car. "I ain't gittin' in the middle of this. We finally got us somethin'. It won't do us no good if we're dead."

"Mrs. Willard," Amy implored. "If it's about the money, I might be able to find a way for you to keep it. There's much more at stake here. Who was Skeeter working with and what were they doing?"

Esty shifted the truck into reverse. She grabbed her purse from the passenger seat and opened it far enough to reveal a pistol. "Lady, I don't wanna hurt you, but if you try to follow me you better be prepared for the consequences." She stared down Amy and then backed out. Amy watched her go. She noted the license plate number, but that wouldn't likely be of much help. Still, she'd give it to Scouten on the off chance that it would help with something.

CHAPTER FORTY-ONE

MY HAD NOT HESITATED TO CALL Scouten and Schreiber to tell them about Skeeter. Schreiber was impressed, but pointed out that it wouldn't do much good unless the money could be recovered. For her part, Amy at least felt confident that the problems of Minnesota Marine were not just a series of unfortunate coincidences.

She returned to her office the next day ready to fight the next battle. Instead, she found an old battle had returned. Sitting on her desk were the documents from a foreclosure action brought by Amalgamated Grain. "What the hell is this?" she thought to herself.

Amalgamated had decided to take it to the next level. It had bought the loan from the bank. As a result, it obtained all of the rights that the bank had, but with the ability to move considerably quicker. The documents in the pile contained a declaration of default, a notice of foreclosure, and a motion for the appointment of a receiver to take over the operations of Minnesota Marine pending the foreclosure sale. The clock was again ticking.

Amy called Tony Drabeck. "Have you been served with the new action by Amalgamated?" she asked.

"Yeah. I sent copies to you. Can you tell me what it's about?"

"I can give you my best guess. Amalgamated hoped to use the Buy-Sell Agreement with Bogardus to get your shares cheap. That didn't work, so they took a bigger step. They've bought your loan from the bank. As a result, they step into the bank's shoes and have all of the bank's rights."

"That doesn't seem right. I've been with the Friendly Bank in Minneapolis for years. Why would they sell the loan out from under me?"

"Didn't Friendly Bank merge with some conglomerate from the West Coast? I think relationships go out the window when those things happen."

"I suppose you're right, but what's the incentive for them to sell the loan?"

"You're a risk. Right now, your loan creates a problem because there is no insurance. By selling the loan, the bank eliminates that problem."

"What do we do?" Drabeck asked.

"You still have rights under the loan. You just have to cure the default before the foreclosure sale. If you do that, Amalgamated will still own the loan, but they won't be able to do anything as long as you keep paying. It'll be a big investment by Amalgamated for a small payoff."

"What about the receiver? What's that all about?"

"A receiver is like a trustee. The idea is to put a third party in place in order to keep anyone from running off with the assets. The Court appoints a receiver to take control of the finances, but you can still get it back in the end."

"How much time do we have?"

"The motion to appoint a receiver is next week. The foreclosure on the real estate will take longer, but the foreclosure on the boats and the other assets can be done in a few weeks. Any luck finding insurance?"

"Not yet. Nobody wants to touch us unless we get things under control."

"I don't know if you heard yet, but I think Skeeter Willard is still alive."

"Where is he?"

"I think he's on the run. That's the problem. Even though the insurance company shouldn't have paid anything, it won't matter if we can't get it back."

"Do you think there's a chance?"

"Of course. There's always a chance."

"What if we don't find him? Do we have a chance in the foreclosure action?"

"Of course," she said with less confidence. Amy tried to give Drabeck comfort, but she wondered whether she was just deceiving him. There were very few defenses available under the loan agreement because banks live by the Golden Rule – the person with the gold makes the rules. The extraordinary losses the company was experiencing defied explanation. Yet, finding an explanation – and a remedy – would be necessary if the company was going to have any chance to survive.

Amy resigned herself to the fact that her weekends were going to be spent at the office. Amy's professional future might be hanging on Minnesota Marine, so her personal life would have to take a backseat.

CHAPTER FORTY-TWO

MY HAD MANAGED TO ASSEMBLE a mountain of documents relating to Minnesota Marine. She had insurance files, including additional documentation that had been retrieved from the archives. She had legal files from G. Garson Graves and a few other lawyers up and down the river. Finally, she had financial records that the company had been forced to produce in the Bogardus shareholder matter. All things considered, it promised to be one of the most boring endeavors imaginable.

She reviewed the financial statements until her eyes glazed over. The insurance documentation was, from her standpoint, mostly undecipherable industry jargon. The legal documents were the only things familiar to her, and they read like the morning paper. Nonlawyers have difficulty comprehending anything in legal documents, but Amy found the structure of such documents to be a welcome way to easily convey information to those with an understanding. Unfortunately, Graves' failure to produce documents that were allegedly confidential left a bit of a gap.

She trudged through several documents and then allowed herself some time to daydream. Her thoughts usually returned to the same thing – Tucker Sheridan.

She only allowed herself a few minutes of fantasy before resuming her review. As an incentive, she would reward herself with imagination time after completing the review of a predetermined number of documents. That seemed a little prepubescent to her, but it also seemed to help get the work done.

Amy found documents relating to the Hendrickson matter that had come up when she was in New Orleans. The records were minimal. The claim file indicated that it was a back injury and that it was the fault of a fellow crewman named Rick Banks. She pondered how she could get more information and managed to find a perfect solution. She'd call Tucker.

He answered after a couple rings. "Hello, Mr. Sheridan," she said in a flirtatious voice. "Amy Prescott calling."

"Hello yourself," he said. "To what do I owe this pleasure?"

"Just business, I'm afraid. I'm up to my eyes in files, and I'm hoping you can help me understand a few things."

"I'm at your service."

"What can you tell me about the Hendrickson loss?"

"What do you mean?"

"The lawyers in New Orleans all think they're going to get rich off the file, but I can't find much about it. What happened to him?"

"I think he fell and hurt his back."

"Well, that's part of what I'm trying to figure out. Why did he fall? We need to figure out if there's a problem with our safety procedures. The file says something about it being the fault of someone named Banks."

"I think the problem was just lack of experience. Banks had hardly any experience, but old man Drabeck hired him and made him a mate."

"Does Drabeck ordinarily handle the hiring? That doesn't seem like it would be his job."

"I don't really know the details," he said. "Maybe Banks was a friend of the family or something, but if you ask me Hendrickson got injured because Banks just didn't have enough experience."

"Do you think his injuries are real?"

"Yes. I visited him, and they're real."

"That was thoughtful of you," she said with enough sarcasm to suggest that his concern seemed out of character. "Do you do that with everyone?"

"Not usually. I was in the area so I stopped by. Drabeck likes to say that he puts the employees first, so it's something he wanted me to do."

"Do you think he puts the employees first?"

"I don't really know. The business has been struggling the last few years, and I was hired to try and get it on track."

"How's that working out?"

"How do you think?" he said. "The company can't get insurance and is being taken over by the bank. I'm just glad I'm paid in cash and not stock."

They were both quiet for a moment. Amy wanted to change topics, but waited to see if he had anything else to say on the business end. "So, how have you been otherwise?" she finally asked.

"Busy. Between trying to save the company and looking for a new job if that doesn't happen, I don't have much free time."

"Speaking of saving the company, did you hear that we busted Bogardus because of your tape of Mick Sterling singing 'Into the Mystic'?"

"I did hear something about that. Nice job, as usual."

"Well, it bought us some time."

The conversation was ebbing. "Do you think you'll be back in Minnesota in the near future?" he asked.

"Actually, we have a hearing next week."

"Well," he said, "maybe we can get together."

"Okay."

"Otherwise, call me if you have any other questions or anything else."

After she hung up, she wondered whether she should have told him that she'd been thinking about him. What she really wanted to know was whether he'd been thinking about her. The problem was that she had already declared a relationship off limits while she was representing Minnesota Marine.

CHAPTER FORTY-THREE

THE NEW LAWSUIT WAS FILED IN Minneapolis instead of St. Paul. That could have been driven by Amalgamated's desire to avoid Judge Pendens or the outcome from the first time around. Because Friendly Bank was headquartered in Minneapolis, the loan documents specifically said lawsuits could be venued there. There wasn't much Amy could do about the choice of location, but she would still try to make some mileage out of the previous victory. At least she could still use her same local counsel.

She had researched every part of the loan documents looking for a defense. In the long run, she didn't see a lot of hope. In the short run, however, she thought the reputation of Minnesota Marine should be enough to eliminate the need for a receiver. Its financial record was spotless, while the record of Amalgamated was less pristine. A reprieve of a couple weeks might be enough to solve the company's problems.

Downtown Minneapolis was considerably more developed than its counterpart in St. Paul. Skyscrapers had apparently been relatively late arrivers, however, as virtually all of them were of the glass tower variety that became popular in the seventies. Amy liked the fact that the city bustled, even though the core did not have the same genteel charm as St. Paul.

She met Drabeck in the lobby of her hotel. To her surprise, Tony brought Tucker Sheridan. She smiled as she shook his hand, but otherwise tried to keep it strictly business.

Tony tried to act upbeat. "Another do-or-die day," he said with a chuckle. "Is this wearing you out as much as it's wearing me out?"

"It's taking its toll," she said. "Just when we think we're in the clear, we start all over again."

"How do you feel about it?" Tony asked.

"To be honest, you should be looking for someone to pay off the loan. Is there another competitor out there that you like better than Amalgamated? Maybe you could make a deal with someone else where they pay off the loan but let you stay involved in the company."

"I think Amalgamated would let me stay involved with the company. They just won't let me run it the way I want to run it. That's the problem."

"Well, I can only tell you that something's got to happen, and I don't think it's within my power. If I can keep the judge from appointing a receiver, you'll have to move pretty fast."

Drabeck seemed to understand the situation, but it didn't appear he had any new ideas. Instead, he was apparently going to rely on Amy.

They met Tommy Steinman in the lobby of the courthouse and proceeded up to the courtroom of Judge Culhane X. Martinson. Mark Cavanaugh was already in the courtroom chatting with whomever would talk to him. He smiled and nodded toward Amy. She had beaten him once, so this was his chance for payback.

Judge Martinson had a reputation for being "by the book" and nononsense. He showed that by convening court promptly at the scheduled time. Some judges make lawyers wait, and appear to do it for no reason other than that they can. Martinson was apparently of a different mind.

The case was called and Cavanaugh was soon arguing his motion for the appointment of a receiver. The issue was simple, he said, as a default triggers the right of the creditor to appoint a receiver. Even though that was the only real point he made, he managed to take ten minutes to say it.

Amy came out swinging in every direction. She didn't have any really strong arguments, so she tried to aggregate all of the small ones. She started by pointing out that Amalgamated had tried to take over the company by virtue of the previous action in St. Paul, and she made it clear that Amalgamated had failed so that "now they're trying a *new* tactic in a *new* court."

Next, she argued that Minnesota Marine had not actually missed any loan payments, and that a technical default didn't justify the appointment of a receiver. Judge Martinson stopped her for a moment to reread the language from the loan documents. "I'm not sure the language of the contract supports you on that," he said. "I think it's an interesting argument, but I don't see a distinction between payment defaults and covenant defaults."

"We think it's a factor that needs to be considered," she pleaded. "Amalgamated has taken some aggressive and inappropriate actions, and we think the Court needs to look at the big picture and be cognizant of the fact that there has not been a payment default."

Martinson nodded to suggest that he would at least keep the distinction in mind.

Amy then addressed the losses. She did not accuse Amalgamated of having caused them, but she wanted it known that it was a possibility. "A court of equity should not aid a wrongdoer," she implored.

Again, Martinson stopped her. "At this point, you don't have any proof of the wrongdoing, do you?"

"Not yet, but we do have some highly questionable things going on."

"Like what, for example?"

"For starters, we lost our insurance coverage because of a crewman who fell overboard and apparently drowned. I believe the crewman is still alive and faked his death. We hope to have more evidence of that soon, and that could change everything."

"Is it your position that the loan documents allow you to cure a default and put the loan agreement back in place?"

"Absolutely," she said. "And given a little more time, we think we will be able to do so."

She waited to see if he had another question and then continued. "Most importantly, your Honor, Minnesota Marine has a long and exemplary record. There is no reason to appoint a receiver because the company has not defaulted on the payments and will continue to make the payments." Amy then proceeded to detail the company history. Hard work and a commitment to excellence and to employees had driven the company to the top, and the recent wave of misfortune should not be allowed to undo that. She was passionate and any listener would have developed an admiration for the company. Unfortunately, that wasn't enough.

"I appreciate your arguments," Judge Martinson finally said, "but the loan documents are pretty clear. Furthermore, if I order the appointment of a receiver, I haven't necessarily ruled against your client. We'd just have a neutral party preserving the assets pending the rest of the proceedings."

Amy's heart sank as she realized the direction things were heading. "I know a receiver is theoretically neutral," she said, "but it's a turning point in the life of a company when control is taken away from the person who built it. Once you take control away from Tony Drabeck, you'll forever change him and everyone's perception of the company. Your Honor, it just isn't fair. He did nothing wrong. Punishing such a good corporate citizen would send the worst possible message."

Martinson was not callous, but he was pragmatic. "You make a good case, but it doesn't really matter. I have to enforce the agreement, and the outcome is not subject to any real dispute. While Amalgamated is not yet entitled to take control, it is entitled to have the finances put under the control of a receiver. From this point on, the collection of receivables and the spending will be handled by a receiver."

Amy felt a tremble in her legs and thought for a minute that she might pass out. Losing was not part of her normal repertoire. She had hoped that Martinson would have at least waited and sent the ruling after a couple days. Instead, she had to lose on the spot.

She heard a chair being pushed back, and noticed Drabeck rising. "Your Honor," he said, "How does that affect the payment of legal fees? Can the company continue to pay Ms. Prescott to represent it?"

Martinson stroked his chin as he pondered the question. "The company and the receiver are authorized and directed to pay the legal fees through today. Going forward, however, the company is being operated for the benefit of whomever becomes the owner. You can continue to handle operations, but the receiver will do whatever it feels is appropriate to protect the assets. As a result, only the receiver can authorize the company to make payments for future legal services."

Drabeck plopped down back into his seat. His look was not one of anger, but of humbled defeat. Amy looked at him and felt like she was going to cry, so she quickly looked away. She couldn't honestly fault the judge for his ruling, but she had somehow expected to prevail despite the overwhelming odds against her. Winning streaks sometimes do that to lawyers.

Amy stood motionless. Judge Martinson asked if anyone had anything else. When there was no response, he adjourned. As soon as he had left, Cavanaugh rushed to the gallery where Amalgamated's people were located. A receiver may have been theoretically neutral, but Cavanaugh was clearly treating this as a victory. That was probably fair, as Amy was treating it as a defeat.

Amy put a hand on Drabeck's shoulder. "I'm sorry, sir. I thought we could hold them off for a while longer, but I guess I was wrong."

"You did your best," he said. "You couldn't help the fact that we're in such desperate shape."

Tucker supplied some support as well. "I thought you were really great. Unfortunately, it isn't always the best lawyer who wins."

Amy knew that was true, but it didn't give her much comfort. "Well, we still have some time before the foreclosure sale. Let's not give up."

Drabeck smiled at her enthusiasm. "I guess you didn't hear. We aren't allowed to pay you any more. It's too bad, because you would have made a great lawyer for the company. Unfortunately, the receiver controls that now. You can go back to doing whatever it was you were doing before we commandeered all of your time."

She thought about her previous caseload and how trivial it seemed compared to the battle she had been waging on behalf of Minnesota Marine. On the other hand, the stress level was certainly lower when the outcome was less significant.

Drabeck lifted his elbows to the table and put his head in his hands. He wasn't crying. It was more like he was trying to squeeze the tension out of his forehead. "Well, perhaps we should go drink a toast to the end of something really great."

With that, they left the courtroom. They descended down the elevator and soon found themselves on Sixth Street, which actually ran under the courthouse. "This way," Drabeck said, as he led them west.

After a couple blocks they were in the midst of some recent additions to the Minneapolis skyline. In the middle of it was a place that looked like it had been there since Vaudeville. An art deco exterior with a neon sign that said, "Minne's, Home of the Silver Butterknife Steak."

Drabeck led them inside. "We used to come here to celebrate the big events at the company. There's not much to celebrate today, but it's fitting that we come here."

The interior was clean and well maintained, but the décor was as outdated as the exterior. To add to the ambiance, most of the waitresses looked like they had started working at the restaurant during the Eisenhower administration. Yet, the restaurant was packed.

Drabeck led them into a small cocktail lounge. The bartender had a broad grin as they took their seats. "Senator. We haven't seen you in years."

"Age will do that," he said. "As much as I enjoyed coming here to celebrate events, the morning after kept getting more and more difficult."

"Please don't tell me you're on the wagon," the bartender said.

"Certainly not tonight," he said. "Beefeater Martini, please."

Tucker and Amy followed suit. After the bartender walked away, Amy said, "Did you use to be a senator?"

Drabeck smiled. "No. That was just a little joke we had. This was once the place where all the movers and shakers came when they were in town. I got a couple of the bartenders to call me that because I figured most people would be too embarrassed to ask if they thought I was a senator and didn't know who I was."

"Were you trying to impress the ladies?" Amy asked.

"No," he assured her. "I just liked fooling people."

Amy had tried to lighten the mood, but it wasn't working. When the drinks came, Drabeck held his up. "I'm proud of everything Minnesota Marine ever accomplished. I never thought the company would end up this way, but I don't really know how else it could have ended. I guess I should have sold when I was in a stronger position."

Amy was choking back her emotions. She didn't feel at fault, but it was tearing her apart to have witnessed the downfall of the company. "I know it's no consolation," she said, "but you must have built something special to cause Amalgamated to go to such lengths to get it. They're not entitled to it, but it reflects well on you."

"Thank you," he said.

Everyone was quiet while Tony endured the moment. Finally, Amy spoke up. "Mr. Drabeck, I think I should go back onto one of the tows. I don't know what's going on, but my meeting with Skeeter's wife pretty much confirmed that there is something."

"That's not a good idea," Drabeck said. "I heard you almost got killed the last time. You were supposed to stay on the towboat, and instead you put yourself in harm's way."

"It was a rookie mistake," she said. "I was just getting comfortable with the operations when Skeeter disappeared. This time I'll go down to Louisiana, where most of the losses have occurred. You don't have to worry about paying me. I'm sure our firm will agree not to charge you unless we get the company back for you."

"No, you'd still be a rookie, just in a new environment. Amy, I really appreciate what you did for the company, but your place is in the court-room."

"I think you're being overprotective. I'm a big girl."

"Really, Amy, if this company had survived, we would have needed someone like you to handle our legal issues. There isn't anything that you can do onboard. We only sent you before because we thought it would appease the insurance markets."

Amy exhaled her exasperation. "Mr. Drabeck, I assure you that I will stay out of danger. You don't really have any defenses to the bank foreclo-sure, so there isn't anything for me to do in that regard. Please. Just let me go back and observe some more."

Drabeck was not budging. "Ms. Prescott," he said with newfound for-mality, "I still control the operations of this company, and as long as I do you are forbidden from getting back on a towboat. Do I make myself clear?"

"Yes, sir," she said.

Everyone was quiet for a long moment. Finally, a somber Tony Drabeck announced he was going home. Given the amount he intended to drink, he said he'd rather be somewhere that didn't require him to drive. He was adamant, however, that Tucker and Amy should have dinner to-gether and charge it to the company. "The judge said 'after today the receiver makes the decisions on spending,' and I interpret that to mean I still make the decisions today." He stood up and patted Tucker on the shoulder. "Amy," he said, "thanks for all of your help. You really were amazing. In the end, we just didn't have a chance. Perhaps if we'd met earlier, we would have never ended up in this mess." He smiled and ambled out the door.

Amy watched him and felt like her heart was being torn out. "That's a tough way to end a career," she said.

After a few moments of silence, Tucker said, "Poor Tony. I think his problem was that he waited too long. The world is changing, and he wanted it to stay the same."

Amy wondered whether that was a bad thing. "Well, at least he reached a point in life where everything was just the way he liked it, and he didn't want things to change."

Tucker blinked in surprise. "Are you saying you're not happy with your life?"

"I'm not saying that I'm not happy, but I certainly haven't reached the point in my life where I feel like I've realized my destiny or purpose. Sometimes I feel like Frodo in 'The Lord of the Rings.' I'm on one long journey and, just when it looks like it might end, there's a whole new sequel."

Tucker studied her for a long moment. "That sounds like someone whose love life is not fulfilling."

She glared at him. "What makes you say that?"

"It stands to reason that a person in a fulfilling relationship would feel like they've found what they're looking for, so at least part of the quest would be over."

"So, now you're a psychotherapist too?"

He laughed. "Let's get a table in the restaurant and have dinner."

She agreed.

The proceedings of the day had weighed heavily on her, but the gin and the company were changing her mood. Tucker's charm was helping as well. He did not have nearly her education, but he could hold his own in virtually any discussion.

As they lingered over dessert, he said, "You know, I was pretty disappointed the way our last date ended."

She smiled and looked down at the table. "It wasn't what I had in mind either, but I felt a professional obligation not to get involved with someone who was part of a case on which I was working."

"Thank God for Judge Martinson," he said.

She stopped to try and figure out his comment. "What do you mean?"

"You're no longer working for the company," he said. "From your standpoint, this case is over, so you have no reason not to get involved with someone from the company."

The same light bulb then went off in Amy's head. "I guess that's right," she said. "Now, if only I found you attractive." The words had barely left her lips when she started to giggle.

The check came, and Tucker put it on his company card. They stepped out into the night and headed for her hotel. After a half block, he reached over and took her hand. They walked the next three blocks in silence. When they got to the hotel, he walked in with her and got in the elevator. After the last dinner date, it didn't appear he was going to ask for permission. He wouldn't need to.

Amy inserted her key card, and Tucker opened the room door and guided her through. His hand on her shoulder gave her a gentle tingle. Amy thought back to their first encounter and her feelings about his behavior. Friction frequently leads to sparks, and this one seemed to have set off a flame. As angry as she'd felt the first time they met, she now felt desire with the same intensity. Tucker seemed to be even more consumed than her.

He gave her a look that made his intentions obvious, and she didn't back away. He reached his hand behind her head and held it as he leaned forward to kiss her. It was long and it was passionate. He did not flail away like a schoolboy. He tasted her like she was a fine cabernet – slow and methodical -- in an attempt to extract every sensory perception the kiss had to offer.

His hands moved to her shoulders and his lips moved to her cheek and then her hair as he continued to absorb her. Amy closed her eyes and let him explore. He had a day's worth of beard, but his delicate touch caused it to merely be a reminder of his masculinity and not a source of irritation.

He began running his fingers through her hair, while unbuttoning her blouse with his other hand. She reached for his shirt, but his arms kept her from being able to reach his buttons. When he had undone her last button, he pushed back her blouse until it hung from her wrists behind her. He unhooked her bra in the front and then pushed the straps over her arms until the bra and blouse fell on the floor.

She reached again for his shirt buttons, but he wrapped his hands around her shoulder blades and pulled her close. He kissed her. Her hands went to his shoulders and then to the back of his neck. She felt his tongue engaging hers in a slow, deliberate waltz. He stayed close to her, but slid his hands to the front of her skirt and unbuttoned it. He put his hands on her hips and hooked his thumbs inside her pantyhose. He pushed skirt and pantyhose past the curve of her behind and let them drop to the floor. She stepped out of her shoes, and he pulled her clothes the rest of the way off. He was still fully dressed, but she stood in front of him wearing nothing but a smile.

He kissed her again, and then took two steps back to look at her. Either the cold or the anticipation was causing goose bumps to rise on her legs. She thought that she would feel embarrassed to be standing naked in front of him, but she didn't. Seeing the effect she was having on him actually felt empowering.

As he eyed her he began removing his own clothes. It was not a strip tease. Instead, it reminded her of the deliberate way he undressed in order to put on the asbestos suit at the fire. His mind was on the purpose ahead – not the act of undressing.

When he was done, he extended a hand. She took it, and he pulled her toward him. He twirled her like a dancer until her back was against him. From the back, he kissed her neck, while his hands caressed her arms and hips. He traced circles around her breasts, and she pushed them out in the hope that his hand or arm would brush against them.

Tucker turned her back to face him. In a soft voice he murmured a question: "Birth control?" It sounded as natural as a Frenchman saying, "Would you like to make love?"

Amy smiled. "That's covered," she whispered. "And I'm assuming neither of us has anything else to discuss."

Tucker gave her a look and shook his head as reassurance. He then backed to the bed and pulled her down beside him. Again, he was methodical. Amy arched her back every time his hand or arm passed over her chest, but he seemed to be deliberately avoiding erogenous contact. She was ready to move to the next level, but Tucker continued to kiss her and stroke her face and hair.

After what seemed like an eternity to Amy, Tucker rolled on top of her and positioned himself with his knees between hers. He kissed her stomach and then kissed a trail to her mouth. Even now, as he approached the threshold, he was not in a hurry. As their mouths connected, he finally entered her. He stopped barely inside and then slowly inserted his length until their hips were touching.

He rotated his hips in a way that caused him to touch as much of her as possible. He was leaning on his elbows and then released his weight on top of her. Slowly he started to rock up and down, in and out. Amy felt a slight numbness in her lip. She had never figured out the explanation for the sensation, but it was a symptom of her arousal. The strokes became longer, but they were no faster or harder.

Tucker propped himself back up on his elbows. He was watching her. All the while, his hips continued at the same rhythm. It was constant and deliberate. Most of Amy's previous lovers had apparently learned pace and technique from farm animals or the Spice Channel. Tucker was not in a hurry.

Amy felt perspiration forming between their bodies and didn't know or care who was the source. As she held him, she noticed a soft fragrance in his hair. Her breath quickened, as he was finding all of the right spots.

She closed her eyes. Several minutes went by and Tucker continued his mission. Amy grabbed his back and squeezed his shoulder blades as the sensation built. She felt herself nearing the moment and started thrusting violently. Tucker released his weight back on top of her and reached down and took a hold of her hips. He held them in place and kept her from flailing while he continued his task.

Amy's breathing slowed for a moment and then became heavier as she again sensed what was coming. She tried to increase the pace, but Tucker again physically restrained her hips and stopped her from seizing the moment. Each time he stopped her, the intensity built. Amy was in a near frenzy, as the blood was building in her head. She was trying for the last bit of friction necessary for nirvana and Tucker kept holding it at bay. Her head felt light as she struggled to complete her journey.

Finally, she lay still and surrendered to it. Tucker continued the same deliberate motion. All of a sudden, she heard a woman screaming, and then realized it was her own voice. She convulsed and gyrated without any sense of control, and felt as if she had left her own body. The sensation was starting to ebb when Tucker completed another stroke and she returned to euphoria.

Panting, she realized that she had either never had an orgasm before or Tucker Sheridan had just invented something new. That surprised her, because she had always thought she had a healthy and complete sex life. Apparently she'd been wrong.

"Holy shit," she said with a heavy sigh.

Tucker smiled at her. "Good things are worth waiting for," he said.

"I never knew there was something like that waiting for me."

"Maybe there's more to come."

She looked up at him and realized he was still going. "Why don't you let me do some of the work," she said. She pushed him onto his back and got on top. She doubted that she'd be able to show him anything new. Just the same, it wouldn't be for a lack of trying.

CHAPTER FORTY-FOUR

TUCKER WOKE HER EARLY IN THE morning to tell her he was leaving. "What's your hurry?" she said. "I would have thought a guy like you would stick around for a quick eye-opener."

"I suppose if 'quick' was part of my technique, that might be the case."

"Listen to you," she said. "Give a woman the greatest orgasm of her life and all of a sudden you think you wrote the Kama Sutra."

He grinned as he absorbed her praise. "We still have important shipments to handle at the company. You may not have anything else to do on this matter, but my work isn't done."

His words struck a nerve. She kissed him and said goodbye, but she lay back down with decidedly mixed emotions. Her love life had taken a big step forward, but her professional life had gone in the opposite direction. The idea of a relationship with Tucker Sheridan appealed to her, but the idea of being a Harbor Captain's wife left her a little short. There was a certain romance in the words of "Into the Mystic," about "When that foghorn blows I will be coming home," but she couldn't see that keeping her candle lit for more than a time or two.

After he left, she got up and showered. She was halfway through scrubbing when she stopped and just let the water run over her. She imagined his hands on her shoulders. She imagined him behind her, running his fingers through her hair. She imagined him touching her everywhere except the last place he touched her when they were together. That would have to wait until they were together again.

As she dressed, the fantasy was replaced by the reality of her professional situation. Minnesota Marine had represented more than just a challenge. Controlling a relationship like that was currency in the quest for partnership. She had other clients, but nothing of that magnitude. Now it was gone. The firm might give her more time to develop new relationships, but the simple fact was that the Tom-Tom Twins would make partner before her. That would be reason enough for her to leave of her own volition.

The trip back to Chicago was soured by her circumstances. She should have been basking in the afterglow of her first night with Tucker, but the loss of the client was dousing that. It seemed her personal and professional life could not reach their zenith at the same time, but her situation was better than when they had concurrently hit the nadir a few weeks earlier.

She took the train in from O'Hare. She decided to go to the office for a couple hours before going home to ponder her future. Valiant was at the reception desk talking to a caller. He held up a hand to stop her. After a moment, he finished his call. "Miss Amy, I was supposed to tell you that Mr. Schreiber wanted to see you as soon as you got in."

"I thought I told you to just call me 'Amy.'"

He leaned forward and lowered his voice. "That's fine when I see you in the hall, but we need a little more professionalism in the reception area. I'm in charge of first impressions at Schreiber, Marko & Meath, and I want our guests to know that we are a first class organization."

Amy accepted that. She walked to her office to deposit her briefcase, and then went to see Mr. Schreiber. "You wanted to see me?" she said as she entered.

"Yes. I take it things didn't go well yesterday."

"I'm afraid not. If I look at it objectively, I guess we didn't have much of a chance. But when I'm representing the good guys, I always believe that I can win."

"It's too bad," he said. "Minnesota Marine would have been a nice client for the firm to have."

It meant even more to Amy. "I know," she said softly.

"Are we all done, or is there something we can appeal?"

"I don't think our chances on appeal are very good. More importantly, the Court has ordered that the company can't continue to pay our bills. So, unless Tony wants to pay us personally, I don't know what we can do."

"Well, why don't you take a break. Go home and come back fresh tomorrow."

CHAPTER FORTY-FIVE

A MY ARRIVED AT THE OFFICE earlier than normal. She decided she needed to spend some more time to see if she could make sense out of what had been happening. She was no longer getting paid for her services, but something inside her was still driving her to find the answers.

She analyzed who could potentially benefit from each loss and whether they could have caused it. Amalgamated benefited from losses in general, but too many losses might damage Minnesota Marine's reputation and its long-term prospects. The union's cause was helped by worker injuries, and general mischief making was not an uncommon practice for some unions. The lawyers, and in particular Graves, benefited from the losses, but their likely sin was the unholy matrimony that apparently had developed with the plaintiffs' attorneys. The insurance broker made a big commission as losses increased, but now stood to lose everything.

Then she laid the files out in an effort to find commonality. She put the cargo losses together, the injured worker claims together, and the property damages together. That didn't suggest an answer, so she organized them by location of the loss. That didn't help either. She added a couple more variables and thought a pattern might be emerging.

She was trying to confirm her hypothesis when she found something peculiar in the insurance files. She found a file where events seemed out of sequence. She decided to again call Ted Hollerback, the broker in St. Louis. After he answered, she said, "Professional courtesy."

"Excuse me?" he said.

"This is Amy Prescott calling," she said. "I was expecting you to ask me why sharks never attack lawyers, and I was just trying to beat you to the punch."

Hollerback had to take a minute to process it, but then started laughing. "I like that. I'll add it to my repertoire."

Amy was pleased she could contribute. "Of course, I didn't call just to help you with your material. Minnesota Marine had a big pollution loss three years ago in Kentucky. In the file, there's correspondence denying the claim because the company hadn't bought the right policy endorsement. But then the file indicates that they did buy the endorsement later, and the insurance company paid the claim. I don't understand that. You can't buy insurance after an accident and then collect for the same accident. How did that happen?"

"If I could explain that, I'd be a rich man." He waited for her to respond. When she didn't, he continued. "I told you that I inherited this account from a broker in Minneapolis. I don't know how he did it, but he could get the insurance companies to pay just about anything. I asked about this one when I first took over the account. Pollution coverage is provided by a separate company that covers only pollution claims. Apparently, the guy told the pollution insurance company that Minnesota Marine meant to buy the coverage and would in the future. The insurance company agreed to let Tony pay the insurance premium after the fact and treated Minnesota Marine as if it had been covered the whole time."

"Why would the insurance company do that?" she asked.

"Like I said, if I could figure that out I'd be a rich man."

Amy was quiet for a moment while she pondered that. "Are there other situations where the company is making money through insurance claims?"

"I wouldn't say 'making money,'" he said, "but there are other times when they benefit from losses. I mean, they have replacement cost coverage, so the fire to the Kay Drabeck meant they got a completely rebuilt and refurbished boat. If the Harbor Captain hadn't gone onboard and turned off the fuel, they might have gotten a brand new boat."

"That's interesting," she said, "but the company doesn't benefit when a worker gets injured, does it?"

"Actually, it does. Minnesota Marine has a death and disability policy on its employees that pays benefits to the company if there's a loss."

"How could that be?"

"Well, the company is harmed because it has to find a new employee."

"That doesn't seem right."

"Well, I don't know what they do with it. I suppose they could use it to defend the lawsuit or something else."

"What about a cargo loss? Can the company make money on that too?"

"Not legitimately."

"What do you mean by that?"

Hollerback was silent for a moment. It's like this: Did you hear the one about the two guys sitting in the hot tub at Vail?"

"Was one of them a lawyer?"

Hollerback paused. "I guess he could be. Let's say it this way. Two guys were sitting in a hot tub at a ritzy hotel in Vail. The first one asks what the second one does. The second one says, 'I was a lawyer for twenty years and then I bought a manufacturing company from one of my clients. We had a fire and I decided to take the insurance money and retire.'"

"Okay," Amy said.

"So then the lawyer says: 'How about you, what do you do?' The first guy says, 'I owned a manufacturing company too. We had a big flood that wiped everything out. I decided to take the insurance money and retire.'

"The lawyer gives the second guy a puzzled look. 'Really,' he finally said. 'How do you start a flood?'"

Amy did manage to laugh, and it wasn't just to be nice. "So, are you saying it could make money by committing insurance fraud?"

"Well, a company could make money if it claimed it was carrying cargo and lost it, but had already sold the cargo somewhere else."

"I'm not following," she said.

"Simple," he said. "The company claims to pick up a load of grain from a customer, but actually sells the grain to someone else. Then it sinks the barge and claims losses for the barge and the cargo. If the insurance is in place, Minnesota Marine gets made whole and it's actually ahead because it already sold the cargo."

"Have they ever done that?"

"Not to my knowledge, but you asked if it was possible to make money on a cargo loss."

Once again, Amy's conversation with the insurance broker yielded a lot more information than she expected. She pondered what he said and couldn't believe that she could have overlooked the obvious. She had been so focused on the union, Amalgamated, and others that she had not even considered the possibility of a fox in the henhouse.

CHAPTER FORTY-SIX

AMY PULLED OUT THE FINANCIAL records that the company had been forced to turn over to Bogardus. She hadn't really studied them before, as the business valuation was the responsibility of an expert appraiser. Her telephone call to Hollerback changed that.

Her financial background was limited, but one thing was apparent. The company had not been particularly profitable during the last few years. In fact, without the money from the insurance claims, it was not clear if it would have been profitable at all.

She spent several hours pondering her next move. She had known what it should be, but she resisted the urge. The time for reflection didn't change her mind, but it may have changed her approach. The fact remained that she needed to get back into the thick of it.

She called Tony Drabeck. "I know we already talked about this, but I need to go back onto a tow," she said. "But I want to go to New Orleans and ride upriver. That's where the most losses seem to take place, so I need to see it firsthand."

"Amy, I told you before. It's too dangerous. I won't allow it."

She had expected that response, and decided it might be time to scrutinize Drabeck. "Why is it that Minnesota Marine collects insurance when its workers get injured or killed?"

"What?" he snapped.

"I'm just trying to put the pieces together, and I don't understand how the company can collect for injuries to its workers."

"Ms. Prescott, I'm not in any mood to talk about the operations of the company. I thank you for your concern, but, according to the court, it is no longer your concern."

She tried to interject another question, but he fended her off and ended the call.

After he hung up, Amy closed her eyes and rested her head in her hands. She had been so charmed by Tony Drabeck's rhetoric about being part of the greatest generation that she never suspected he might be part of the problem.

Amy wasn't giving up, so she went to see Mr. Schreiber. "I need to talk to you about Minnesota Marine."

"Have a seat," he said. "What's on your mind?"

"I want to go back onto a tow. There's something suspicious going on, and we're running out of time."

"Okay," he said. "So, why are you talking to me?"

"Drabeck says he won't allow it. He thinks it's too dangerous."

Schreiber's expression changed upon hearing Drabeck's directive. "Well, that's the end of the argument then. If he doesn't want it, he's still in charge of operations."

"But, we don't have any other options."

Schreiber then became Drabeck's advocate. "We sent you onboard before. Look what that got us."

"Sir," she said, "I think that whole thing was a set-up. I don't know what purpose it served to send me on a wild goose chase, but it's becoming clear to me that nobody wanted or expected me to find anything. Since you insisted that I go, I can only assume that you're in on it."

The blood drained from Schreiber's face as he jumped up and closed his office door. He walked back to his desk and stared at her. "Just what do you think I'm in on?"

"Look," she said as her voice began to rise. "You insisted that I go on-board even though you could have sent Jackson or Bethany or any other man in this office. You had to have thought that a woman would be afraid to leave her cabin, so I wouldn't see anything. I don't understand what the motive could be, but nothing else makes any sense. Now that nobody will let me go back onboard, it just confirms it. I was chosen because you thought a woman would be too timid or inept to find out what was going on."

Schreiber pulled off his glasses and rubbed his palm over his eye. He sat quiet for a long moment, but then began to chuckle. "Amy, I had you handle this case because I thought it needed a real lawyer. I couldn't send those other dipshits. What do you call them, the Tom-Tom Twins? I couldn't send them because they would have either cowered in their cabins or tried to negotiate a piece of whatever illegal activity was going on. This wasn't a job that called for bozos or ass kissers."

Amy was suddenly forced to reconsider her strategy. "I'm not sure I understand. You must have had a reason for insisting that I go and then trying to convince me to stay on the towboat where I wouldn't likely see anything."

"Isn't the fact that you're the best lawyer we've hired in years enough of a reason?"

Now she was really on her heels. "I don't recall you ever telling me that."

He shrugged his shoulders. "Can you blame me for wanting to keep you hungry? People who think they have something to prove are usually a more valuable asset."

"So you assumed I would disregard your directive to stay in my cabin?"

He shook his head and smiled. "Amy, I'm not clever enough to use psychology on you, much less reverse psychology. I told you to stay out of harm's way because I was concerned that something could happen to you. Somehow, I knew you'd manage to handle things."

"Well, I appreciate your confidence, but I'm not sure it paid off. I didn't see what happened to Skeeter, so I'm not really able to help."

Schreiber leaned back in his chair and looked at her through the bottom of his glasses. "Do you really think there's anything to be gained from going back onto one of the tows? What would you be looking for?"

"To be honest, I don't know. But I do know something's not right. As far as I can tell, business has actually been bad, and the insurance claims might be the main thing keeping the company going. There are a lot of pieces to this puzzle, and I can't put them together from an office in Chicago."

"I won't stop you," he finally said. "But I don't see how that matters. I can't order anyone to let you onboard."

"Who can?"

Schreiber picked his teeth while he considered the question. "I can only think of one person. Do you have the name of the receiver?"

Amy's face lit up at his suggestion. She rushed to her office to grab her file and returned with the information. Jim Schreiber telephoned the company that had been appointed to oversee the financial affairs of the company. He explained the situation for a long time. He also reminded the receiver that the receiver's job was to preserve the assets and that they seemed to be at risk. Finally, he clinched it with his favorite sales pitch. "Have you ever heard the saying that nobody ever got fired for buying IBM? This is the same deal. If you don't hire us and something goes wrong, everyone will be pointing the finger at you. If you hire us and something goes wrong, you can point the finger at us. And if you hire us and nothing goes wrong, who's going to blame you for being conservative?"

That was all it took. The receiver was now the client, and the receiver gave authorization for Amy to go back onboard.

CHAPTER FORTY-SEVEN

AMY HAD NOT RECOGNIZED A PATTERN to the losses until she saw a master schedule for the fleet. She then realized that she had made a mistake in trying to find a common cause to all of Minnesota Marine's losses. The fact of the matter was that barge companies always have some level of claims. The issue was not, therefore, what was causing all of the losses. It was what was causing the additional losses.

The majority of the Company's operations were on the Mississippi, but losses occurred regularly on the Ohio and Tennessee Rivers as well. The losses were distributed according to a recurring pattern for many years, but in recent years the losses on the Mississippi had spiked. More specifically, there had been an increase in upstream losses on the lower Mississippi. That was the place to look.

Because the upper Mississippi was closing for the season, a larger percentage of the boats were now working on the Ohio or the Tennessee. She was grateful for that because it narrowed her search.

Of the boats that were working the Mississippi, only a couple would soon be heading northbound from New Orleans. That was the part of the river with which she was unfamiliar, and that was the part she wanted to see. More importantly, she decided she might be able to observe more if the rest of the crew didn't know she was there for that purpose. As a result, she decided to review the crew rosters to make sure none of her previous river acquaintances would be on board. As she scanned the second list, the names were, "Cadle, Beckley, Landgraf, Ramstad, Maahs, and *Banks*." She looked closer to check the last name. It appeared to be the same person involved in the notorious "Hendrickson claim" that she learned about from the meeting between G Garson Graves and Marcel. That clinched it. That would be the tow she would join.

She still needed a reason to be onboard, so she arranged for the receiver to reassign the cook and send Amy in her place. She had to dig deep into her wardrobe to find suitable attire for a towboat cook. The only things that fit the bill were left over from her days on the farm. She found a few pair of bellbottom jeans, and she packed whatever tee shirts she could find that had beer logos or rock and roll groups on them. In addition, she started experimenting to determine how she could make her hair look bigger.

Amy reported to the Minnesota Marine facility in New Orleans. This wasn't like going for a boat ride the way it was in Minnesota. It wasn't just a matter of walking out on the dock and onto the towboat. Some barges were being loaded at terminals and then moved into the tow. Others were being loaded directly from ocean vessels that had brought their cargo to the United States. Somehow, several different towing companies managed to navigate the confusion at the same time.

She met the captain, a somewhat portly man in his fifties. She explained that she'd only worked for the company briefly, having cooked on a boat on the upper river. He welcomed her aboard, but suggested that she wear looser fitting clothes. Unfortunately, most of her high school wardrobe had little choice but to fit tightly.

Once onboard, she surveyed her cabin and the kitchen. The boat was somewhat larger than the one she'd been on while on the upper river, but the layout was similar. The menu plan and the provisions had all been taken care of, so she only had to cook and observe. She consciously decided that she would do everything she could not to look like she was trying to get information, and that meant that she'd leave it to others to initiate conversations.

The dining schedule was a little less haphazard than the first time. Crew shifts changed every six hours starting at midnight. Thus, breakfast was served from 5:30 to 6:30 to accommodate the crew that was about to start its shift and then the crew that ended its shift at 6:00. The same thing happened at lunch and dinner.

The tow departed in the afternoon, so Amy's first chore was dinner. As the men trickled in, she greeted them and explained that she was the new cook. "I hope y'all are hungry," she said in a southern accent that she had subconsciously decided to adopt.

These men were a little more rugged, to put it nicely. She had quickly felt comfortable with Sean and Peanut, but this was like being on a whole boat full of Skeeters. She spoke briefly while she was serving, but otherwise remained quiet as she tried to listen to the men. Occasionally, she'd hear them lower their voices and then let out a big laugh. She could only assume they were making sexual jokes, and perhaps they were about her. She started to reconsider whether the future of Minnesota Marine mattered enough to her to justify what she was doing.

After dinner, she went on deck to read. She had brought romance novels and some gossip magazines, so as not to arouse suspicion. She didn't really plan to read them, but they allowed her to observe without being noticed. Unfortunately, she wasn't sure what she was looking for. The most important thing, therefore, seemed to be eavesdropping.

Amy got up early the next day to start her routine. She checked the crew roster to see Bank's assignment. He started at 6 a.m., which meant he'd come in for breakfast about 5:30. At the appointed time, a handful of men appeared in the galley.

"Well, I s'pose I should learn y'all's names so that I know what ta call ya," Amy said.

The responses weren't enthusiastic, but each man gave his name. Amy was listening so hard for Banks that the other names all but deflected off of her. Finally, the last man identified himself as Rick Banks. He was average height and rather pudgy. He did not look like a man who labored for a living. It wasn't that he looked like a white-collar worker either. Instead, he looked more like someone who lived off of an insurance settlement or his girlfriend's social security benefits.

"Pleased ta make yer acquaintances," Amy said as she continued her faux accent. "Y'all don't be shy if ya got anything ta say about the food. I do my best, but I ain't really use ta tryin' ta satisfy so many different tastes."

"I dunno about these other guys," one of the men said, "but I'd rather eat your meals if I could look at you then have to eat one of my wife's meals while lookin' at her."

That brought a big laugh from the peanut gallery. Amy showed little reaction. "I'm sure it's easy to talk smart now, but I'll bet you feel a little different after you've been away from home for three or four weeks," she said.

The same man responded. "That may be, but it's only because I start to forget what she looks like."

Again, the crowd went wild.

Another man joined in. "I don't know what yer talkin' 'bout, Rufus. Zeke here takes breakfast at yer house most times when you're gone and he ain't never complained about the way yer wife looks in the morning." And so it went. Banks laughed along with the crew, but he didn't participate. Amy assumed that his relationship with the others probably did not go back far enough to allow him to join the insult parade.

Amy walked back to the stove to start preparing for the crew whose shift would soon be ending. She could hear the conversation, but wasn't learning anything worth remembering. As the other shift arrived, she repeated the introduction process. Again, she tried to remember the names, but it wasn't like she was anticipating a long-term relationship with any of them.

Later in the morning, she took a break to admire the scenery. She noticed Banks and another deckhand walking on the tow. She counted thirty-five barges in all, and the distance from back to front was more than double the distance of the tow she'd previously ridden. The front barge always seemed to extend to the next bend in the river. She was glad that she had already satisfied her curiosity about walking out on the tow.

In the afternoon, some of the crew were in the dining area playing cards. Amy didn't recognize the game, but it seemed to be some sort of poker. There did not appear to be much strategy, and the winner seemed to be determined merely by the flip of a card. The players would start to cheer and encourage the card as if inanimate objects could respond. "Come on, baby," one of the players kept saying.

Banks was a little more animated than he had been in the morning. "It's my turn!" he said. After saying it several times, he yelled, "Donde esta dinero!" One of the other crewmen cracked up when he heard that.

Then they both started chanting "Donde esta dinero" as they waited for the cards to be flipped.

Amy had learned a little Spanish from the Latin Americans who had worked on the farm when she was young. Whenever they wanted to know where something was, they would say, "Donde esta," followed by a word or a pantomime. Amy understood "Donde esta" to mean something like "where is," or "show me." Thus, she recognized the crew's chant as a Spanish version of the Jerry Maguire catch phrase, "Show me the money."

The game meant that there wasn't much to hear that might interest her. She only hoped that there wouldn't be any more Spanish, as her vocabulary had already been almost exhausted. Considering that neither Banks nor the other man looked Hispanic, she assumed they had nearly reached the end of their bilingualism as well. Given the nature of the rest of the discussions, it really didn't matter what language they were speaking.

CHAPTER FORTY-EIGHT

THAT NIGHT, THE RAIN STARTED. The lightning and thunder always seemed to be in the distance, but the rain was relentless. From Amy's perspective, it meant a pleasant night's sleep. The crewmembers that worked outside apparently had a different opinion, however, as there was no end to their swearing.

The rain continued through the morning with no sign of letting up. Amy was taking a break after the morning meal when something caught her attention. A small boat was speeding upriver towards them. She watched as it pulled up alongside the towboat and someone threw a rope to a crewman. After a moment, a man climbed off the small boat onto the big one. Amy couldn't see the man under his rain hood. He walked along the port side until he got to the stairs. He flipped down the hood. Amy felt the hollow feeling in her stomach that comes with fear. It was Dudley Raymond.

Amy's mind began to race. Drabeck must have found out what she was doing and sent Ray to make sure she didn't find anything. That confirmed in her mind that there must be something to find. If Drabeck had financed a faltering company by faking insurance losses, he had obviously taken it too far.

Amy walked up to the bridge to hear Ray report to the captain. They arrived at the bridge at the same time. Ray gave her a flirtatious wink and a big metallic grin, but didn't say anything to her. Instead, he turned to the captain and said, "The boss wants me to take over for Cadle. We have a boat to take him back down river."

"That's fine," the captain said. He then turned to Amy. "Was there something you wanted to see me about?" he said.

She struggled to find words. "I just wanted to check t'see if anyone had any complaints about the food. Y'all don't have to be nice just cause I'm kinda new."

The captain smiled. "It's fine as far as I know, and I'd tell you if it wasn't."

Amy thanked him and went back to the galley. She worked for a while, and then went back out on deck to look around. The rain was still falling, but it was much lighter. She was enjoying the clean smell that came after the rain when suddenly she noticed someone looking at her from a deck below. It was Ray. When she saw him, he just smiled and nodded and then began walking. If he was trying to pretend that he wasn't spying on her, it wasn't working.

Evening came and the rain stopped. That didn't prevent everything from still feeling wet. It was overcast and cool, so nothing was drying out in a hurry. Amy put on her Pink Floyd sweatshirt and went out on deck.

The sun had dropped below the horizon, but there was still a hint of illumination. Amy saw someone walking out on the tow. She couldn't tell who it was or what they were doing. Instead, she saw little more than a shadow moving around about halfway down and on the starboard side. She waited, hoping to get a better look. Someone was systematically walking around the perimeter of the barges and doing something. She just couldn't tell what it was.

The spotlight on the bow of the towboat came on, but it didn't help much. The long narrow beam was focused on shore markers a mile or more ahead. As a result, the illumination of the tow was minimal. Furthermore, the tow didn't drive with the spotlight on. Instead, it was used to mark a spot and then turned off until there was a need to locate the next navigational marker.

As she watched, she felt as though someone was watching her. She looked around, but didn't see anyone. She went back to trying to see what was going on out on the barges, but then swung around in the hope of catching someone spying on her. Again, she didn't see anyone. Perhaps she was getting a little paranoid.

She finally decided that it would seem suspicious if it looked like she was spying, so she went to her quarters. She listened, hoping to hear footsteps or voices, but the drone of the engine negated most of the random noise. Something didn't seem right, but the answer was not coming to her.

She pulled out her cell phone and hoped for a signal. There wasn't one. She pulled out her navigational map and started looking for the next metropolitan area. Marianna, Arkansas looked to be the next city of any size, but she didn't really know where they were at the time. Frustrated, she sprawled across the bed. In no time, she fell asleep.

W HEN SHE WOKE UP THE NEXT MORNING, she immediately went out to look at the tow. The sun was coming up, but there wasn't enough light yet to see much. She went about her breakfast duties and did her best to act bored.

After breakfast, she went back out on deck. Banks was on the tow. She watched him lumber around the perimeter opening the manhole covers on the wing tanks. She stared for a long time, and then heard a door unlatch. She turned to see Ray smiling at her. She gave him a cursory smile and hurried back to her quarters.

She again checked her phone. Three bars, and that should be enough. She called Tucker Sheridan.

He answered after the second ring.

"Tucker, it's me, Amy."

"Hi there," he said in a tone that presumed the call was to praise his lovemaking skills. "What's going on that you'd be calling me?"

"I'm on a tow coming north, and I'm sort of working undercover. There's something going on, but I don't think I can handle this myself. You need to send the Coast Guard or something."

His tone turned serious. "Okay, okay," he said, "you better tell me what's going on or what you think is going on."

"Ever since I started working for Minnesota Marine, I've been trying to connect all of the losses in order to figure out what was causing them. I couldn't find an answer. Then I finally stopped to think about it. Minnesota Marine always had a certain level of losses, so assuming that all of the losses were the result of the same thing was a mistake. Instead, I had to figure out which losses were out of the ordinary."

"That makes sense," he said, "but I don't know how you would determine which was which."

"It was a matter of finding any correlation between the increased losses. The reports usually didn't sort by upstream or downstream, but the jump seems to have been in upstream losses."

"Okay," he said, "but you still haven't told me what you've found."

"I'm not sure I've found anything yet, but I have some hunches."

"Are you going to share them with me?"

"For one, I always assumed that the losses were intended. Then it dawned on me that maybe nobody is deliberately causing the losses, but that they are the unintended consequences of some other activity. I need some help, however, so we need to call in the authorities."

"I think you might be moving a little fast. What are we going to tell them?"

"I think someone is smuggling something in the wing tanks. I don't know what or who is involved, but I'm afraid Drabeck might be doing the John DeLorean thing of trying to save the company by smuggling drugs."

"Wow," he said. "That'd really be a story. What makes you think that?"

"For starters, some of the crew have been using Spanish phrases, and they are clearly not Hispanic or the type of people who learned extra languages in school. They were saying, 'Show me the money,' except they were saying it in Spanish. I think they learned it from whomever they're dealing with."

"Okay," he said. "I guess that's a start."

"On top of that, some of these barges were loaded directly from ships that came from South America. That would make it relatively easy to smuggle the goods into the country by loading the wing tanks at the same time."

"I don't think that would be as easy as you think, but I s'pose it's possible."

"Then, we had a lot of rain, and Rick Banks was out on the tow doing something, and I think he was checking on the cargo to make sure it wasn't wet. He took the covers off the wing tanks, and I think he did it so that whatever was inside would dry out."

The line was silent for a moment as he formulated a response. "If there is something going on, maybe we should try to catch people in the act. I mean, if I get the authorities out there, we might find something, but we'd have a hard time figuring out who was involved."

"I know who's involved," she said. "Drabeck didn't want me coming here. His business is going down the drain, but he didn't want me finding out it was his own fault."

The line was silent for a moment. "We have some time," he replied. "That tow won't stop before Paducah, so there won't be any place to unload it before then."

"What do you propose we do when we reach Paducah?"

"I'll fly down and get aboard before that. I know it might look a little suspicious, but I'm still the Harbor Captain. I'll come up with an excuse as to why I need to ride the tow north for a while. That tow will be split in Paducah and some of the cargo will go up the Ohio and some will go up the Mississippi. I'll have to get aboard before then."

"That sounds like a plan."

Tucker's voice turned tender. "Will you be okay until then?"

"Yes. Just knowing that you're coming should be enough to keep me going."

"All right, then. I'll see ya soon."

CHAPTER FORTY-NINE

THE WAIT FOR TUCKER SEEMED to take forever. With no locks on the lower Mississippi, there were no interruptions. The flip side was that there were no breaks in the routine and just a constant trudge upstream.

She started watching for Tucker. This wasn't the pining-for-a-lover watch. Instead, she was waiting for her protector. Amy started to worry that Drabeck had gotten wind of the situation and diverted Tucker or, worse, fired him.

Amy was feeling the first pangs of panic. If she had not been expecting him, she would have felt reasonably comfortable making the rest of the trip. His failure to arrive, however, set her mind to working all sorts of nefarious schemes.

She went to her cabin and pulled out her cell phone. She pushed the button to light the screen, but there was no response. *Shit.* She'd forgotten to turn it off and the power had drained out of it. Even if she'd thought to bring her charger, the boat operated on a direct current. Her only chance at communicating was the boat's radio, but that didn't seem like much of an option.

She waited until dark and then decided to take matters into her own hands. She had decided she would get off the boat the first chance she had, but in the interim she needed to know for herself what was going on. She grabbed a penlight from her keychain and donned a life jacket. She was going out on the tow.

When the shifts changed, it was customary for the crew going off duty to make a report to the crew coming on. While that was part of the formal protocol, it also seemed like a time to socialize. Amy relied on that and left her cabin to coincide with the midnight shift change.

She walked to the front of the towboat and crouched behind some gear. She waited for the searchlight to come on and find a navigational marker. When it went off, she stepped off the boat and onto the tow. She went to the column of barges farthest to the right and began walking along the side. She wasn't next to the water. Rather, she was on the inside edge of the most starboard barge. Walking at night was even worse than walking in the day. Fortunately, there was a full moon, so she didn't need to use her flashlight to navigate.

When she got to the third barge, the spotlight came on and shot over her head up the river. She lay motionless on the deck until the light went off. She got up and walked down to the fourth barge. She found a wing tank cover and lay on the deck next to it. She positioned her penlight in one of the gaps and looked in. She saw an inch or two of water, but nothing else.

She moved forward to another cover and did the same thing. Again, there was nothing, so she tried the adjoining barge with the same result.

This was the approximate area where she had seen Banks. Covering the entire tow on her hands and knees was not something she was prepared to do. Perhaps she'd have to wait and watch when the barges were being unloaded. Unfortunately, it was likely that different barges would be unloaded in different places and that would make it impossible to observe.

She was far enough from the engines to hear another boat approaching on the starboard side. Its spotlight suddenly came on, and she hit the deck. The small boat was apparently only getting its bearings and distance from the tow, however, as the spotlight went dark in a matter of seconds. She lay still until the boat had passed and then went to the fifth barge in the column, which was now the front barge.

Being at the front of the tow, she felt much more vulnerable to being caught in the spotlight. Rather than move more quickly, she decided the best thing to do would be to move more slowly and simply lie still when the light went on. She hoped that her dark clothing would keep her from being noticed even if some light caught her.

Her inspection of the wing tanks was not yielding results. Every one was empty. She realized what she had to do, and she wasn't looking forward to it. She was going to have to check the wing tanks on the side next to the water.

She crawled along the front of the barge to the other side. She wasn't crawling to avoid the spotlight. She was crawling because she was afraid to stand up for fear of losing her balance. Even lowering her center of gravity didn't completely alleviate her fears of slipping and going over.

She got to the first cover and shined her light in. Nothing. As she moved to the back, she repeated the drill with the same results. The spotlight came on and she lay still. While prone, she wondered why she should care enough about Minnesota Marine or anything else to take the risks she was taking. Natural curiosity and a penchant for justice should only take you so far, and this was clearly beyond that point.

She got to the fourth barge and resumed her search. She shined the light in and then jumped back. There was something moving in the wing tank. She positioned herself above the opening in the cover and turned her light on again. All of a sudden, she was looking at the faces of several young Hispanic women. The wing tanks were only about the width of a person, but this one was full.

She moved to the next cover and found more women. The closer she looked, the more they looked liked girls. *It wasn't drugs that were being trafficked, it was women.* Amy wanted to say something or ask them about what was happening, but her Spanish wasn't up to it.

The spotlight came on and she again lay flat. She decided she'd seen enough. When the spotlight went out, she started for the towboat. As she looked up, she was startled by the silhouette of a man.

"What are you doing out here?" The voice was Tucker's.

"Where've you been?" she snapped.

"Something came up and I couldn't leave any earlier without arousing suspicion. I just came aboard a few minutes ago. When you weren't in your cabin, I got worried you were doing something foolish."

Amy let out a long gasp. "You won't believe what I found. It's not drugs. The wing tanks are full of women being smuggled into the country."

Tucker's expression was not one of surprise or interest. He was struggling to find words. Finally, he said, "Why did you have to be so nosey? Couldn't you have just been a good girl and minded your own business."

The blood drained from Amy's face. "What?"

"You heard me. Why did you have to be so hell bent on this? Couldn't you just leave well enough alone?"

"So, you're in on this? You and Drabeck are buying and selling women into prostitution?"

"Be serious," he said. "Tony Drabeck is stuck in last century. He wouldn't have the foresight to trade the most demanded commodity of this century. These women want to get to the United States, and there are people who will pay a lot to help them get there."

"You mean 'pay a lot to own them.'"

"Hey, I just provide the transportation. I don't speak the language well enough to interview the passengers about their intentions once they're in the United States."

Her heart was pounding and talking was the only thing that might give her an opportunity to delay what she assumed was coming. Tucker was standing between her and the towboat and she didn't have another avenue of escape. "Did this have anything to do with the losses, or is it just a coincidence?" she finally asked.

"Probably a little of each," he said. "I think that moron Skeeter probably started the boat fire. He was supposed to deliver the girls and bring back the money. I think he had some gambling debts and lost the money trying to win enough to pay everything off. When that didn't work, I think he thought he could delay his day of reckoning by sabotaging the boat."

"So, is he still alive?"

"He was the last time I checked. I think he faked his death to keep our Latin American partners from killing him. I sent someone to find him, and he promised to cut us in on his insurance settlement if we didn't kill him."

"What else?"

"Well, you were right about Banks. He didn't have any experience on the river, but I hired him for his other skills. That led to some losses because he didn't know what he was doing and injured another crewman."

Amy desperately tried to keep him talking. "But he's just one man. There were way too many other accidents."

"They were treated as accidents for insurance purposes, but that doesn't mean they weren't intended by someone. You're not the first person who had to be silenced. That, and I think we were sabotaged on occasion by elements of organized crime that saw us as competition. Believe me, I didn't want the losses to happen because they brought too much attention to our operations. I guess I should have focused more on the real business."

"So, what now?" she asked.

Tucker was quiet and shook his head. "I don't know why you couldn't stick to the courtroom. Do you always try to help when nobody wants you to?"

She didn't have an answer, but struggled to find something to say to keep the conversation going. Finally, Tucker spoke again. "Do you want a piece of this action?"

Amy was dumbstruck. "What?"

"Forget it," he said. "I don't think I could buy your silence."

"Don't be so sure," she said, trying to at least buy some time.

"No. I'm afraid you're about to be the latest and last Minnesota Marine casualty. Skeeter probably jumped off the back of the boat and that's why he lived. If you go over here and nobody yells to shut off the engines, you're pretty much history."

Amy was having trouble getting her breath. "You won't get away with it. The women in the wing tanks will know what happened."

"So what? They aren't about to go to the police."

"I'll scream."

"And what? Hope that somebody other than Banks hears you over the noise of the engines. Believe me, I'm sorry I have to do this on account of you were about as good of piece of ass as I've had."

Amy looked at the water and considered her options. She could get up and run the opposite direction, but she was about as likely to fall in the water following that route. She turned and started crawling over the barge cover. Tucker grabbed her leg and pulled her back down.

She thrashed around trying to free her foot. She kicked at him with the other foot, but couldn't reach him. She was lying on the deck with him standing over her. Suddenly she heard a loud crack. Tucker stood motionless for a minute, and then dropped to his knees with a dazed look on his face. As he fell, he revealed the cause. Standing behind him was a man holding something that looked like a Billy club. It was Dudley Raymond.

"I realize that might not seem sporting," Ray barked at Tucker. "But you're at least thirty years younger than me, and I needed to make sure the girl got away." Ray tossed the club overboard and held up his fists like an old-time prizefighter.

Tucker put his hands out for balance. He started to get to his feet, but he was still unsteady. "You son of a bitch," he said as he started toward Ray. His balance wasn't there, however. He took a step and then he wobbled. He sat down on the barge cover. "What kind of a man attacks someone from behind?"

Ray stood up straight and lowered his hands. He stared a hole through Tucker Sheridan. "What kind of a piece of shit attacks a defenseless woman?" he said. "I told you I needed a little advantage, but take your time and when you're ready I'll be happy to kill you with my bare hands."

"Don't," Amy said, "it's not worth it."

Ray looked at her and then back at Sheridan. "It's not up to me," he finally said. "I'll do whatever I have to do."

Tucker was rubbing his head trying to regroup. He was taking deep breaths and they kept getting deeper. Finally, he rose to his feet and sneered at Ray. "You should have held onto your club, old man. Everybody knows you can't swim so good, and there'll be nobody there to save you this time."

Ray resumed his fighting pose. Tucker moved toward him, but he was still unsteady. He tried to throw a punch with his right hand, but he missed. His momentum carried him forward toward the edge of the boat. He fell to his knees and tried to grab a cleat. He missed and fell overboard.

Ray walked to the edge and looked into the water. "Damnation," he said. He ran along the side of the tow toward the towboat. "Man overboard," he yelled repeatedly. The engines were too loud, however, and nobody heard him until he got to the bridge.

The Captain killed the engines and the crew hustled out on deck to look for someone in the water. Everyone was hollering, but nobody was hollering back. A couple deckhands went to the back of the towboat to see if anything had surfaced. Nobody reported seeing anything.

Amy was still numb. Tucker Sheridan had given her feelings like she'd never had before, and now he was probably dead. Sadly, that was the outcome she thought was probably for the best.

CHAPTER FIFTY

MY MADE HER WAY TO THE BRIDGE and plopped down in a chair and closed her eyes as tight as she could. When she opened them, Ray was standing over her. "Are you okay?" he asked.

"I'm not hurt, but I'm a little confused."

Ray rubbed his eye with his three-fingered hand. He smiled until the gold on his teeth caught the light. "I'm not sure I can help ya. Why was he tryin' ta kill ya?"

Amy still had not figured out what she thought of Ray or whether he could be trusted. "Weren't you put on board by Drabeck to keep tabs on me and to keep me from discovering whatever has been going on?"

He chuckled. "Not really. I was put on board to look after you. Mr. Drabeck was afraid you'd be in danger if you discovered that something was actually going on and sent me here to protect you." Ray shook his head in embarrassment. "I almost didn't come through."

"I don't get it," she asked. "Did Drabeck know that Tucker was using the boat to smuggle girls for prostitution?"

"I don't think Mr. Drabeck had any idea what was going on. He knew something wasn't right, and he probably thought you were smart enough to figure it out, but he sent me in case there was trouble."

"So, why you?" she asked.

"I guess because he knows I'll do anything for him and the company." He let out a long sigh. "I owe a debt that can't never be repaid."

Amy was obviously warming to the man who had just saved her life. "That's the part I don't really understand. The guy who got hit by the train – the one that you went to prison for -- wasn't that Drabeck's son?"

Ray gave her a quizzical look. "I don't know where you got that idea. That prison time happened before I ever worked for the company."

Amy was perplexed. "I thought you were involved in some way with the son's death. What am I missing?"

Ray sat down on a chair next to her and leaned his elbows onto his knees. He was quiet for a moment. "I guess you have a right to know." He sat up and reached in his pocket for a tin of Copenhagen. He pinched a bit and slid it under his lower lip. "I was involved in Tony Junior's death, but I didn't cause it."

She didn't want to force it out of him, but she needed to hear more. "Go on," she said softly.

"Y'see, Mr. Drabeck is really the salt of the earth. A lot of guys wouldn't give an ex-con a chance, even when they committed a crime like mine, but Mr. Drabeck is different. He doesn't care where a fella's been. He only cares about where he's going and how he's going to get there. He gave me this job and I loved it, and I guess I loved him for it."

Ray spit a stray piece of the tobacco and then continued. "The thing is, this is a dangerous job and Mr. Drabeck was always concerned about the people who worked for him. The company even had insurance policies to provide extra benefits to anyone who got hurt or died. When Tony Jr. was in his twenties, Mr. Drabeck wanted him to learn the business from the bottom up, so he had him spend a year doing all of the different jobs on the river. We all thought Mr. Drabeck was crazy for having his son work such risky jobs, but he wanted his son to realize the danger so that he'd keep the interests of the workers first when he was running the business."

Ray's eyes were starting to glisten as he talked. "Anyway, we were headed up river near Wabasha. We'd just gone through the locks and I was rechecking the lines. All of a sudden, we hit a barge that was adrift in the channel. I lost my balance and fell. I hit my head on the deck and then fell in the water. I don't really remember it happening. I just remember coming to in the water."

Ray's voice was becoming quieter and he was having trouble continuing. "We were only a little ways above the dam, and I can't swim that good. Next thing y'know, I see Tony Jr. running full blast down the length of the barge and diving into the water. Can you imagine that? A piece of shit like me floating in the river and this kid with everything in the world going for him risks his life for mine."

The tears were now running down the old man's face, and he wasn't bothering to wipe them away. "Anyway, he grabbed me and pulled me toward the tow. The other guys got a line down and hooked it under my arms. In all the commotion, I guess everyone lost track of the stray barge. We were turning, and the current was pulling, and all of a sudden I was on board and the stray barge crashed into us again and then Tony Jr. was nowhere to be found. He was a good swimmer, but I don't think anyone's that good."

Amy's eyes were now glistening as well. "Is that why you got upset when I said suicide bombers had courage? When you said you had witnessed real courage, were you talking about Tony Jr.?"

He paused and wiped his face with his sleeves. "Yeah. That's why."

"Because you think he was someone who loved life."

"I know that for a fact. He was always a great kid, but he had just told me that he was getting married. You shoulda seen the look on his face when he was telling me about her. He was a young kid with a big future in front of him, and he'd met the woman he wanted to spend the rest of his life with. You can't love life more than that kid did."

Amy put a hand on his shoulder to comfort him. "That must have been pretty hard for the fiancée."

"I don't think anyone will ever know."

"What do you mean?"

"Nobody had ever met her. He was going home to tell his family about her, but nobody knew who she was."

"He didn't tell you her name?"

"He might have, but it wasn't anything I'd be likely to remember. I didn't even know where she was from."

"That poor woman," Amy said. "Did you tell Mr. Drabeck?"

Ray was quiet again. "I couldn't really even face him for a long time. Nobody ever blamed me for Tony Jr.'s death, but I always felt a little responsible. After enough time passed, I thought it wasn't worth mentioning."

"I can understand that," she said, "but it's too bad about the fiancée.

"I really wanted to do something," Ray said, "but I didn't know where to start. I suppose I could have gone from town to town up and down the river."

"That's a lot of towns," she said. "Besides, what would you do when you got there if you didn't know her name?"

"Well, I had one clue. Y'see, I think they were getting married because they had to. When I say 'had to,' that's really just an expression, 'cause Tony Jr. was just as excited about being a father."

"So, what would you do – search all the birth records? How would you even know what to look for?"

"Well, it woulda been a long shot, but it might have worked. Y'see, Tony Jr. told me that if they had a girl, his fiancée was going to name her 'Chardonnay.' I doubt there's too many girls with that name."

All of the wind went out of her. Memories of her childhood rushed through her consciousness. All of the days as a little girl, when she sat in the tire swing or on the bluffs and wondered why her father didn't want her and why he had abandoned her to a world in which she never fit. Tears welled up in her eyes and her lip quivered. Finally, Chardonnay Amanda Prescott spoke. "I think you may have just repaid the debt that can never be repaid."

♣ POSTSCRIPT ♠

This book is dedicated to the memory of my great uncle Ray, who, for reasons I never knew, we called "Uncle Dudley." He was a storyteller and, ever since I was little, I remember him holding court just about everywhere he went. Some of the humorous anecdotes in the book were adapted from some of his yarns. I always admired him and wanted to emulate his talents.

I also want to dedicate it to him as someone who knew that a real man is not merely someone who is rich, handsome, or good in bed (kudos to any readers who noticed the reference to Ray's "woeful countenance" in Chapter Thirteen and remembered that Don Quixote was dubbed the Knight of the Woeful Countenance). The story about the abusive husband killed at the railroad crossing is half true. There was a man who lived near Ray who abused his wife and died in the manner described, but Ray had nothing to do with it. In his later years, I'd occasionally drive Ray places and every time we went past the location of the collision he'd retell the story. Invariably, he'd conclude with a statement about the husband's abusive tendencies and express gratitude that "the son of a bitch got what he deserved."

I would not be a good lawyer, however, if I drew conclusions from just one piece of evidence, and I think the most telling thing is this: Ray did not marry until he was in his sixties. His wife was a widow of about the same age who had had five children with a man who apparently had not shared Ray's philosophies about how to treat women. When she became ill and it appeared likely that she would die, her five children came to Ray and asked that she be buried next to him, because, in their judgment, she had been happier during the years married to Ray than all the years married to their father.

ACKNOWLEDGEMENTS

I would like to thank Terry Becker for his technical help, the folks at the Prairie du Chien Library for their historical help, and all of my test readers, including Linda Wendt, Karin Wendt, Shawn Moren, Tom Haider, Cary Johnson, Paul Maahs, Bill Bartkowski and, of course, my family.